CONFESSION OF
A HIRED KILLER

Books by Elsinck:
  Tenerife!
  Murder by Fax
  Confession of a Hired Killer

CONFESSION OF A HIRED KILLER

ISBN 1 881164 53 5

Printing History:
 1st Dutch printing: 1992

 1st American edition: 1993

Cover Design: Based on an Idea by Studio Combo (Netherlands)
Typography: Monica S. Rozier
Manufactured by BookCrafters, Inc., Fredericksburg, VA

CONFESSION OF A HIRED KILLER

by

ELSINCK

translated from the Dutch by H.G. Smittenaar

INTERCONTINENTAL PUBLISHING

Somewhere, well hidden in the darkest corner
of our soul, resides a merciless avenger.
Just barely held in check by civilization,
justice and . . . cowardice.

The Investigation

Nothing has happened and I dare to hope again. What I feared yesterday is not forgotten, but I am no longer preoccupied by it. It no longer rules me. I feel capable of winning and am able to think about you again and to fantasize about later. Who knows, everything may yet be resolved and perhaps there will be time for many things, perhaps I will be allowed to grow old with her. I imagine that I will then tell her, every day, about a day of my life when we were apart. And she will be able to tell me about one of her days. Every day we shall have something new to talk about. It will take at least twenty years before we run out of things to talk about. I will be 76 and she will be only 60. But together we will have at least forty years of memories. Memories we can argue about, whenever we mix up the dates. Together, we will spoil our grandchildren and sneak them extra pocket money, despite your protestations. She will tell me not to whine about my little maladies and infirmities and I take her on short trips with the car. For the last time we shall travel to the places where our memories were formed and where we can recognize nothing. Once a week she will dress in her best clothes and I will proudly show her off in the best restaurants. The doctor will still allow us to eat anything. People will look at us and wish that they, too, could grow old as gracefully as we. She will scold me about the size of the tip and on the way home I take the wrong turn. I will hold her hand when we cross the street and I will have a little list, written in her own dear hand, when I go shopping. She makes sure that I wear a scarf when it is cold and I will squeeze fresh orange juice for her, when she is in bed with the flu. Daily we will tell each other that time flies and you will tell us not to be boring. She will decorate the house with fresh flowers from our garden and I polish the car once again. In Spring, I paint the picket fence and together with her I

✳1. Serifos: Sunday, May 27, 1984

Catarina was the first person in the small mountain village who wondered what had happened to the "foreigner" who had lived for years in the small house next to hers. She had not seen him for days but she knew he was home. He was a strange, lonely man, nice, he always greeted her in a friendly manner, but there had hardly been any real contact during the ten years he had lived next door. Actually, he had no friends in the village at all, with the exception of Petros. Everybody knew Petros and was more or less familiar with his background. What was not known had been added to by imagination and gossip. A few hundred people lived on the mountain top and all were, in one way or another, related to each other. But Petros was from Spetsai, an island to the west of the Peloponnisian Peninsula. And those from Spetsai were different. That had been established centuries ago and had remained that way.

She wondered if perhaps she should not investigate. First she discussed it with her sister, who lived in the street above. Her brother-in-law had told her to mind her own business, but her curiosity would not be denied. The house was so strangely quiet. A different quiet. She was used to see him leave, from time to time, for an errand and she was used to hearing music. Usually classical music with lots of violins, ponderous, slow. Somebody had told her it was Bach. Anyway, she did not really care about that. The music never bothered her and that was enough. After all, they were used to hearing everything from each other, her whole life long. The small houses were close together and the walls and roofs were made of stone and the streets were narrow. Every sound echoed between the high mountain walls and the white painted rocks of the sidewalks. It was really never quiet. With just average hearing one could recognize the footsteps of the mailman when, early in the morning, he started his daily rounds at the bottom of the village.

Everyone who passed was observed and every passerby could be heard from a distance. She had tried to peer through the cracks in the closed shutters, she had even mustered the courage to knock softly on the door, but had left again because there was no answer. Sometimes he drank too much. She knew that from the grocer in the village, the sole source of liquor on the island. He was a good customer, the grocer often said so. Also, you could hear when the trash bin was emptied in the cart that collected garbage. The emptying of his trash bin made a different sound from that of others.

After four days she became uneasy. She had not seen Petros either, for all that time. She had heard that they had left together about ten days ago on the sailing boat of the "foreigner". The boat had not returned and neither had Petros. Just the "foreigner" had returned, four days ago. She had seen him at the bakery on the day of his return. A little later she had seen him with a load of bottles.

The fifth day, it was Sunday, May 27, she knocked on his door and after several attempts to elicit a response, she carefully turned the knob and found the door unlocked. It did not surprise her. Nobody locked the doors in the village. Even if you went to your family in Athens and were gone for days, you would not lock the door. Shyly she entered and called his name, but there was no answer. The shutters in front of the small windows were closed and heavy curtains in front of the windows closed off all light. It was dark inside. She searched for the light switch, felt the wires which were mounted on the wall, followed them with her right hand and turned the old-fashioned switch. Her scream of horror resounded through the narrow streets and caused the first curiosity seekers to leave their homes. In a panic she left the house and fled in the direction of the stairs that led to the street where her sister lived. A few moments later her brother-in-law left the house hurriedly and stormed down the stairs that descended between the houses to the square where the small police station nestled against the

12

church. There was but one, solitary policeman on Serifos island, one of the fifty six islands of the Cyclades.

*2. Serifos: The same day.

The village policeman entered while the two women and the brother-in-law remained outside and a number of neighbors watched from a distance. He switched on the light in the space immediately behind the front door and saw it. The foreigner was bent over his typewriter on the desk. He was dead, that was obvious. His head rested at an angle on his left ear and his arms hung down. His face was covered with blood and lacerated. A white cloth had been placed in front of his mouth and tied at the back of his head. His shirt was torn and red weals were visible on the back, interspersed with burn marks where cigarettes had been pressed in the skin. The butts were in an ashtray on the desk. There was still some blood on the butts. The constable had no experience with this sort of case. He had read about it in the papers, from time to time, and in the past, a dim past, it had been mentioned during his training period. But that was the extent of his knowledge. The only thing he knew for sure was that he should not touch anything. He went outside again and asked the brother-in-law to guard the door and to take care that nobody entered. He walked down the stairs that served as a street, picked up the telephone in his office and called Athens.

About ninety minutes later, it must have been around ten thirty, a helicopter landed on the terrain normally reserved for soccer matches. Four men emerged and walked in a crouch toward the local constable who awaited them next to the white Lada with the police emblem on the side. They shook hands and when the rotors and engine of the helicopter shut down, they could understand each other's names. A few suitcases were unloaded and they all got into the car. The Chief Inspector, a corpulent, middle aged man sat in front and the three others, more slender and younger, shared the back seat. During the ten minutes it took to drive the distance over the twisting road, the constable related what he knew. When they arrived at the house, half the village had gathered. The brother-in-law stood rocklike in front of the door, fully aware of his responsibility and importance.

The first stories were already starting to live a life of their own and everybody had suddenly something to say about the "foreigner" who had lived among them for more than ten years and who now had been found dead over his typewriter. The five men emerged from the car and all conversation ceased. Impressed, the crowd parted to let them through and opened a path to the front door. The local constable marched in front with big steps and a determined look on his face. This was his day, a day that would increase his respect from the village, where nothing happened and where for more than thirty years he had been known for writing a few unimportant tickets and for the enforcement of insignificant trifles and meaningless futilities.

Chief Inspector Spiros Karatzis from the head office in Athens, entered the room and looked around. Everything in the house was in disorder. Drawers had been removed and thrown on the floor. The contents were spread around. The two drawers from the desk were upside down on a small table in the middle of the room. The books, once lining the wooden shelves along the walls, had been removed and thrown helter-skelter. Nothing remained in place in the small kitchen and in the bedroom the mattress had been cut open. Around the chair occupied by the "foreigner", the blood had been absorbed by the white carpet and on the desk it had coagulated. Chief Inspector Karatzis leaned over the corpse and pointed at the neck.

"That was the *coup de grace*," he said.

Inspector Janis Tselentis, his regular partner, looked at the bullet wound and added:

"That's for sure."

14

"He's been beaten, cigarettes have been extinguished on his back, look here and here," he pointed at a few spots. "They just left the butts."

"You think what I think?"

"They were looking for something, something important. When they didn't find it, they went to work on him. Eventually they killed him."

"Perhaps he told them something."

"Possible. In any case, he knew something. It remains to be seen if he told them."

"It's not a regular case, sir, I'm sure of that."

"You're right, that's certain. Listen, for starters, go to the office of the local constable . . . eh, what's his name again?"

"Takis."

"Oh, yes. Takis . . . Go to his office and call Athens while I talk to him. You know the drill. We need a doctor, he needs to be moved and from the smell that's already long overdue. Talk to the boss, tell him this is not a normal case, perhaps he'll want to come. Anyway, you know the routine. The photographer is here already, so he can get started. Andreas can start with the fingerprints, so *he'll* be busy for a while. Call the pilot and tell him to return at once to Athens to pick everybody up."

"All right, I'm on my way."

"One more thing. Call my wife and tell her I'll be here for a while. Ask her to throw some stuff together, enough for a few days. Have somebody from the office pick it up. I'd do the same, if I were you."

"Nice, paid vacation in the Greek Islands."

"Hard enough to come by, you know that."

"I can hardly believe our luck."

"I thought the same, at your age. Go on with you, now."

The two specialists began their work and the Chief Inspector walked over to constable Takis.

"Who found him?" he asked.

"The woman next door."

"What did she tell you?"

"Nothing, she left in a panic."

"Well, let her calm down, it can wait. Let's find a quiet spot and talk."

"Would you like to drink something?"

"Coffee, a capital idea. You have coffee on this mountain?"

"They have the best coffee in all of Greece in Bar Poseidon."

"Impossible, my wife makes the best coffee."

Laughing, they descended the stairs in the direction of the square. The villagers stared after them.

They sat down at the only table on the terrace of Bar Poseidon. A fat man with a gleaming bald head and a soiled apron came outside to take their order. His eyes were curious as he looked at constable Takis and it was obvious that he was just barely able to restrain himself from asking questions.

"You know the victim?" the Chief Inspector asked Takis.

"Of course, he's lived here more than ten years."

"Permanently?"

"No, he's often gone. He travels a lot, I think."

"You mentioned a name, Roberto . . . eh, . . ?"

"Dubour. Actually his name is Robert, but here they call him Roberto."

"Belgian, you said?"

"Yes, born in Antwerp. He's 56 years old. But I have his complete dossier in the office."

"That can wait, tell me about the man himself. I want to form a picture of him."

"He arrived here about ten years ago, with his boat, the *Christina*, a wooden boat, old, but well-kept."

"The boat is moored here, at the dock?"

"Please wait, sir, I said . . . that is, I would like to start from the beginning, the boat comes later."

"Sorry, go ahead."

"At first he lived in Livadi for several months, on his boat. Papers were in order, the harbor police had nothing to complain about. Just a tourist, like many others. Nice, quiet guy, nothing remarkable. He spoke fluent Greek and got along fine with the locals. But you know how the islanders are, very clannish, so he didn't have any real friends. I don't think that bothered him. He was a loner. He went his way, talked to anybody, was friendly, but that was the extent of his involvement with the island. Then, after a few months, he bought the house, from a cousin of mine, as it happens. He fixed it up himself. That took some doing, because the house had been neglected. My cousin helped him with the work for a few weeks . . ."

He was interrupted by the proprietor, who served them their coffee. After they had been served, the constable continued:

"He has no debt in the village, always paid on time and in full. His residency permit, too, was always renewed in a timely manner. I never had to ask for it. Probably wouldn't have. He caused no problems and then you're inclined to take it a bit easy with the red tape. But, every time he had been to Athens to have the permit renewed, he'd make it a point to stop by and show it to me. As I said, nothing to criticize. The harbor police, too, were always paid on time. In short, a first class person. Alone, as I said, very much on his own. He was nice, friendly, but you couldn't get to know him. Not really. The *Christina*, his sailboat, although I call it a boat, it's a good size, was maintained by Petros. A former merchant seaman, who rented a house in the street adjacent to the quay. He's from Spetsai. He's on a pension and lives here alone. At least, I understand he has no family left. Another loner."

"What else do you know about Petros?"

"Well, you know, nothing in particular. Used to be a captain, Panamanian papers. The usual. A little bit of smuggling in booze and cigarettes, especially just after the war. Negligible offenses. Used to work for one of the less respectable companies owned, via dummies, by Onassis, or Niarchos, who knows. You know the drill, rust buckets with a high insurance value. I don't think he's ever been involved with taking a ship 'on her last voyage', if that's what you mean. Petros and Robert Dubour used to go away together, on

Roberto's boat. About two weeks ago they left together. According to the neighbor, Roberto returned about five days ago, alone. The boat has not returned, nor has Petros. It's a bit strange."

"Did he ever have any visitors, I mean Roberto?"

"Never, as far as I know."

"Have you noticed anything peculiar, please think carefully."

"Yes, well, you see, when I saw him this morning, I asked myself the same question, but I can't think of a thing."

"I take it you noticed that this isn't your ordinary murder?"

"Well, that sort of thing just doesn't happen on the island, normally, so I've got little experience with it. But even I could see that it was more than the usual sort of thing. The only suspicious thing about the victim, so to speak, is that there's nothing suspicious about him."

"He was just right, very correct?"

"Yes, but Northern Europeans are always a little bit more organized, worry a lot more about rules and so."

"Did he get any mail?"

"I suppose so, but we would have to ask Fotis, he delivers the mail."

"Did he keep money in the house?"

"I don't think so. He used to pay cash, but it was never a lot. Now that I think about, he once asked the grocer if it would be all right to pay a bill a little later. He had to go to the bank to get money, he said. Yes, yes, I remember it well. That was about four months ago. So, he couldn't have had a lot of money in the house. But I didn't think he was exactly poor. He had some nice equipment in his house and he wore an expensive watch. No, he wasn't poor."

"So we can rule out robbery?"

"You don't believe that yourself, especially when you look at what they did to him and how they messed up the place."

"You're right. Could it have been people from the island?"

"Impossible."

"How could one get on the island without being noticed?"

"There's a daily ferry, but it never carries much traffic. To land without being noticed would be difficult."

"Is the quay guarded at night?"

"No, of course not."

"Does anybody live on the quay, or in a boat?"

"No, nobody."

"There are a few restaurants along the quay, until what time are they open?"

"They're not open at all, yet. They're only in business during the summer. At right angles to the quay there's a bar, next to the grocer, the supermarket, actually, but it closes after the last bus departs, around ten at night. You see, during the summer it's a little busier, tourists mainly, but at this time of the year there's little going on."

"So, it would be possible to arrive quietly by boat, walk quietly to the top of the village and quietly kill the man, walk back and depart?"

"You would not necessarily be seen by anybody."

"Over the next few days I would like to talk to some of the people who live near the quay. You know them all?"

"For over thirty years."

Inspector Janis emerged from the police station across the square, noticed his superior on the terrace with the local constable and crossed the square toward them.

"Everything is taken care of, chief, the helicopter is on its way to Athens, they'll be back in about an hour with the doctor and the paramedics, clean underwear and tooth brushes."

"You're staying here?" asked Takis.

"At least for the night."

"Then I'll reserve a room for you at the inn below."

"Two rooms," added Inspector Tselentis.

"I'll go and do that now and then I'll gather all the documents about Roberto." He stood up and walked to his office across the square.

19

The two inspectors from Athens climbed the stairs once again and returned to the house of Robert Dubour, the Belgian. The Chief Inspector noticed that the photographer had finished and said:

"The helicopter will be back in about an hour, with the doctor. Please give me some close-ups when the doctor is here."

"I'll take care of it, chief."

"What did you find, Andreas?"

The fingerprint expert from the Dactyloscopic Service was treating the kitchen doorknob with a large, soft brush.

"As far as I can tell," he answered, "there are quite a few fingerprints. That always gives hope."

"Did you see the letter in the typewriter, chief?" asked the photographer.

"Yes, I saw it, but I want to wait for the doctor, before we move the corpse."

"Here's his dossier, Inspector," said Takis, who arrived a few minutes later. He handed a sheet to Spiros Karatzis, who began to read:

Name: Robert Dubour; Nationality: Belgian; Born: August 13, 1927 at Antwerp, Belgium.

He interrupted his reading to ask a question.

"How much longer do you need, Andreas?"

"At most another hour, chief."

"Good. When the helicopter arrives, I want you two to go back with it. You can make the office by about three thirty. Make sure that we get a photo, fingerprints and other data to Interpol in Brussels. Ask for further details as soon as possible."

They started to search the house methodically. No detail escaped them. Every book was searched and every scrap of paper was read. Meanwhile the helicopter had arrived and constable Takis entered with the doctor and two men in gray uniforms who carried a body bag between them. After greeting each other, the doctor opened his bag and took out a pair of rubber gloves which he carefully put on. He looked at the victim, touched him and said:

"He's been dead for a while."

"Yes, we thought so. Can you estimate how long?"

"Well, yes, a few days . . . three or four. Thank God it isn't too warm at this time of year. The house is pretty cool, as well. Otherwise it would have been a much worse job."

"What about the neck wound?"

"I shouldn't have to tell you, fired from close by, that's clear. They probably pressed the barrel against the flesh, probably with a silencer."

"I thought so. Can we move him for a real good close-up of the face? I would like to have all details on their way to Interpol in Brussels, today."

"I can think of cozier pictures, but go ahead. Let's put him down on the floor."

The two paramedics came closer and stretched the body on the floor. After the photographer had made his close-ups, he and Andreas took off for the helicopter which would carry them back to Athens.

Then Karatzis had a closer look at the letter in the typewriter and removed it.

*3. Serifos: The same day

Catarina and the two policemen from Athens were seated at the large, wooden table in her kitchen.

"Would you like a pick-me-up?" she asked and placed a large bottle of ouzo on the table.

"Ma'am, I'm on duty," said Chief Inspector Karatzis. "My colleague and I are strictly prohibited from drinking while on duty. But headquarters, and Athens, are a long way off and my partner needs me for a good evaluation of his performance, he'll be quiet. Also, we'll be on the island overnight. So, please, we're happy to

21

accept your kind offer." Karatzis settled himself comfortably on the chair.

"What a terrible situation, sir," said the woman. "He was such a nice man."

"Did you know him well?"

"Well, knowing, . . . knowing is perhaps too big a word. But I saw him almost every day. To be honest, he didn't seem a happy man."

"Why do you say that?"

"To be honest, he was a lonely man. No children, no family, nobody."

"Did you ever talk with him?"

"Yes, you know, the weather and things."

"Did you ever see anyone else there? I mean, visitors?"

"Never. I've never seen anyone else and he's lived there more than ten years. Yes, of course, except Petros. To be honest, I wasn't too thrilled about that. We have a nice neighborhood, you understand?"

"How's that?"

"To be honest, I've never trusted Petros. But he was the only one to stop by, from time to time. Never anyone else."

"What did he do?"

"He played a lot of records, classical mostly. During the summer he was away a lot, with his boat. And he used to run. He was very good at it. He drank a lot, that was too bad. But I could tell from the bottles in the garbage. I counted them, once. And lately he used to make a lot of noise with his typewriter. He had never done that before, that is, so often and so long at a time."

"What do you mean by so long at a time?"

"Well, at least three weeks, every night."

"This was the first time?"

"Oh, yes. He used to work on his typewriter before, but never for long. A letter or something. You can hear that. I mean, he used those short, sharp raps, you can hear that very well. Especially during the summer, when all the windows are open, the sound carries, you know. But recently he used to type at night and it is so still, you hear everything. To be honest, I was about to ask him to stop. But, you know, he was already gone, then."

"He was gone?"

"Yes, for about eight days, or so. That happened regularly."

"He was gone often?"

"Oh yes, quite often."

"For long?"

"Sometimes for longer, sometimes for shorter."

"Give me some idea."

"Well, he was never gone less than a week. Let's say about two weeks, on the average."

"How often did that happen?"

"Well, yes, I couldn't say, off hand."

"What was the last time he left?"

"Well, let's see. He came back about five days ago and at that time he'd been gone for about a week. Shortly before that, he was away as well."

"You mean, he was home only a few days between trips?"

"Yes, wait a moment, let me think. He left the day after my sister's birthday, so that was the 27th of April. He went away that time for, let's say, a week. Then he came home again, because the typewriter started up again. Every night. That lasted about a week, maybe more. But when I started to get upset about it and wanted to say something about it, he was gone again."

"So, about ten days?"

"Yes, it seems that he and Petros left with the boat, as I heard later. And Petros hasn't come back yet, is that right?"

"That's right."

"To be honest, I believe Petros did it."

"Did you hear anything, during the night, about five days ago?"

"No, I don't think so."

"As far as we've been able to determine, he would have been typing at that time."

"Go on with you! Really? Strange, it didn't wake me. It probably wasn't too long."

"No, ma'am, it was just a short letter, to be honest," said the Chief Inspector and winked at his partner.

✳4. Serifos, Monday, May 28, 1984

The air in the inn, next to the bay, was still damp and humid. Chief Inspector Spiros Karatzis and his partner, Inspector Janis Tselentis, were the first guests of the season. The eight rooms of the inn had not been aired since the previous October, when the last guest had left the island. But the couple that ran the inn were friendly and hospitable and did everything in their power to make the stay of their two visitors from Athens as comfortable as possible. They had even provided fresh bread for breakfast from the baker who lived near the top of the mountain. And that was a trip of at least half an hour up the mountain and along the twisted stairs with more than a hundred steps and another half hour back again. There was also fresh feta cheese on the table and the coffee was strong and good.

"What do we have so far?" asked the Chief Inspector. "One corpse with something to hide about which we haven't a clue. We also don't know how important it is to the party that put a bullet through his head, or whether he spilled anything about it. It is possible that the balance of the letter he began to write has something to do with it. How did you evaluate that letter?"

"Sad, he seemed a nice guy."

"Where is the person to whom the letter is addressed and what has the victim done with the previous letters?" asked Karatzis thoughtfully.

"They probably were looking for that."

"Possible, but not necessarily. Anyway, the tone of the letter doesn't fit. It's a loving letter about a woman he hasn't seen in years and has been unable to forget."

"Intended for someone else."

"Yes, most likely a son, or a daughter, that seems a likely conclusion. How did he write that again? 'Daily we will tell each other that time flies and you will tell us not to be boring . . .' That proves, to me, that it must have been addressed to a child of both of them. But what could possibly have been written in the rest of the letter that he had to be killed for it? What else do we have?"

"A nice guy, nothing to complain about, no debts."

"Yes, indeed, his name is Robert Dubour, he's from Belgium, he has a sailboat, the *Christina*, and he left on her about ten days ago, accompanied by his friend, Petros."

"He's been tortured by at least two people who are experienced in that sort of thing. We found fingerprints of the victim and possibly of the perpetrators, no passport, no driver's license, no other identification."

"He loved to drink, but was never seen under the influence."

"And that's about it, Janis. It's nothing yet, but I've a feeling that there's more behind this than we can possibly suspect at this time. You know what makes me especially suspicious?"

"What?" asked Janis.

"His papers here are perfectly in order. Every tee crossed and every eye dotted. I don't have to remind you what an effort that takes in this country. It's almost impossible and nobody even tries. I don't know of a single Greek who's ever managed it. Let alone a foreigner? Have you any idea what a foreigner has to go through to get a Residency Permit? But he had everything! *He* did! You know what that means, Janis?"

"That, at all costs, he wanted to avoid trouble with the authorities."

"Very good, my boy. But why did he want to avoid that?"

"Perhaps because he was being sought and had found a safe haven here."

"Exactly! But that doesn't mean that some sort of authority was after him. It could have been someone else."

"Mafia?"

"For instance."

"Could he have been a *padrino*, or some sort of important boss?"

"No, they always find a way. That sort isn't going to hide on top of a mountain for ten years. No, it's something else. The only thing I'm sure of, is that this was some sort of settling of accounts, an execution. Everything points to it."

"What do we do next?"

"We'll visit the Harbor Police."

Spiros stood up, wiped his mouth one more time with the napkin, threw it on the table and walked from the breakfast room, followed by Inspector Janis Tselentis. They walked along the un-paved, dusty path toward the water. They passed the quay with the fishing boats, the sole supermarket and souvenir shop of the island and the bar with the terrace on the corner. To the right was the high mountain wall where several villas had been built. They afforded a magnificent view of the Bay around the village of Livadi. From this vantage point the barren, undulating mountain area was on the other side of the water and to the left, on the side of the mountain, the white smear of the *chora** of Serifos, where the dead man had been found at his desk. The village was indeed no more than a white smear against the ocher background of the massive moun-tain. No more than the faint brush stroke of a painter who wanted to accentuate the contour of the mountain. The *chora* was an idyllic village. The houses were all painted white and the flagstones in the narrow streets were outlined with white paint. Transport was im-possible. If anything heavy had to be delivered, a donkey was the only option. A new refrigerator, or a TV set meant that one had to hire a donkey to do the moving. Every bag of cement for small

---

* A *chora* is the village with the same name as the Greek island on which it is situated. i.e. Naxos on Naxos. Tinos on Tinos, etc. Here: Serifos on Serifos. ---trans.

repairs or remodelling jobs, had to be conveyed on donkey's back. The bus that daily made the trip to the top of the mountain had only a single stop at the top. When passengers got on, or off, the entrance to the village was blocked.

Below, near the concrete quay, to the south of Livadi, where the ferry moored, was the small office of the Harbor Police. They entered. A constable was seated behind the desk in a sparkling white uniform that had recently been ironed by his wife. The desk itself was an old, wobbly piece of furniture, vaguely in the shape of a table. It was covered with undetermined pieces of paper and several ticket books.

"Good morning," said Chief Inspector Spiros Karatzis.

The man did not look up, but growled something, while he laboriously tried to fill in a form with Greek letters, without knowing for sure what the purpose of the form might be.

"We're from Homicide in Athens and we would like to talk to you about the *Christina*, a sailboat."

The man jumped up and stood at attention.

"Good morning, Chief Inspector," he said and introduced himself. "I've some items ready for you."

"Let's all sit down."

The constable busily unearthed two old chairs from the next room and placed them in front of his desk.

"What can you tell us about the boat?" began Spiros.

"Not much, sir. The boat had been docked here in the harbor for at least ten years and we've never had any trouble with her. He was a nice guy."

Spiros looked over the information the constable had given him and asked:

"English flag?"

"Yes, sir, home port Southampton."

"I notice that he wasn't the owner."

"Yes, that happens a lot. The boat belongs to a friend of his and he had the use of it. He was the captain. Look, here's the agreement."

27

"Hm, Neville James Footman, born December 11, 1934 at Kirkby-in-Ashfield, Great Britain. Has the friend ever been here?"

"Never, because we would have known. Here is the complete record of the *Christina*, arrivals, departures, payments, passengers . . ." He handed the folder to Spiros who glanced at it and then passed it on to Janis.

"I would like to take the file with me."

"As you say, but I must ask you to sign for it."

"When did she last leave?"

"That's right here, sir. Let's see, . . . yes, . . . here, look. May 14, 1984, destination Aiyina."

"I want to know if the boat did indeed arrive."

"I can find that out for you, sir, but it'll take a little time."

"Try to do it as soon as possible."

"About an hour?"

"That would be nice. Also ask for particulars. If somebody left, or if they took on additional passengers. In short, all possible information they have. And ask particularly if they noticed anything out of the ordinary."

"I'll take care of it, sir. Terrible case, ain't it?"

"You might say that."

"Nothing ever happens here and now, just like that, a murder. Do you know anything, yet?"

"Nothing yet. But another question. You and your people check the arrivals and departures of the ferry, don't you?"

"Yes, sir."

"You don't keep names of the passengers?"

"No, we don't have that."

"How many of you are there?"

"There's three of us, sir."

"Who was on duty, let's say, in the last six days?"

"Me of course, and George. Nicolas is on vacation."

"Can you tell me anything about the passengers that have arrived and departed during the last week?"

28

"I kinda figured you wanted to know that, sir. My partner and I talked about it in detail, yesterday. You know, it isn't the tourist season yet and this is but a simple island. We're not exactly a tourist attraction, such as Mikonos. The kind of tourists we get here are usually young people, with backpacks, you know what I mean. There's only about eleven hundred people on the island. Over the years you get to know almost all of them personally. If there's a stranger among them, you notice it right away. Especially young people with a backpack. The islanders seldom travel at this time of year. If we have a total of twenty departures or arrivals per day, I probably exaggerate. We would have been certain to notice a strange face. Perhaps you can miss it once, but if a stranger comes by ferry, he's got to go back and he'd have been on the quay at least twice. But we can remember no strangers, except for the 'foreigner' himself. He arrived on Monday."

"Did you talk to him?"

"No, he didn't see me, because I was on the other side."

"Didn't you think it strange to see him arrive by ferry. After all, you knew that he had left with his own boat?"

"No, I never gave it a thought. And if I had thought about it, I would have assumed that his boat was in the wharf, to paint the bottom, or something. As you know, that has to be done every so many years. It has happened a few times since he first docked here. Nothing unusual about it."

"Then there remains the possibility to arrive at night with a fast boat and disappear again, after the murder."

"There's no other way, if you ask me."

"Athens is seventy-three nautical miles from here?"

"Yes, sir."

"How was the sea during the past week?"

"Calm, easily navigated by a power boat. Especially at night, the sea is like a mirror, then. When there's no wind, of course."

"Was there wind?"

"No, hardly. Here are the weather charts for the last week. As you see, an average of 1 to 2 on the Beaufort scale, that's less than ten knots. And at night the wind dies down, ideal weather for a speed boat."

"How long would a speed boat take from Athens to Serifos?"

"Well, it depends on the boat, of course, but an average of forty knots should be feasible."

"That means it would take about two hours?"

"But he has to get back, chief. Does he have enough fuel?" asked Janis.

"That's a good question, my boy. What do you think?" Spiros asked the Harbor policeman.

"Four hours total, at top speed, say eighty liters per hour and that is a lot, would make three hundred and twenty liters. That type of boat easily has a tank of some five hundred liters. It could be done."

"Let's say they depart from Athens at about eleven and arrive around one in the morning. I heard that there's nobody left around here at that time, is that right?"

"Yes, sir. Especially at this time of the year."

"A boat like that, it would make a noise, right?"

"They could have been going at top speed until the entrance of the bay and then at slow speed into the basin. These modern engines are very quiet and the engine space is well isolated. You probably wouldn't even hear it in the houses right along the water's edge."

"So, it's possible?"

"I think it's the only possibility. I wouldn't know any other way. A plane would be noticed."

"All right, they moor and walk to the top. Takes about half an hour. It is then one thirty. Let's assume they were busy for about an hour, that's two thirty. Half an hour back down again, that's three o'clock. Into the boat and away. They could be back in Athens by five in the morning."

"It could have happened that way," agreed the constable.

"Another thing, though," continued Spiros. "Starting the engine makes a lot more noise than just running it, am I right?"

"Yes, you're right. You always have to give extra gas when starting. You can hear that."

"That would mean that it's possible that somebody in the area might have heard something."

"Yes, that possibility exists, chief," said Janis. "But how can that help us, even if we know it? The only result is that we then know for sure that they arrived by boat and we already know that because all other possibilities are eliminated."

"Very good, Inspector Tselentis. But, maybe, somebody woke up and looked out of the window and maybe they saw the boat. May I call Athens from here?"

"But of course, sir," answered the constable and pushed the phone in his direction.

While Spiros dialed the number he said:

"Let's take a look along the quay, Janis. Maybe we'll get lucky."

He finally reached the operator and asked to be connected.

"This is Spiros Karatzis. Listen I would like you to do the following. Inquire around the marinas in Athens to see if a fast speedboat has left there during the last few days. No, I don't have a name. I've got nothing. It should be a boat capable of at least forty knots and with a range of at least two hundred nautical miles, understood? Next. Send a telegram to Interpol, London. I want information regarding a certain Neville James Footman, born December 11, 1934 in Kirkby-in-Ashfield, Great Britain. I'll spell it for you . . ."

*5. Serifos, the same morning

They left the office of the Harbor Police and spoke to a few people who lived closest to the harbor. Disappointed and without tangible results, they gave it up after about an hour and sat down on the terrace of the Corner Bar. When the owner served them their coffee, Spiros gave it one more try.

"May I ask you something?"

"But of course, sir. You're the policeman from Athens, isn't that so?"

"Yes, apparently you knew already."

"New travels fast around here, we don't have that many secrets. You're here for the murder of the 'foreigner', isn't that so?"

"Yes, a bad business. You live here?"

"Oh, yes, we have an apartment over the bar."

"Where's your bedroom. At the front, or in the back?"

"In front, why?"

"Did you happen to hear anything, about six days ago, during the night from Monday to Tuesday?"

"No, not as far as I know. What should I have heard?"

"The starting of a speed boat, a speed boat with large engines, or perhaps the arrival, or departure of such a boat."

"No, I really wouldn't know."

"You're a heavy sleeper?"

"You could say that. As soon as I hit the mattress, I'm dead to the world."

"Good for you, but too bad for us. Ah, well, it can't be helped."

"But you know, I'll ask my wife, she's a very light sleeper. I'll go get her."

He went inside and reappeared several moments later accompanied by a motherly woman, who clearly had come straight from the kitchen. She approached, still wiping her hands on her apron. The man resumed the conversation, introducing her in an offhand manner.

"Vasso, these are the gentlemen from the police, from Athens. They want to ask you something."

Spiros stood up, shook her hand and said:

"Your husband just informed us that you live above the bar and that your bedroom is in the front of the house."

"That's right, sir."

"Well, your husband told us that you're a light sleeper and I wanted to ask you if you heard anything strange during the night from last Monday to Tuesday?"

"Between Monday and Tuesday?"

"Yes, between Monday and Tuesday. I assume it's usually quiet on the quay, at night?"

"Yes, nothing much going on."

"Please think carefully."

"Well, now that you mention it, I *did* hear something, but I can't be sure if it was Monday night, or Tuesday night."

"Really, ma'am, the day isn't all that important. But tell me, what did you hear?"

"Yes, well, let me think . . . Yes, I remember. I heard something and I thought at first that it might have been a truck, or a bus. I'd been sleeping, of course, I wasn't really awake yet. I remember waking up and thinking: Is it already so late? Is the bus here already? The bus starts at six thirty, you know, and it always wakes me up. But when I looked at the clock I noticed that it was only three thirty."

"So you heard an engine?"

"Yes."

"Did it sound like someone started an engine?"

"Yes, now that you mention it, it sounded like that, yes. Yes, well, I didn't think much about it, at the time, I went back to sleep."

"And that was about three thirty?"

"No, not about three thirty, it was *exactly* three thirty. *That* I remember very well."

"Ma'am, you have helped us immensely. Thank you very much."

"At your service, gentlemen," she answered and left the terrace.

While they were still theorizing about what they had just heard, the Harbor Police constable came to the terrace and said:

"I expected to find you here."

"You found something?"

"Nothing important, but it's something." He took a piece of paper from a pocket and started to read: "*Christina* was in Aiyina on May 15th, same crew, no particulars. She departed on the 16th at five in the morning and took passage through the Corinthian Canal, same crew, no particulars. Apparently she proceeded from there to the Island of Keffalinia, because they delivered a Transit Log to the Customs in Argostolion. That means she went to a foreign country, most likely Italy."

"Sicily?"

"Possible, but it's a good distance."

"How long did they remain in Argostolion?"

"One night."

"How was the weather?"

"I asked that too. Calm sea, Beaufort 3, or less, from the North-Northeast. Excellent sailing weather for Sicily."

"Well, we know for sure, then," concluded Inspector Karatzis. "To me it's as clear as day. Destination: Mafia!"

*6. Brussels, the same day

The Captain of Police Headquarters in Brussels arrived at his desk at exactly nine o'clock in the morning and looked at the reports that had accumulated during the course of the night. He was a precise man, obsessed by the thought that administration and paperwork could never be complete enough. He prided himself on finishing everything the same day it came in. When he left for home in the evening, his large desk was totally bare, with the exception of a small box along one edge wherein he kept three pens. The first thing he looked at in the morning was the waste paper basket. If it was empty, he knew that the cleaning crew had been through the office during the night. It had become second nature to him to check and double check everything. He felt it could often be a matter of life and death that everything was handled completely, precisely and accurately. No detail was to be ignored and every little fact, no matter how seemingly unimportant, had to be placed in the overall scheme of things. That which was dismissed as trivial at one moment, could, perhaps, the next moment provide the vital clue to a solution. He read every file with interest and concentration, whether it was a report of a stolen bicycle, a bank robbery, or a mugging. He had a fantastic, near photographic memory, for names. Thousands were stored in his memory and usually he was able to connect them to a particular offense. He sorted reports according to kind and importance in separate piles. Then he suddenly noticed a telex message, a picture and a fingerprint form, transmitted by Interpol in Athens. The Captain read the documents with his usual concentration and picked up the telephone. A moment later there was a knock on the door and an Inspector, cigarette in the corner of his mouth, entered. He noticed the look on his superior's face and was suddenly aware of his smoking. Feeling caught, abashed, he murmured "Please excuse me, sir," went back into the hall and extinguished his cigarette in the large ashtray outside the door. When he entered for the second time, the Captain said:

"You all smoke too much."

"You're right, sir."

"If you know I'm right, why don't you quit?"

"I wish I could."

"Just quit. But enough . . . I have a request from Interpol in Athens."

"Is it urgent?"

"Of course it's urgent. We have to show our international friends that Belgium is capable of more than just drinking beer."

There he goes again, thought the Inspector, the same story. As if everybody in the department had nothing better to do all day, then twiddle their thumbs. With a friendly face he answered:

"But of course, sir. I'll start at once. I'll get back to you as soon as possible."

He took the papers and left the room, happy to be able to light up again and to sit down at his own desk, among his own mess of papers, empty coffee cups and other odds and ends. He looked intently at the photo and the fingerprints, read the name and stood up. He took an elevator and went to a room filled with VDTs, printers, modems and all kinds of equipment that went far beyond his comprehension. For more then two years he had a terminal on his own desk, but could never muster the patience to understand it. He was one of the old-timers, came up through the ranks by dogged and patient determination, a "hands-on" policeman. Of course, all that modern equipment was fantastic. What took weeks in the old days, those bastards would spit out in less than ten seconds, but himself behind a keyboard, no, he was too old for that. His ways were set. He approached a woman in front of one of the screens and gave her the name he had received from the Captain.

"Angela, would you please find out about this guy. Who is he, where does he live, what does he do. In short, anything you can find out. It's for Interpol, so it's urgent."

"Can't you do it yourself?"

"You can do it so much better."

"Hypocrite! Are you going to be at your desk?"

"Of course, just knowing you might call me, will glue me to my chair."

He went back to the elevator and pushed for the third floor. I should really cut down on smoking and walk more stairs, he thought when he arrived at the floor above. He went to the Dactyloscopic Service. Behind this door resided the latest technological marvel, developed by the American firm of De La Rue Printak. Years of research and development had gone into the completion of this latest computer. It was the most important development in fingerprinting of the twentieth Century. It could compare more than 4,000 fingerprints per second. They had explained to him how it worked and he had learned the information bulletin by heart in order to appear informed, but he really did not understand the machine.

"Marcel," he addressed one of the people in the room, "I've got something for you. It's from Interpol in Athens, so the boss says it's urgent."

"The boss labels everything urgent," answered Marcel.

"Here it is." He showed the fingerprint form. "Make sure you don't wrinkle it. Do not spindle, fold, staple, or mutilate. The boss wants it back in his files in the same pristine state."

"The boss can go to hell. Let's see it."

"Usable?"

"Excellent even."

"Here's the name."

"You have a name? Then you don't need me!"

"Check and double check, my boy, you should know that. Trust everybody, but always cut the deck, or, as Lenin used to say: 'Trust is good, but control is better'. The boss wants to make sure the fingerprints match the name."

"Yes, yes, I get it! I'll see what I can do."

"About an hour?"

"Since we have the name, you can wait for it."

Marcel sat down behind the deceptively simple keyboard, typed in the necessary instructions, was rewarded by a few requests from the computer and finally typed in the name of Robert Dubour. He added the date and place of birth: August 13, 1937 and Antwerp.

It took several seconds before the name on the screen was replaced by a set of fingerprints.

"Well, he's in the files, let's compare."

He studied the screen, flipped through a number of computer "pages" and compared the fingerprints from Athens.

"Well, that's obvious," said Marcel, pensively looking at the screen. "You don't need me for that, you can see for yourself."

The Inspector looked intently at the screen and after a moment he said:

"They don't match."

"Very good. This is someone else. There isn't a single point of congruence."

"Dubour has different fingers, my friend."

"So, the old nitpicker upstairs is right again. Where did they get the prints. Can you look that up?"

"Of course, just a moment."

Marcel's fingers flew over the keyboard and new information emerged on the screen.

"Military service. This is a print from 1958 and it's the only one we have."

"That could mean he has no criminal record."

"It could."

"But now I'm really curious about the identity of the guy we're looking for."

"That's going to take a little longer, but with a little bit of luck, I should be able to tell you in about an hour."

"I'll be at my desk, please give me a call."

"You can get it on your own terminal," answered Marcel.

"I don't even know how to turn that thing on. No, I'll call you, I can do that much."

"You must really get used to modern communication methods, my man," said the computer expert.

"I'd be crazy. If I did, I'd get square pupils, just like you."

* * *

At his desk, surrounded by his comfortable and familiar mess, he called the Captain and told him about the discovery.

"I say it again and again, we can't check enough," concluded the Captain.

"I know, sir."

"Call me when you know more."

"You can get it on your own terminal, sir," said the Inspector with a smile around the lips that again surrounded a cigarette.

"Just call me," growled the Captain.

38

About an hour later the phone rang and the Inspector heard the voice of Marcel.

"I found him. There's no doubt about it."

"Go on."

"The corpse in Greece is Jean Louis Dupre. Born in Brugge on February 22, 1935. Mother: Maria Magdalena Shivers, born May 13, 1906 at Antwerp. Father: Carl Stephan Dupre, born September 9, 1903 at Brugge. That's all."

"Where did you get that information?"

"Military records again. 1955, no further entries."

"Thank you." He broke the connection and dialed another number.

"Angela, what have you found so far?"

"Nothing much is known about Dubour. Father and mother died shortly after each other. No dates, that's strange. Shortly after WW II he signed as volunteer for the Congo. Sergeant First Class with the *Force Publique* in Leopoldville. Honorary discharge in 1960 after the Congo became independent and became Zaire. After that he was all over the place, around the world. He regularly renewed his passport at various Belgian Embassies and Consulates. Latest renewal was three years ago in Athens. No known address. We haven't any addresses for him at all. Very strange."

"Any criminal records?"

"No, nothing."

"Do you have a photo?"

"Should be there, but you'd have to get that out of the archives at the State Department."

"Please make me a print-out and I'll come and get it."

"See you."

"But I have another one for you. Jean Louis Dupre, born February 22, 1935 at Brugge."

"I'll call you back."

"Thank you, darling, I wouldn't know what to do without you."

"Good thing your wife can't hear you."

After hanging up, he looked for, and found, the number for the Department of Passports at the State Department. He reached an official and requested the file on Dubour. A motorcycle policeman was dispatched to pick it up and half an hour later the file was on his desk. He looked through the file and compared Dubour's photographs that had been collected over the years. The original request for a passport came from the Embassy in Pretoria and was dated October 3, 1961. The latest was from Athens and was dated September 30, 1981. He compared the photos and looked at the face that gradually grew older. The latest one he compared to the picture sent by Athens and he had to conclude that there was no doubt. The pictures were all of the same man. There was an interval of five years, the regular period, between a request for a passport, or renewal. There was no information from before 1961. That meant that the details would have to be in the Registrar's Office at the place of birth, Antwerp, or perhaps with the Defense Department. He called around and again a motorcycle policeman was dispatched. This time to the Registrar's Office in Antwerp. That was about 35 miles from the center of Brussels. The motorcycle cop would be back before one in the afternoon. At a quarter to one, the phone rang. It was Angela.

"Your Dupre is a strange one, too," she said.

"Tell me."

"Also military service in the Congo. Also volunteer."

"They were all volunteers at the time."

"Well, anyway, he also joined the *Force Publique* under General Janssen in Leopoldville, but he deserted in 1960. It is assumed that he became a mercenary, he might have joined the mercenary army of Jacques Schramme. Does that mean anything to you?"

"Yes, that name rings a bell, loud and clear! Schramme and his so-called mercenary army were no more than a bunch of bandits. They worked for Tsjombe when he wanted to secede the province of Katanga."

"Before my time, but you're right. As far as we know he was with the mercenaries only during the first attempt at secession, because he was arrested in Pretoria, in 1963, for currency smuggling. He spent three years in Pretoria Central Prison. There was an attempt to have him extradited to Belgium because of the desertion, but that never happened. After that we lost sight of him. He never asked for a passport, or anything. He just disappeared."

"No death certificate?"

"Nothing. Nobody reported him as missing, either. You got yourself a couple of loners there."

"It isn't a couple of guys, Angela, it's just one guy and he's dead."

*7. Palermo, the same day

It is usually hot and busy in Palermo. As in every city with too many cars and too little space. Loud people and small collisions are the dominating sounds. Behind the large doors of the old houses that all resemble museums are the court yards. *I cortili*, in the vernacular. Peace and quiet reigns there and small, secluded splinters of paradise have been created in the busy city. Palm trees, banana trees and tall cypresses rise above the rooftops. Their only purpose to be decorative and grow older. Most of the court yards are paved with hand-hewn flagstone and a fountain is seldom missing. Imposing stairs lead to dark, cool upper floors. Rubbing and polishing is the order of the day and all the family heirlooms are treasured and preserved. The silver and the pottery, the furniture and the linen. Large, frozen interiors where never, since time immemorial, has a single piece of furniture been moved from its appointed place, where the curtains, hand-made by father's great-grandmother, are still displayed in all their splendor. A tradition that could be admired, if the presence of that other Sicilian tradition was less terrible.

41

Headquarters of the *Carabinieri* in Palermo is probably the most heavily guarded police station in the world. The *vendettas* that have become a part of the island's tradition are not only applied to the traitorous members of the various Mafia families, but are also, increasingly, aimed at the representatives of Law and Order, the judiciary and the police force. The killing, often in broad day light, of police people, judges, lawyers, or politicians who oppose the Mafia, has become an accepted fact of life. The offices of potential victims and their families are constantly guarded.

The ugly, semi-modern building at the Corso Vittorio Emanuele looks like most government buildings in Italy. In a country that is considered to be the trend setter for form and elegance in most things, the designs for government buildings seem to be merely dusted-off originals from the time of Mussolini. There are no palm trees in the courtyard of the police building, only police cars, most of them with bulletproof windows and also a number of armored cars. The windows of the building are always closed and covered with heavy bars. The entrance is guarded by a squad of officers who are required to wear bulletproof vests. Their automatic weapons are always at the ready. Inside the building it is cool and the ceilings are high.

Inspector Giorgio Bergarmi read the message from Athens and spoke to the man opposite:

"Alberto, look at this. Perhaps we should pass this on to the *Circondario Marittimo*."

"Is it important?"

"Interpol."

"Well, I would perhaps involve the Water Police, but I wouldn't let them have overall jurisdiction," he answered while reading. "I mean, if you'd like some nice, fresh fish tonight, they're probably just capable of handling that, but you shouldn't expect much more from them. And this is really rather important, apparently."

"Well, the Greeks get a bit excited, at times."

"Yes, maybe. But look what it says here. This was a sizeable boat and just two guys aboard. It wasn't a pleasure cruiser."

"Could be a couple of queers," laughed Giorgio.

"Two homos in an old boat?"

"Yes, it doesn't seem very urgent. Plenty of real work, here."

"A Belgian and a Greek. One Robert Dubour and a Petros Theologitis. The owner is someone else: Neville James Footman. English registry. Rather international, don't you think?"

"You may be right."

"A lot has happened among our dear family members lately. Quite a few have found a new resting place."

"I'll call Luigi," said Giorgio. Then, after a moment he spoke into the telephone:

"Buongiorno, Luigi, Giorgio here . . . yes, everything's fine here . . . calm . . . *i tuoi stanno bene* . . ? Just a question . . . did an old sailing boat put in over there, around the seventeenth? *Christina* . . . British registry . . . yes, please, I'll hold while you check . . ."

He placed his hand over the mouthpiece and said: "You wanna bet he's going to be curious?" He continued speaking into the telephone, removing his hand:

"You found it? When did the ship arrive? . . . No, we don't know that . . . no, nothing the matter, for the time being . . . the message came from abroad . . . what do you care where it came from, I only want to know when she made port . . . May eighteen . . . Did you prepare the *certificato*? . . . In Messina, aha . . . crew? . . . Luigi, please, just tell me what you know, you sound like an old woman. . . . No, I'm not keeping anything from you, we don't know anything ourselves, yet . . . two in the crew, two men, yes, that's right . . . Dubour and Theologitis . . . yes, we knew that . . . Where did they go? . . . What's the number of your guys in Trapani? . . . 36287 . . . *Grazie*, Luigi . . . Si, si, Luigi, if it's important we'll let you know . . . Goodbye for now, *arrivederci*."

He threw the receiver back on the hook and remarked:

"He's really nosy, you know that?"

43

"Well, at least you'll keep him awake tonight. Anyway, they went to Trapani?"

"Yes, I'll ring them, too." He dialed the number.

"Hello, *Carabinieri* Headquarters in Palermo. Inspector Giorgio Bergarmi here. I would like to verify the arrival of a sailboat on the eighteenth, the *Christina*? . . . Yes? . . . Any particulars? . . . Two men, right . . . a Greek, Theologitis, and a Belgian, Dubour . . . British registry . . . yes, that checks . . . Anything else? . . . Si . . . si . . . a letter . . . how do you know? . . . Si . . . si . . . the next day . . . *Grazie, arrivederci, capitano.*"

He replaced the receiver, a lot more gently this time, and addressed Alberto.

"One of the guys from the boat asked the Harbor Master for directions to the Post Office and the Harbor Master walked over with him. The man from the boat sent a letter, a fat envelope, according to the Harbor Master. Again, according to the same source, the guy from the boat spoke fluent Italian with a Sicilian accent. The crew indicated that they would leave for Favignana the next day."

"It's really starting to become a little *too* international."

"I'll call the Greeks, why don't you call Favignana."

Both grabbed a telephone and dialed. They concluded their respective conversations almost simultaneously and looked at each other to see who would start.

"Go ahead, you start."

"No, you start, my news is much more interesting than yours."

"*Christina* did indeed arrive, but stayed at anchor in the bay next to the harbor. Next day the ship was gone, but a tender was found in the harbor."

"That could mean that whoever left the boat did not return aboard."

"*Ecco*, exactly, because it was too far to swim. What's your news?"

44

"A corpse. The Belgian has been killed on a Greek island near Athens. Tortured and a bullet through his head. The Greeks think it's vengeance. The killers tore the place apart. It's certain that they were professionals. They were looking for something, but apparently didn't find what they were looking for. The Greeks are sending a picture and additional information. What do you think? Any ideas?"

"The envelope from Trapani!"

"Exactly, they were looking for the contents of that envelope."

"I think we should inform the boss."

"Good idea."

* * *

The Chief Inspector was in his office with the high windows at the front of the building. It was the only office with daylight. The glass was bulletproof and an armed guard, machine gun at the ready, was on permanent duty at the door. They entered and the Chief Inspector looked up from what he was reading over the top of his half glasses and pointed silently at two chairs against the wall. Giorgio told the story while the Chief Inspector looked out of the window, presenting an impression of total disinterest. When Giorgio stopped talking, his boss did not react but kept staring out of the window without saying a word. It created an uncomfortable, strange atmosphere. After several minutes of deadly silence, the Chief Inspector finally turned in his chair, looked at them and said:

"Go to Favignana, but *prego*, be careful."

He then continued his reading.

"If I didn't know from personal experience," Alberto said when they were outside the office, "that he is the nicest, most loyal and most trustworthy person on the island, I'd probably like to kick him, sometimes."

"Yes, he's different, you can say that again, but he's a rock."

"What's the plan? It's now quarter past five and it's at least an hour's drive. It'll be dark by nine. Well?"

"I think we'd better leave in the morning, around eight. That way we'll have the whole day."

"I agree."

"I keep trying to remember what the saltwater cop from Favignana said and now I do. From the nineteenth to the twentieth, was the boat there, or not?"

"Yes, she was there, during the night of the nineteenth."

"Do you know what else happened that night?"

"No."

"Well, that's the night that Joe Bacelli, a respected businessman, our good friend and much esteemed tourist from New York, died of a heart attack in the house of Alfonso Franchi, at Favignana."

"Well, that's a coincidence."

"And you wanted to hand the case over to the Harbor cops."

*8. Pretoria, Tuesday, May 29, 1984

The Warden of Pretoria Central Prison read the telex from Police Headquarters in Johannesburg, placed the file of Jean Louis Dupre in front of him and started the report for which he had been asked.

Report concerning Inmate # 29570
>   Name: Jean Louis Dupre
>   Born: February 22, 1935 at Brugge, Belgium
>   Incarcerated: June 14, 1963
>   4 Years incarceration, economic delict
>   Early release on June 14, 1966 for good behavior

General impressions:
Prisoner 29570 was a quiet man who served his time in an exemplary fashion. No difficulties were reported during his incarcer-

ation. It was clear from the first day of imprisonment that he separated himself from the other prisoners and went his own way. On the second day he indicated a desire to study and he submitted a written request to that effect on June 18, 1963. This request was presented by me, the undersigned, to the governing authorities who granted the request as witnessed by a letter, dated July 3, 1963, which was made a part of the record. It was noted that prisoner 29570 was fluent in English, French, Dutch, Italian and German. During his infrequent conversations with the black prisoners, it became evident that he had more than a cursory knowledge of Swahili.

After consulting with the proper authorities, it was decided to assign prisoner 29570 to a single cell. Upon request, duly granted, he was permitted the use of a typewriter, a desk and a modest amount of writing supplies. The assigned Parole Officer visited regularly and supplied the prisoner with books, newspapers and magazines in several languages. The prisoner studied Greek, economy, anthropology and geography. Prisoner 29570 completed a series of studies during his incarceration and obtained a number of A-Levels from Cambridge University, England. Prisoner 29570 did not receive visitors, received no personal mail and did not send any letters. The undersigned, as well as other prison personnel maintained cordial relations with the prisoner. He was trustworthy, was aware of his past failings and prepared himself for the future.

Pretoria, May 29, 1984

This is a true and accurate statement and hereby so attested and signed:

Willem Jan Streijtbos
Warden, Pretoria Central Prison

*9. London, the same day

Immediately after receiving the call from his Superintendent, the young inspector, nattily dressed in a gray three piece suit, picked up his note pad and walked in the direction of his superior's office. The way in which he walked betrayed his past as a rugby player for London Welsh. He had been one of the best players on the team, a feared defensive lineman who usually stopped his opponents. He had had the opportunity to become a professional and had even had an offer from the United States, but had given preference to his studies. Rugby was now nothing more than a hobby, reserved for week-ends. He trained a junior team. He knocked gently on the mahogany door with the brass plate that shone like gold because of the incessant polishing. He heard the voice of his superior and entered.

"Good afternoon, Thomas," said the Superintendent with a friendly voice that retained a trace of the accent of his birthplace and always sounded somewhat lilting.

"Good afternoon, sir, you called?"

"Yes, my boy, sit down." The Superintendent pointed at a chair. He looked intently at the young inspector and said: "You look fine, my boy, that's a nice suit. I like that. You haven't been with us long, but you know what's what."

"Thank you, sir."

"How long have you been with us?"

"Six months, sir."

"You know, I like it when people in Special Branch look good. I'm proud of our department, Thomas, I don't mind telling you. The world around us degenerates, but I would like to hold on to the old traditions, Thomas, and *one* of those is that we dress properly. We owe it to ourselves. New Scotland Yard isn't just any police station, you know, New Scotland Yard is an institution, a legend. Jeans don't belong here."

While he continued in this vein, his pet subject, he stood up and went to stand in front of the windows, hands on his back.

"Jeans belong in New York, San Francisco. Don't think that I look down on the Americans, not at all, they are professional policemen and fantastic colleagues, but we're different. We're British, we have traditions and we mustn't forget them. Why do I carry on like this? I didn't call you for that, that can wait. I'm telling you all this, because you are one of the newer members of our force. I've read your reports, your older colleagues are happy with you and I would like you to continue that way. I hope you'll be with us a long time."

"I intend to, sir."

"I understand. You're of the generation that one day will lead this department, our department, and will determine the way in which it will be perceived by the public. I'll be leaving in about two years, my job will be done. But, let's discuss the case for which I called you."

He sat down at his desk.

"I've received a telex from Interpol in Athens, a photograph of a victim and a name. Look at it." He leaned forward and handed the papers to Thomas.

"Find out who that is. I don't think we'll be involved, but you never know. I talked to Athens and they assume that the killing is probably a vengeance action of organized crime. Keep at it, keep in contact with the people who are working on it. It's of vital importance that we keep an eye on these kinds of crimes. They have a way of settling in, not unlike the large multinationals. Before you know it, we have them on our doorstep. I added the name of the contact person in Athens."

"Do you want me to keep you personally informed, sir?"

"For the time being."

"I shall start at once, sir."

Young Thomas Cowley stood up and left the room with the high ceiling and distinguished wainscotting. He read the name when he returned to his desk: Neville James Footman, born December 11, 1934 at Kirkby-in-Ashfield. He looked at the dead face in the photo and shivered. That was still allowed if you had only

49

been on the job a mere six months. He took his trench coat from the hook and left the large building in Whitehall to walk in the direction of the Passport Office which was only a few blocks from New Scotland Yard. He showed his badge to the doorman and a little later he was talking to a friendly man. He gave the name supplied by the Superintendent, sat down at one of the desks and waited for the file to arrive.

When he received the file, he compared the passport photo with the photo of the dead man, noted the dates on which Footman had applied for a passport and the numbers. The first one had been issued on November 5, 1965. The address was listed as 57 Wagon Road, London North and had not changed in twenty years. The birth certificate, required before the first passport could be issued, was also in the file. He left the building and took a cab to Wagon Road. It was a commonplace street with low, identical houses on either side. He told the driver to wait and approached the door of number 57. There was no bell, but a large brass knocker in the shape of a fist. The name plate on the door announced the domicile of John A. Williams. He heard footsteps inside in response to his knocking and a little later the door was opened by a middle-aged lady. Again he showed his badge and said:

"Good afternoon, missus, I'm Inspector Cowley from Scotland Yard."

The woman looked at him in panic and asked:

"Oh my God, is something the matter?"

"No, missus, don't be alarmed. I just want some information."

"Is it about my son?"

"No, ma'am, it's not about your son. It's about this man."

He showed the photograph.

"Is 'e dead?" She looked with horror at the photo.

"Yes, ma'am. Do you know this man?"

"No, I've never seen 'im."

"Does the name Neville James Footman mean anything to you?"

50

"No, never 'eard of it. Should I 'ave?"

"According to our information, this man is supposed to live at this address."

"Well, as you can see, 'e doesn't live 'ere. Are you sure you 'ave the right address?"

"Do you know anyone in the neighborhood with this name?"

"No, never 'eard of it."

"And you have never seen this man, you are sure?"

"Positive."

"How long have you lived here, ma'am?"

"More than twenty five years. My son was born 'ere and 'e's already twenty four."

"Did you ever receive mail addressed to this name?"

"No, never. Really. I 'ave never 'eard the name before."

"Thank you very much, ma'am. Sorry to have bothered you."

"Sorry I couldn't 'elp you."

Cowley went back to the cab and directed the driver to Somerset House. In one of the departments of this building were stored the death certificates of millions of Britons. He already knew what he was going to find regarding the mysterious Mr. Footman, but nevertheless, he wanted to be sure.

He returned an hour later to the Yard and rang the Superintendent.

"Please excuse me, sir," he said in response to the voice at the other end of the line.

"Go ahead, Thomas."

"The usual story, sir. Neville James Footman died on March 15, 1935, at the age of three months as a result of pneumonia."

"I had a feeling about this, Thomas. The entire system of registry we use, is wrong. Any criminal with a modicum of brains can obtain a British passport within a few weeks for the mere expenditure of a few pounds."

"I am sorry to have to agree with you, sir."

"Well, put it on the telex and dispatch it to Athens."

"I shall, sir."

"And keep in contact, Thomas, I want to be kept informed."

"Very good, sir."

Inspector Thomas Cowley of New Scotland Yard replaced the receiver on the hook and went to the Communications Center.

*10. Favignana, the same day

At eight o'clock in the morning Giorgio Bergarmi and Alberto Logoluso departed in their Alfa Romeo for the small island of Favignana, to the west of Sicily. An hour later they stood in front of the ferry that was to bring them to the island. The small harbor where they entered was dominated by a large, deserted building from the previous century that had once housed a canning factory before the tuna in the Tyrrhanian Sea had been wiped out. A bleak building that evoked memories of bloody scenes and long work days in the killing heat for meager wages. Across the harbor was the snobbish house, square and symmetrical, that had once been the domicile of the family that had bought the island over a century ago and had been the only employer for the population. The paint had peeled on the extravagant decorations and the shutters were broken and crooked. Somewhere in Italy, no doubt, there was an heir who managed the family fortunes, but who had no interest in maintaining the old house.

The old men in the village could remember it well. How, on Sunday, they deferentially doffed their caps and made a bow when the family passed. It was a time of cast-down eyes and folded hands. When the sea had been emptied of fish and the tuna disappeared, the younger men and women departed for better regions. All that remained were the old men who in times gone by had gutted the tuna with bloody aprons as their only protection and the old women who had lost their youths on the assembly line. Today they sauntered aimlessly through the gray streets, in a village that had nothing to offer, on a forgotten island.

In the center of the village was a bronze bust of the man who had lived in the big house, but nobody looked at it. A small, neglected quay jutted about a hundred yards into the sea and had become the gathering place for a chaotic assembly of boats. A few tourists visited during the summer, because someone else's poverty is idyllic. A few hundred yards from the sea, away from the poverty and neglect, there were a few modern bungalows, belonging to wealthy families from Naples and Rome, to let them escape the summer heat in their respective cities. The deserted, stately homes next to the old vineyards, that originated from *before* the building of the cannery had been transformed into small palaces with high fences and automatically locking gates. The owners were seldom seen and did not mingle with the native population.

The two inspectors drove off the ferry in the direction of the village and stopped in front of the decrepit office of the local *Carabinieri*. The corporal, in his best uniform, all shined and spruced, was waiting for them and greeted them exuberantly.

"You had a good journey, signori?" was his first question.

"*Perfetto*, ispettore."

That "ispettore" was received well, because it was several ranks above that of corporal, several ranks higher, in fact, than he would ever reach.

"What can I do for you. You have only to say. I've kept the entire day free for you, I can help you in anything."

"We would not have expected otherwise, ispettore, in Palermo they know that you have things under control, here."

"We never have problems, here," was the serious answer while he made a deprecating gesture with his right hand, sticking his underlip forward in the manner of Mussolini.

"You know why we're here?"

"That I know, but I wonder what you hope to find,"

"The boat we're after, the *Christina*, seems to have called here," said Alberto.

"Not in our yacht harbor," pointing at the neglected quay.

"We understand. The boat seems to have anchored outside the harbor."

"I told you that over the telephone. Myself, I've not seen it. There was a tender and I confiscated it, as soon as I knew that Palermo was interested."

"How did you know the tender belonged to the yacht?"

"It was in the harbor for about ten days and nobody knew who it belonged to. When you gave me the date of the *Christina*, yesterday, I checked when the tender was discovered and the dates matched."

"Did anybody see the man who came ashore in it?"

"That investigation I set aside, for the time being," he announced ponderously. "I only heard about the case yesterday, so I first chained up the tender. It could be evidence, isn't that so?"

"Very shrewd, ispettore."

Every time he was addressed as "ispettore" he felt himself a little more important and he started to speak more formally.

"Why don't we take a look," suggested Giorgio.

Together they walked toward the quay where the inflatable tender was moored. The oars were still in the boat.

"Who told you that *Christina* was anchored here?"

"That was Francesco. Look, there he is, in his boat." He pointed at an old man who was working on some nets.

"Francesco!" he hailed the man. "Please come here a moment. These are colleagues from Palermo and they want to ask you about the boat you saw."

"What they want to know?" asked the old man suspiciously, without making any move to leave his boat, or come closer.

"Just come here a moment, they want to know what you saw."

"I've said everything that I knew," answered the fisherman sullenly.

"Just come here, these people have a job to do."

Slowly and reluctantly Francesco stood up, climbed onto the quay, approached them and told his story in one short sentence:

"The boat was anchored around the headlands, Sandro, I sailed past her, more I don't know." He started to turn around.

"Was it the *Christina*?" asked Alberto pleasantly.

"Yes, that was the name on the bow, English flag."

"Did you notice anything particular?"

"No."

"Was anybody on board?"

"I didn't see anybody."

"What time was it?"

"About six, it wasn't dark yet."

"And you haven't seen the yacht again, after that?"

"No, because I went fishing the next day and she was gone."

"Do you remember what day that was?"

"The same day that somebody in one of the big houses had a heart attack."

"How can you be so sure?"

"Everybody was talking about it."

"And the next day you found the tender?"

"Yes, when I went fishing, just around the bend."

"So, it wasn't in the harbor?"

"No, around the bend, I told you."

"That's where you found it?"

"Yes, it was pulled up to the shore."

"What did you do then?"

"At first I left it there, but when it was still there, the next day, I took it along. There's no law against it."

"In retrospect, didn't you think it a bit strange? First you saw a ship that disappeared the next day and then you find her tender."

"I wouldn't know and I could care less what people do with their property, I leave them alone. I found the dinghy and I claim it as salvage."

"You didn't think it necessary to inform Sandro?"

"I told you, I mind my own business." There was a petulant tone in his voice.

"What was the weather like that day? At sea, I mean."

"The first day I passed it, it was calm, but there was a bit of a breeze during the night."

"Can you tell me exactly where you found the tender?"

"I told you, just around the bend, in the bay."

"So, it wasn't visible from the harbor?"

"No, of course not, otherwise I would have known about it," interrupted the corporal importantly.

"What sort of bay is it. Are there houses?"

"No, nobody goes there. Just steep rock walls, nothing else."

"And nobody lives nearby?"

"No, nobody."

"This is a small village. Everybody knows everything about everybody. Did you hear nothing at all about the sailboat? Did anybody mention it?" Giorgio asked.

"I heard nothing."

"Ispettore, could we take a look there?"

"Well, yes, that's a bit difficult. We do have a patrol boat, but it's being repaired. We've been waiting more than three months for parts," answered the corporal.

"Signor Francesco, would you be so kind as to take us there?"

"Listen, I want nothing to do with it, also, I'm almost out of fuel and . . . eh, . . . I should be fishing."

"Just tell me how much it would cost."

He thought a moment about this unexpected fortune and after he had mentioned an amount that was much too high but that the "gentlemen" from Palermo could only accept, they agreed to leave in two hours. The fisherman disappeared to fill a jerry-can with fuel and the policemen walked in the direction of the village. In the village they sat down on a terrace. The bar owner looked a bit strangely at the unexpected visitors, but suspected them to be police.

"You must be here for the boat," he remarked.

"How do you know?" asked Giorgio.

"Well, that's logical. If a nice little tender is found in the harbor and nobody even so much as touches it for ten days and when at the same time an American tourist with an Italian name happens to die of a heart attack, what would you think?"

"No idea," said Alberto.

"Well, it's probably too hot to steal."

"You mean, nobody wants to take the risk."

"Si, si, you figured it out," said the bar owner derisively.

"Do you happen to know what happened to the sailboat?"

"You're from the police, aren't you?"

"Yes."

"Palermo?"

"Yes," answered Alberto and showed his identification.

"I know nothing," answered the owner and turned to walk away.

"Hey, wait a moment, you must hear some things, I think."

"Too much, sometimes," came the curt reply.

"So, what do you know about the boat?"

Reluctantly the man took a chair, straddled it backward, placed his arms on the back and whispered: "Let me put it this way, it was a nice funeral. A nicer funeral then we're used to on this island, or can afford."

"Did you see the funeral?"

"Of course, and a lot of well-known faces."

"Did you see this man?" Giorgio showed the photo of the corpse from Serifos.

The man studied the photograph with care.

"Perhaps," he said finally.

"What do you mean 'perhaps', was he there or wasn't he?"

"It's possible, but I didn't look that carefully." Again he wanted to leave.

Giorgio raised his hands in a gesture of despair.

"What use is that? Do you recognize him, or not?"

"Listen, Mister Inspector, or whatever you are," answered the bar owner, "we're just common folk here. We ain't got nothing, all of us. Everything I own you can see by just looking around. And I'm one of the lucky ones. The rest, on this island, have even less.

This island has been squeezed like a sponge. And that's exactly the way we feel ourselves. Most of Italy has been squeezed like that. But we're still alive and we make the best of it. That's the only thing we've got left. We're still alive. And that they'll take away too, if it suits them. You should know how it is, here on Sicily. What does it get us, if we help you? What guarantees me that I can trust you? Who guarantees me that you won't get a secret call tonight so that you can tell them who has said too much, here? Nobody here will talk, ispettore, you should know that. We're used to turning our backs when something happens that's better not to know. Even worse, if we can pick up a few thousand liras by saying what they want us to say, we do it like a shot. Because that means that you can perhaps pay off a loan from some shark that has nailed you to the wall for life, just to make the interest payments. And they know that, you understand, Mister Ispettore? They know that! And that's the way it is on *this* island."

"Yes, it's a bitch," answered Alberto dejectedly. He rested his head on his hands and closed his eyes.

It remained silent for a long time. Nobody made a noise.

"But anyway," the owner said suddenly, less vehemently, "I heard that the boat was anchored in the bay. Somebody heard an explosion that night and saw a fire. I don't know any more." This time he rose resolutely and went behind the bar. Without a word, Alberto placed some coins on the table and they left.

* * *

The ancient, single cylinder engine of the fishing boat puffed peacefully when they left the harbor. The bay was to starboard and within twenty minutes they reached it. The fisherman knew the waters like his back pocket and sailed slowly along the steep rock formations and the narrow shingle of gravelly beach at the foot. As everywhere, here too, the narrow beach had been polluted by plastic remnants of packing material without which the modern world seemed unable to ship, or sell, anything. Alberto asked the fisherman to sail as close as possible to the shore and the old man complied carefully. When they heard the gentle scraping of the bottom against the keel, the man stopped the engine and threw an anchor over the side. Giorgio and Alberto took off their socks and shoes, rolled their trouser legs above the knees and went over the side. The "ispettore" reluctantly did the same and followed them to the shore. They walked over the sand and gravel and looked at the junk around them. Alberto was the first one to find a piece of wood.

"Come and look at this," he said and showed his find to his partner.

"Yes," answered Giorgio pensively. "I know what you think and I'm afraid you're right."

"What color was the boat?"

"We never got that information, but it was a wooden one, that's certain."

"How certain are you?"

"She was built in 1929 and she was a Colin Archer."

"What does that mean?"

"You know little of boats, Alberto. The Colin Archer is a famous design of Mr. Archer from England and they were all made out of wood. After the war, the same design has also been built in steel, but most certainly not in 1929. If I'm wrong, I'll eat the boat."

"Francesco!" called Alberto, "what was the color of the ship you saw here?"

"What!?"

"The color, what color was she painted?"

"Black with a white border and varnished upper works."

"Well, you see," observed Alberto, "this is a piece of the hull. It's painted black on one side."

"There's a piece of one of the ribs, copper nail." Giorgio pointed at the detail.

They searched the beach some more and found other pieces presumably originating from *Christina*. Then they went back aboard the fishing boat.

Four hours later the fast, gray boats of the *Carabinieri* in Palermo were anchored in the bay. Divers went over the side and a small army of detectives searched the beach in detail. Toward evening the wreck had been found and remnants of torn clothing had been located. They did not find a trace of Petros. A body that remains for ten days in the Mediterranean is gone, eaten by fish.

The same fish caught by Francesco.

*11. Athens, Wednesday, May 30, 1984

At half past nine in the morning, after a well deserved night's rest in his own bed, Chief Inspector Spiros Karatzis reached his office at police headquarters. The two nights in Pension Serifos had been a disappointment. The beds were hard and the sheets had been dank and clammy. He went through some mail and then went to the Communications room, where he took a number of telex messages from his designated bin. While he walked back to his office, he looked at the names of the senders. In passing he called for Janis Tselentis to join him and together they returned to his office.

Silently they sat opposite each other and read through the messages.

"An interesting corpse," said the Chief Inspector.

"I agree," remarked Janis.

When they had both finished reading, Janis was the first to break the silence:

"His real name is Dupre. But we know him as Dubour. So . . . who's the *real* Dubour?"

"I think that the real Dubour has been dead for some time. Most probably killed in the Congo," said Spiros.

"But Brussels maintains he received a honorary discharge in 1960."

"Yes, but there was a mercenary army at the time, led by Schramme, according to the information on Dupre. They know that Dupre was a member. But that has to be a coincidence. I doubt if there is complete documentation available on the mercenaries. It consisted of the outcasts of the world. Criminals, ex-Nazi's, deserters from the Foreign Legion, you name it. What sort of future did Dubour have in Belgium? He stayed in the Congo. The only thing he was good for, at that time, was to be a soldier. He figured he could make some real money with Schramme, joined up and was killed. Perhaps he and Dupre were buddies. Dubour is killed, so Dupre decides to call it quits. He deserts, but takes Dubour's papers. He knew very well that a corpse in the jungles of the Congo would be unrecognizable after just a few days. He deserted under his own name, Dupre, from the official Belgian army, according to Brussels. The Belgian government even asked Pretoria for extradition. So, Dupre was wanted and stood a chance of being court-martialed. But he knew that Dubour had a honorable discharge. Because they were buddies, he probably also knew that Dubour had no family to report him as missing, or to create any other sort of trouble. Thus he just used Dubour as an alternate identity, in case his own name, Dupre, became too hot. He was not wanted in South Africa under the name Dupre, so he remained Dupre. Dubour's papers were just in case. Every five years he dutifully renewed Dubour's passport. Dubour had no police record and was not wanted anywhere. Under that name he could live quietly on Serifos."

"And he used Footman for his activities, whatever they may have been," added Janis.

"I wouldn't be at all surprised if we unearthed a few more names for him."

"He disappeared on Favignana."

"Yes, he disembarked. Petros is dead, that's just about certain. The divers have found all sorts of evidence that still needs to be researched in the lab and we'll know for sure in a few days. But

I'm certain that Petros stayed with the ship. Nobody leaves a vessel at anchor in a strange bay without at least one person on board."

"The tender that was found, definitely belonged to *Christina*."

"Yes, Palermo identified the model as Narwal and the Greek transit log lists a Narwal as tender for *Christina*. Thus, it's the same boat. Anyway, the serial numbers check. He left the *Christina* and didn't go back, of course, because she exploded, or was exploded. In the telex it states that explosives have most certainly been used. Mafia methods."

"So he had an assignment. But what kind of assignment?"

"Bacelli died that night of a heart attack. The same night the boat blew up. That's too much of a coincidence. Everybody in our profession knows Bacelli as a *capo*. Often arrested, but always set free for lack of evidence."

"But he died naturally, Chief, heart attack."

"Listen, Janis, Bacelli was visiting someone on that island. He was there either on 'business', or he was on the run, or he was hiding. That is also in the telex. Let's just assume, for the moment, that the man from the *Christina* killed him. In that house, in bed even, surrounded by his own people. The next day they find him. Do you really believe they would call in the police?"

"No, of course not."

"But you know what they *will* do? They summon a tame doctor and for a few thousand dollars they have him write a death certificate with 'heart attack' as the cause of death. Next they call an undertaker who also knows how to keep his mouth shut and who, incidentally, is an artist in making bullet wounds in a corpse disappear. Two days later there's a beautiful funeral and everybody is happy. The gang, one way or the other, meanwhile discovers the identity of the killer and they dispatch a small revenge expedition to Serifos."

"It sounds very plausible, Chief."

"I'm almost certain that that's the way it happened."

"So, what can we do?"

"For starters, you'll be going back to Serifos with a good crew. You do a thorough search of the house. I want every stitch taken loose, I want every page read, look for notes, indications of some sort of code, whatever. The last time we did that, we weren't fully apprised of the ramifications. Everything that man wrote is going to the code room. In short, you tear everything apart, you lift and move everything, you pull everything off the walls and you don't overlook a thing. Anything you find, no matter how unimportant it may seem, you let me know at once by phone. There's *got* to be something to be found in that house. He was a clever bird, but nobody is ever clever enough. They all miss, or forget, something. Whatever it is, I want it found. Meanwhile I'm going to have a long conversation with Palermo."

"Well, he could be as cunning as you say, but then why did he return to Serifos, after the murder?" asked Janis.

"That's a good question, Janis. I thought about that, but it may be possible to explain that. You know that they searched his house?"

"Yes, they were looking for something."

"Exactly, they were looking for something, but we don't know if they found it. Our corpse on Serifos knew he was in a key position and felt completely safe. He had something, or knew something that could be fatal for a lot of people in the underworld. Look, the man didn't belong to the mob, or a particular 'family', I'm almost certain of that. That's a different kettle of fish. Also, as I said before, somebody from the Mafia isn't going to hibernate on Serifos. He doesn't do that and he can't afford to do that. If you belong to the mob, then it's your life. You need almost daily contact. You can't live in a vacuum. It's business, business all the time. It's almost like running a chain of stores. The merchandise they sell is a bit different and if you don't meet their price, you get a bullet through the head. But that's about the only difference. Some are in charge of 'businesses' with hundreds of 'employees'. But not him! He lived alone. That means, to me, that he had an extraordinary position within the organization. The type of position that was so unique, that he felt untouchable. And that's the answer to your question. He has, or rather *had*, something in his possession that made him immune. At least, it made him think that he was immune, untouchable, but this time he made a mistake. The gents have become a bit nervous, in recent months, after the arrest of about eighty members of the club, last April. I am convinced that he had something to do with that, he was the connecting link between something, or somebody."

"You think he might have been a hired gun, a hired killer?"

"Yes, I think we have to think in those terms. A hired killer with a very special kind of client, and very special conditions."

"Well, it's still a puzzle to me, but I believe that it's a workable theory. I'll get ready for Serifos," answered Janis and stood up.

"Do that and keep me informed, minute by minute."

"I will, Chief."

He walked to the door and left Spiros to his musings.

The Chief stared out of the window for several minutes and then, while he dialed the number for Palermo, he murmured to himself:

"Who was that nice, friendly, polite, lonely man on the mountain, in the *chora* of Serifos . . . and what did he do for a living?"

*12. New York, the same day

"Goddamn, you guys fucked it up!" said the distinguished man with the gray hair, seated behind the enormous desk. He looked like the personification of the ideal grandfather. "I told you to find out what he knew. Follow him. That's not the same thing as killing the fucker!"

"It was a mistake, Riccardo, I told you," answered a skinny man in an expensive suit with a mismatched, too obvious tie.

"Mistake, mistake!" yelled the man. "Go to hell with your mistakes! You were fucking around. You picked the first couple of motherfuckers you met to take care of things. I told you to get good people, professionals. You knew that. It started with the stiff in the train. Do I have to watch everything? I made you rich, Mario, you owe me! You knew how important Dubour was and you fucked it up! That's my fucking thanks?"

"Yes, but listen, Riccardo, he'd just knocked off your own cousin, Joe Bacelli. He fucking killed him!"

"Joe Bacelli was just another cocksucker. A bastard without real balls. He was my cousin, so what!? I don't have people because they're family, they fucking better be able to perform. And Joe Bacelli was a fucking pimp, just like that fucking Luigi Alfara. Joe had only one purpose left and that was as fucking bait! He didn't have to do anything for that and he couldn't possibly fuck that up too. But he did! He even fucked that up! Probably was fucking somebody's broad he'd picked up."

"I didn't know you thought that way, Riccardo."

"You don't know what I fucking think, nohow! You just do as you're fucking told and no more. You just leave the fucking thinking to me. Now get the fuck out, because I got to straighten out the fucking mess you made. I got to get it back under control."

The skinny man left the room and the man who had been waiting by the door wanted to follow him.

"Carlo, stay!"

"Ok, boss," answered the man with the low forehead and the broken nose.

"You didn't hear a fucking thing, get it?"

"Yessir," his expression was even dumber than usual.

"In that case you say 'nossir'!"

"Oh, nossir."

"You have Mario's address?"

"Yessir."

"Make sure he doesn't get home, tonight."

"OK, boss." The man smiled as if he had been promised a special treat.

"And now get the fuck out."

"Yessir." The bruiser left the room.

* * *

Cosa Nostra boss, *capo familia*, Riccardo Mannucci stood up, walked over to the wall of glass that formed two sides of the large room and looked down from the thirty fourth floor, high above Manhattan. He saw how people, antlike, crawled through the streets below and was revolted. That's all they were to him: ants. They could be smashed, if it was convenient. The floor of which the enormous room was a part, belonged to the Cambry & Mullins Real Estate Corporation. Fifty five people in the other offices on the floor worked behind terminals and had no idea about the real purpose of the business for which they worked. Riccardo Mannucci was the modern *padrino* of a mighty family that had financially penetrated a wide variety of legitimate businesses. The big money came from drugs and the latest activity of the family was the swindle in chemical and nuclear waste. The rich, industrialized countries, faced with mounting quantities of dangerous waste, who did not know where to store it or dispose of it, had become an ever increasing source of new revenue for the future. A future with un-heard of profit possibilities.

The industrialized countries spent billions in order to dispose of the waste in an ecological sound manner, but every day tons of the various substances were left over. A mess that nobody wanted. The international hypocrisy that surrounded this problem was a gift from heaven for people like Riccardo Mannucci. He and other like him had the right relations and the necessary funds to help dispose of the problem with a minimum of trouble. Almost seventy five percent of the world was ruled by dictators and petty tyrants who could all be bought. A great number of these people engaged in a veritable reign of terror over a starving population that died like rats in the regions and cities where normal life was impossible. In those places there was plenty of room for all the nuclear and chemical waste that were such a bother to the industrialized nations. An avalanche of paper, forms, assignments, bills of lading and transfer permits formed an abundant veil behind which the politicians could wash their hands in innocence and which allowed them to assure their democratically elected governments regarding the concerned care with which they had disposed of the unsavory by-products that afforded such a high standard of living.

Riccardo Mannucci was one of the caretakers. The vision of a "Godfather" in a rocking chair on the porch of an old villa in Sicily only existed in the imagination of Hollywood. But the *system* had not changed and was not about to change. The traditions of the *vendetta* (vengeance) and *omerta* (silence) that had been a part of daily life for hundreds of years, were nurtured and maintained. In scores of Italian villages the larger part of the male population was simply not there, as a result of the vendetta. The long tables surrounded by large families, the *padrino* at the head of the table in the gardens, colored purple by the reflection of blossoming bougainvillea had been replaced by luxurious offices in the glass and steel skyscrapers of Manhattan. But otherwise everything had remained the same.

He picked up the telephone and dialed a number in Rome: "Riccardo here. Can I talk? Then listen. I take it you know what happened? They killed him . . . The Good Lord knows why, but they weren't my people. . . . No, I gave no such orders, Giovanni Lovallo, you should know that! . . . The plan was to blow up his boat, just to tickle him a little, that's all . . . Mario took care of that . . . Yes, Mario . . . But probably he contracted it out . . . Yes, I wish I knew who it was, he says he took care of it himself but I don't believe him . . . He's such a lazy cocksucker . . . Yes, I know, I shoulda taken care of it sooner, but he *is* family, Gianni! . . . He married my sister . . . Yes, I know, he's a disgrace to the family, but we all fuck around sometimes, Giovanni Lovallo! . . . Listen, forget Mario, that'll be taken care of today . . . Yes, yes, you can count on it.

67

. . . But what next? You have to use your contacts, Gianni, we *have* to know if they found the list, because that's possible . . . And if they don't have it, we must know where it is . . . That list MUST disappear! . . . And I tell you that there *is* a list! . . . That man kept records for more than twenty years, about everything, about everybody! He knew more than you and me together, you can be fucking sure of that! Nobody knew where he holed up . . . I've never seen him and neither have you, you know that. I didn't *want* to see him, know him . . . that was agreed . . . And how many times have *you* called him, over the last few years, Gianni? Ten times, twenty times? I don't need to know, I don't want to know, but we better stick together right now! Everybody's on our ass, ever since that fuck-up in April. Shit, even the FBI is after my ass. You've *got* to stop them in Sicily, Giovanni! Make sure they drop it! . . . How do I know? . . . Do you live in Rome, or do I? Goddamn, Gianni, you've got your connections in Rome, right? What about that fucking judge? You've paid him enough, it's about time he earns it! Order him to drop the fucking case altogether . . . All right then . . . Go and talk to the sonofabitch . . . I think you're pissing in your pants, Gianni . . . and that doesn't fucking help us . . . Listen, we have to know what happened to that list! If we don't find that list you and me and maybe four hundred other family members are gonna be in a lot of fucking trouble . . . And we ain't got nobody to blame but ourselves, Giovanni, we should have watched it a lot closer . . . You know we used than man for more than twenty years for jobs we couldn't let our own people do. He was to be fucking *trusted*! . . . And he still was! . . . Then that fucking business on the train to Rome! Carlo Barinne was ordered to follow him, for chrissake! He wasn't supposed to fucking *kill* him! And that's exactly what he tried to do, the sonofabitch. They found the bullet holes in the door of the crapper on the other side of the car. Nobody ordered him to do that . . . you didn't and I didn't . . . So, who was it, Gianni? I don't know who stiffed Barinne . . . you should never have used Barinne . . . Barinne was a dumb fucker, no brains. Just another fucking butcher, that's all . . . What? . . . Yes, the man from Serifos could have done it himself, but it could just as easily have been another family . . . In any case, when I talked to him on the phone, after that fucking train incident, he didn't say a word about it . . . Anyway, it doesn't seem too fucking smart to shoot somebody full of holes in the middle of a crowded train, now does it? . . . and then to leave the stiff just lying there . . . And that man was too smart to make that kind of fucking mistake, I tell you . . . We only wanted to talk to him, find out what he knew, you *knew* that . . . The sonofabitch wouldn't have talked to the cops, believe me, he was much too fucking vulnerable himself . . . The list was his insurance policy, no more. And can you blame him? But we had to let him know that we knew, that was *our* insurance. That was the only fucking reason. For all I care he could have stuck that list up his ass. It would never have come up if we had left him alone. They just shouldn't have fucking *killed* him! Now there's no telling who has the fucking merchandise! . . . Because we've been betrayed, that's for sure, and Barinne was part of the plot . . . That's the result of all that fucking around! . . . Whoever has the information can make us, or break us, all of us . . . The man from Serifos should have died of old age, in his bed, then he wouldn't have bothered none of us. Apparently he just lived on his Greek island, didn't mess with anybody, with us neither. That man was safe! . . . What!? . . . Don't give me that bullshit, Giovanni, you don't think you could have killed him, just like that, without consequences? . . . That sonofabitch is laughing himself a fucking hernia from the grave. He knows he's got us by the short hairs, Gianni. Find that list, goddammit, before it winds up with the *Questura Centrale* . . . put somebody on it who knows what they're doing and find those two cocksuckers, because if there *was* a list, they've got it . . . OK, call me. Ciao, ciao."

*13. Serifos, Thursday May 31, 1984

The police helicopter touched down at ten thirty on the soccer field at the edge of Livadi. Inspector Janis Tselentis and two other detectives from headquarters in Athens disembarked and walked toward the white Lada, where Takis, the local constable was waiting for them.

"Good morning, gentlemen," he said and approached with outstretched hands.

"Good morning, here we are again. We just can't forget you, as you've noticed," answered Janis heartily.

"I don't mind, Mr. Tselentis, nothing else ever happens here. It's a pleasure."

"These are my colleagues, Cristopoulos and Kontos."

They shook hands and after Tselentis had agreed with the pilot about the time of pick-up, they got into the car and drove up the mountain to the *chora*.

"And," asked the constable, "did you get anywhere with your investigations?"

"It was an exceptional man who lived here for ten years. That much I can tell you."

"Tell me more, or is it a secret?"

"No, no secret, you're entitled to know. Just don't mention anything to the press."

"But of course, Mr. Tselentis. They won't hear anything from me."

"To begin with, the man had three names," and he related briefly what they had learned so far.

When Janis finished speaking, the constable said: "My God, but how is it possible? It's hard to imagine, he was such a nice man, I can assure you."

"Do you know if Petros has any family, anywhere?"

"No, but I can inquire. Why?"

"We're almost certain he's dead."

70

The constable braked abruptly, pulled the car over to the side, set the hand brake and turned toward Janis.

"What did you say? Petros is dead?"

"Yes, the bastards blew up him and the *Christina*."

"Has he been buried?"

"No, there was nothing found to be buried."

"Well, dammit, what did Petros ever do to deserve that? You know, Mr. Tselentis, I always felt a bit sorry for him. He was a good guy, but he had no contact with the people here, as I told you. They didn't like him, because he wasn't one of them. All kind of stories used to go around that meant nothing at all. He was a lonely man. In the bar he was always by himself, off in a corner. Supposedly we're such a friendly people, according to the tourist propaganda. But the hate and loathing between the different islands is the same as when Sparta and Corinth were still waging war on a regular basis. They're hard. Islanders are only friendly if they can make money from you. The only thing that counts is their own family. Everything outside can go to hell and doesn't matter. The foreigner was the only one who associated with Petros. I think they were friends. He and Petros . . . that melancholy man." He looked sadly out of the window, engaged the gearshift again and drove the rest of the way up the mountain. Silently.

The first thing they noticed upon arrival was that the lock on the door had been forced and that the door was half open.

"How is that possible?" asked Janis.

"It must have happened last night, because I checked everything as recently as yesterday evening," answered the constable.

"Has anybody been inside?"

"But who? I take an oath that it wasn't somebody from the island. Under normal circumstances you don't even have to bother to lock your door. And they wouldn't dare enter a house where a murder has so recently been committed."

One of the detectives took several pairs of white gloves from a briefcase and passed them around. They entered the house and looked at the chaos inside. It had been a mess when they first en-

71

tered the house, a few days ago, but a second search had been conducted and nothing was left in one piece.

"They've been back," concluded Janis.

"They're looking for something," added Cristopoulos.

"Yes, they're looking for the same thing we are. It must be damned important."

"Yes, the opposition seems in a panic. It's starting to become really interesting."

Amazed, they did the rounds of the small house that again had been searched from top to bottom, even more thoroughly than the last time. Even the speakers of the sound system had been cut open. The amplifier and tuner had the cover plates removed and the pieces were tossed in a corner.

"I don't think they found anything."

"Why do you think so?" Takis asked Janis.

"Because of the simple reason that *everything* has been searched. Everything has been moved, cut apart, opened, nothing has been left untouched. Look, if you're looking for something and you find it, then you stop and there's always stuff that remains untouched, for which there is no further interest. Nobody destroys everything just for the hell of it, that wasn't the reason for the visit. They wanted to find what they were looking for and then take off as soon as possible. They didn't find anything here, because everything has been searched."

"You know what I think has disappeared, Janis?" asked Kontos. "The cassettes. There's a cassette player, but there are no tapes and that's strange."

"You're right. They were there the first time we searched. I'm certain of it. At least eighty, or a hundred."

"So, maybe just vandals, after all?"

"No, positively not! If the corpse knew something that could be damaging to the Mafia, he didn't have to write it down, he could have dictated it on a tape."

"You're right, Janis, very shrewd," said Cristopoulos. "Especially if you use a regular tape for that. A commercial tape of Tina

Turner, or whoever, with the original cover and labels. You place it with the other tapes and nobody will know the difference."

"Exactly, you can go crazy looking for paper."

"So, theoretically it's possible that they now have the information?"

"Possibly, but I don't think so. We know from Sicily that the man dispatched a fat envelope from Trapani. *We* know it, but they don't! I believe that they're going to be wasting their time, listening to all those tapes."

"Let's say eighty times fifty minutes is four thousand minutes, that's about seventy hours, that'll mean they won't bother us for about three days," said Kontos.

They laughed heartily for a few moments and then Janis proposed to leave things as they were while he called Athens for instructions. They would have to take new fingerprints, because there was a chance that some would be found after the second visit. That was the domain of the Dactyloscopic Service and they would have to do their work first.

A little later Inspector Janis was in the office of the local constable and spoke into the telephone.

"Yes, Chief, they didn't miss a thing."

"Then it's most certainly of extreme importance, whatever it is they are looking for," said the Chief Inspector from Athens. "The man was a hired killer, that's become more and more clear. He kept records, or gathered information during his career and the mob have gotten wind of that. The whole bunch is a bit excited after the thinning of the ranks, last month. They're afraid, really afraid and that's a delightful thought, Janis. Those bastards have taken us for a ride time and again, they've been laughing at us, but now they're running scared. Heavenly!"

"But what do you want us to do?"

"Go ahead as planned. You never know, you might find something. I'll send the finger boys over. Call me in a few hours."

"Ok, Chief."

73

Janis walked back to the bar on the square where everybody was waiting for instructions. He drank black coffee and settled the bill. Together they walked back to the house. While his colleagues began with the search and carefully sifted through the damaged and destroyed inventory, Janis had another conversation with the neighbor.

"Did you hear anything at all, last night," he asked from the door opening.

"No, not a thing."

"You haven't seen anybody, during the last few days?"

"No, really, to be honest, I would have noticed."

"Did anybody pass though the street who seemed to have more than the usual amount of interest in the house?"

"Yes, of course, to be honest, the whole village has passed by. They came from as far away as Kithnos and Milos."

"Yes, well, thank you for your cooperation, ma'am."

"It's my duty. To be honest, you don't have to thank me."

Janis went back to the house. Cristopoulos saw him approach and immediately caught his attention.

"I think I found something, Janis," he said. He showed a small piece of paper.

Janis looked at it.

"It could be a phone number."

"I thought so, too. The number starts with 1 and then 212 and then 8921943. One is the United States and 212 is the area code for New York. This could be a New York number."

"Where did you find it?"

"In an old pair of jeans, in the small pocket, just above the pants pockets."

"You're a genius, Inspector Cristopoulos. I'll call it in at once."

He ran down the stairs, went into Takis' office and called his Chief in Athens.

*14. New York, Friday, June 1, 1984

The telex connection of Interpol in the communication room of the FBI office in New York started to rattle and produced a long, detailed report from Athens, signed with the name of Spiros Karatzis, Chief Inspector. He had worked until deep in the night to finish a complete report, incorporating all the information gathered from Serifos, Sicily, Belgium, England and South Africa. He had not left out a single detail, because his intuition told him that New York could be an important link in the chain of events that would lead to the solution of the case. Early in the morning, one of the certified translators had been summoned to the office to translate everything into English. A number of photographs accompanied the report via separate fax connection. It was four o'clock in the morning in New York, when Karatzis dispatched his report from Athens. It was then ten o'clock, local Greek time. The first thing the FBI Bureau Chief found on his desk when he entered at nine o'clock was the long ream of paper that almost reached to the floor. After pouring his first cup of coffee, he took the telex and started to read the content intently. While he was looking at the pictures he called a name into the intercom. After a short pause, there was a knock on the door and one of the Special Agents, assigned to the New York office, entered.

"Read this." He handed him the telex.

"Goodness, a copy of the Dead Sea Scrolls."

"Look at the pictures."

"Hmm, a strange case."

"What's your opinion?"

"Could be a reaction to the April actions. Maybe we overlooked a few important guys and they're getting worried. Bacelli slipped through our fingers, as you know, and we should have had him."

After months of preparation they had succeeded, during the first part of April, in cooperation with the police forces of Spain, Switzerland and Italy, to roll up one of the largest international drug smuggling rings in history. More than eighty arrests had been made on April 8, thirty-one of them in the United States. A number of major players had found themselves behind bars. Various Mafia leaders, used to escape the consequences of their actions, had been caught and could look forward to stiff sentences. The most important catch, Don Gaetano Badalementi, was probably one of the last of the really important Mafia *padrini*. The Pizza-Boss had been personally responsible for scores of murders and other major crimes during his forty-year career. But not a single indictment against him had ever before resulted in a conviction. But, according to the Italian police, they had been able to secure incontrovertible evidence against him during his latest arrest.

The so-called "Pizza-Connection" was the most important drug link between North Africa, Europe and the United States. During a five year period the organization must have smuggled a wholesale value of more than $1.6 billion of heroine into the United States. The street-value of that quantity was considered to be astronomical. Pizzerias in New York and the MidWest acted as distribution centers for the drugs. Don Gaetano Badalementi was the most important link between the Mafia in Sicily and the Cosa Nostra in the United States. The Sicilian airport Punta Raisa, within the influence sphere of the Badalementi family, was the primary storage and transfer point for the drugs, destined for export to the Cosa Nostra families in the United States. While a gangster war developed in Italy between the Badalementi family and others for supremacy in the international drug smuggling trade, Badalementi, who was called "Don Tanau" in Sicily, was arrested in Spain, together with his son.

"But they did put out a contract on Bacelli," said the Bureau Chief.

"He was dangerous, he was about to spill the beans."

"This could be the beginning of the next major success for us."

"Yes, they're in a panic. The corpse on that Greek island

knew something and it doesn't look like he took his secrets to the grave with him."

"He left something behind that's life-threatening to them."

"And we must find it first."

"We have a phone number."

"Want to call?"

"No, wait just a moment, let's find out who's number it is."

He manipulated the terminal on his desk and then looked at the text that appeared on the screen.

"It's a non-existent number," said the Bureau Chief, disappointed.

"Probably a temporary, clandestine hook-up."

"Put the three names of that Belgian through the computer."

"Just New York?"

"No, nationwide. Start with the usual, then the IRS, real estate records, who knows, he might have had an address here, somewhere."

"That will take a while." The Special Agent left the office and went to the documentation department. The computers there were all interlinked with most data banks in the United States, through FBI Headquarters in Washington, DC. Information regarding taxes, criminal activities, traffic violations and everything else that, in the eyes of the FBI, was worth recording, concerning more than 250 million American citizens, could be accessed within minutes.

About half an hour later he was back. The Bureau Chief looked up and asked:

"Found anything?"

"The names of Dubour and Dupre are unknown. But Footman owns real estate. He owns a house in Berkeley, California. 2859 Shattuck Avenue. It was bought on January 12, 1971 for $45,000.00. No mortgage, or other loans, so it was a cash transaction. The house is rented to a lady by the name of Anita Lucas, born May 25, 1945 in New York. She still lives there with her son, Jon-Jon Lucas, born November 30, 1970. Father unknown. Ms. Lucas is not married. I called Berkeley. It's a nice, quiet neighborhood, mostly middle class. Ms. Lucas works part-time. According to bank records, she receives a monthly payment of approximately $2,500.00 per month. The amount is adjusted each year according to the Cost-of-Living Index. The sender is unknown, from abroad. It sounds like alimony. There are no court records regarding such a transaction, or agreement. Apparently it's a private, mutual agreement, no lawyers were involved."

"So, Footman, also known as Dupre, must be the father."

"That seems obvious."

"She must be the woman he mentioned in the letter."

"Yes, and the son is the child to which the letter is addressed."

"Visitors?"

"No idea. According to the office in Berkeley, there is nothing to report about the woman. She's a good-looking woman, but, as far as is known, she doesn't have a lover."

"You think Footman might have visited from time to time?"

"I don't know, the best thing, I think, is that we have a little talk with her."

"All right, send all the information from Greece on to Berkeley and ask them to follow up."

"I'll handle it."

∗15. Favignana, the same day

While the report from Chief Inspector Spiros Karatzis was carefully being studied in New York, Giorgio Bergarmi and Alberto Logoluso from police headquarters in Palermo, had gathered in the small cemetery of Favignana, next to the fresh grave of Joe Bacelli, the man who had died of a heart attack in the house of his friend. It had taken a lot of trouble to get the necessary permissions for the exhumation, but now they finally had the satisfaction of seeing the wilted flowers and wreaths being removed. The purple ribbons with the dutiful cliches expressing sorrow about the untimely demise of the dear departed and assurances of eternal remembrance were soaked in the mud next to the grave. The grave site itself was three rows removed from the mausoleum of the man who had owned the cannery and the big house. He and his wife rested there in a miniature marble palace, large enough to house two families comfortably. A cross decorated the cupola and a white marble angel, with folded hands, testified against the man who had ordered the construction of this eternal symbol of conceit and bad taste. A little distance away was the high wall in which caskets had been stacked like apartments in a high-rise. There were entombed the nameless dead who had once contributed to the snobbish mausoleum, the large cross and the white, marble angel.

Four men lifted the marble slab from the grave and pulled the casket into the light of day. They broke the seals while the forensic expert opened his bag and pulled on a pair of rubber gloves.

"Do you want to take the corpse to the laboratory?" asked Giorgio.

"It depends on what we find."

After the four man had opened the lid, they removed themselves to a respectful distance and looked curiously at the doctor who leaned over the corpse. He removed the shroud that concealed Joe Bacelli's face and looked at the head. The dead face had the same unsavory expression as during his lifetime. A criminal face that even death could not soften. A man who had killed people without mercy, or had ordered them killed. Who had grown rich on the misery of others and who handled women as whores, or made them into whores. A man who had made dope addicts of children by ordering his subordinates to hand out free samples to high school kids and even grade school children. Thousands of young lives from New York to Los Angeles had been ruined, or terminated by this man. A man for whom nothing was too base and who had left a trail of human misery during the fifty two years that he

79

had walked the earth. Now he was buried, under a marble slab, decorated with a cross and a Bible text in gold letters. The priest had officiated and the grave had been closed in the presence of his friends and accomplices, none of which were any better than he. A blessing had been said over the corpse, because they were all Roman Catholic. In exchange for a generous donation to the church, forgiveness and compassion was being promised, but He who had seen it all had turned His head in sorrow and had become reconciled to the fact that His Creation had gone to Hell.

"I always take two showers after I've examined a bastard like this," said the pathologist.

"You're afraid of infection?"

"Not exactly, but a face like that always turns my stomach."

"Now, now, doctor, speak no evil of the dead."

The doctor did not answer, felt the head and turned it slightly.

"Here, look at that, a bullet through the head. That's your heart attack. Of course, the heart stopped after that. Natural death! Bullshit!"

The two inspectors looked at the spot the doctor pointed out.

"Death was instantaneous. Too bad! I would have wished him a long, slow and painful death. As long as possible and a shortage of pain killers. That would have been a nice death for him."

"Can you say anything about the weapon, at this time?"

"Of course not, but I'll look into it. I take him with me. Now that I've seen him, I can't do without him, anymore."

*16. Berkeley, the same afternoon

A red Schwinn bike with thick tires leaned against the white picket fence that surrounded the house. A brown Pontiac Safari station wagon was parked in the driveway in front of the garage. The yard around the house displayed the love and care that had been lavished on it. The grass was luxurious, the borders were carefully edged and there was an abundance of colorful flowers and healthy shrubs. A small hothouse, filled with roses and more exotic flowers, had been constructed on one side and a modest pool had been installed back of the house. Two pillars, in a mock Colonial style, decorated the small porch to the front door and the large windows had the small square panes typical of that style. The overall effect was early American, but also a bit English. The occupant was a friendly woman with a nice face and a good figure. She had been born in New York, but on her eighteenth birthday, after the early death of her mother, she had left for California to escape her alcoholic father. Other than that, she had no family. Probably there was an aunt, somewhere on the East Coast, but she had never been in contact with her. Fourteen years ago she had met the man who was still daily in her thoughts. He was the father of her son. She had not seen him, or heard from him, until the day that two detectives rang her doorbell.

"Ms. Lucas?" asked the first man.

"Yes, that's me."

"My name is Bristol, detective-sergeant Bristol, and this is my partner, Trendell." He showed his badge.

"We would like to talk to you, ma'am, if it's convenient."

"Well, you'd better come inside, then."

She led the way into a large kitchen and offered them chairs. She wanted to know if they would like something to drink, but they declined.

"Ms. Lucas, we would like some information," began Bristol.

"I hope it's nothing serious."

"No, not at all, don't worry. We're involved in a case and we would like to ask you some questions, that's all. You live alone, is that right?"

"With my son."

"Of course, your son, how old is he?"

"Thirteen."

"Ma'am, does the name Footman mean anything to you? Neville James Footman?"

"That's the owner of this house. The landlord," she answered.

"Have you ever seen him?"

"No, never."

"He never came by? You never had to talk to him? Repairs, or something?"

"No, never. I wouldn't even know where to find him. I've never needed any large repairs, because when I first rented the house it was still brand new."

"And you've lived here for fourteen years?"

"Indeed, you've done your homework."

"Don't you think it strange that Mr. Footman never contacted you?" asked Trendell.

"Yes, a bit. But I always assumed that he bought the house as an investment and he's just biding his time. And he isn't wrong, because if he were to sell today, he'd make a lot of money."

"Ms. Lucas, we want to show you some pictures. A couple of passport photos and a picture of a man who was murdered on an island in Greece. They're not pretty pictures, I must warn you. Would you look at them, please?" He placed the photos in front of her on the table. She looked at the familiar face that stared up at her and she felt the tears in her eyes.

"That's Robert," she said.

"Robert Dubour?" asked detective Bristol.

"Yes, Robert Dubour, he's dead," she said. It was not a question. She made a statement as if she had long since counted on it.

"Yes, Ms. Lucas, he's dead."

She began to cry softly and wiped away the tears with the back of her hand.

"I'm sorry," said Bristol, feeling clumsy.

Both men remained silent. They pitied her. This was one of the aspects of their job that was always most difficult.

"I'm sorry," she said after a while and looked at them.

"Do you feel able to talk to us some more? We can come back some other time, if you prefer."

"No, no, it's all right. Ask your questions."

"You know this man?"

"I knew him, I should say. I haven't seen him for fourteen years."

"What can you tell us about him, Ms. Lucas?"

"What can I tell you? I met him, here in Berkeley. We lived together for six months and suddenly he disappeared."

"Did you quarrel? Or did you not get along?"

"No, nothing like that. We loved each other. There was no reason."

"He's the father of your son?"

"Yes."

"Did he know you were pregnant?"

"Yes, we were going to get married."

"Did he ever tell you who he was, where he came from, or what he did before he met you?"

"Robert was born in Belgium, in Antwerp. His mother died when he was still a child and he didn't have any contact with his father. That's all I know. I was nineteen and in love. We lived from day to day and everything was peaches and cream. You know what I mean."

"What did he do for a living?"

"He told me he had been in the Army, in Africa. He had done some business and had been able to save some money."

"Did he ever tell you that his real name was Jean Louis Dupre?"

"No, never. Is that so?"

"Yes, Ms. Lucas, that was his real name. Jean Louis Dupre, born February 22, 1935 at Brugge in Belgium. He was also your landlord, Mr. Footman."

"Oh, no, what does it all mean?"

"You don't have to worry, there was no way for you to know. We just discovered it by pure coincidence. Did you ever have any inkling what he did for a living? I mean, during the time you lived together, did anything happen that, after all, seemed a bit strange?"

"No, never. He did a few odd jobs, here and there, but he didn't really like any of them. He had some plans to start his own business."

"Did anything ever come of that?"

"Well, yes, I think so. He was in negotiations with a Real Estate agent regarding a storefront, here in Berkeley, near the University. The boss for whom I worked at the time, a Dutchman, had given him a tip. He had plans for a Travel Agency. But suddenly he was gone."

"You're still receiving a monthly allowance. Did you arrange that with him?"

"No. After he left I suddenly received a deposit in my checking account. I went to the bank to check it out, because I couldn't imagine where the money came from. But the bank couldn't tell me a thing. They told me that the money came from a numbered account in Switzerland and there was no way to trace the owner of the account. About a month later I received a letter from Robert, the only letter he ever wrote me."

"Do you remember what it said?"

"It was just one sentence: 'The money comes from me, take good care of our child, I love you, Robert.' That was all. I still have the letter, if you want to see it."

"That can wait, Ms. Lucas. How did you learn about Footman's house? Where you contacted by an agent?"

"Yes, I was still so young, I thought I was just lucky. But later I had my suspicions. You see, at the time I wasn't even looking for a house. An agent called me one day and told me that he had a nice house for rent, belonging to a Mr. Footman."

"Weren't you curious to know who that Mr. Footman could be?"

"Yes, of course, but as I said, I was young, pregnant, I had no friends, Robert was gone, I didn't think all that clearly. It *was* a bit strange, though, such a nice house and such a low rent."

"How much was the rent?"

"One hundred dollars per month. Ridiculous. And I still pay the same amount. The rent has never been raised. I wasn't too sure about it, at the time and I talked it over with my boss, the Dutchman, William was his name. Anyway, he had the contract checked by a lawyer. William and his wife helped me a lot, during that time. They were real nice people. We've been friends for years. But when he died, she went back to Holland. Their son and daughter still live here. She usually comes once a year, for about six weeks, and she usually stays here, because of the room."

"And Robert, let's keep calling him that, never returned?"

"No, never."

"He also didn't call, or inquire, about his son?"

"No, never."

"Did he know the child was going to be a son?"

"I don't know."

"Have you ever been approached by anybody, a private detective, or somebody, who wanted information?"

"Never."

"A strange business, don't you agree?"

"Yes, in a way. I don't know what to think myself, anymore. But it's the truth."

"You never married. Why not?"

"I always hoped that he would come back, but that's over now, of course. Please tell me, sergeant, who was Robert Dubour and what happened to him?"

"Do you really want to know?"

"Yes, I want to know. Who *was* the father of my son?"

"Robert Dubour, Ms. Lucas, was murdered on Serifos, an island in Greece. We don't know everything, yet, but we assume that he was a hired killer."

"A hired killer?"

85

"Yes, Ms. Lucas, it's almost certain that he was a hired killer, a murderer. He had connections with the Mafia and the Cosa Nostra, but was not one of them. Now that you know that, do you find it strange?"

"It's incomprehensible to me. He was the last man in the world whom I would suspect of being capable of killing another human being. Did he do that already, when I still knew him?"

"We're not sure, but it's probable. I assume you have spoken the truth, but I must ask you an unfriendly question. You say you have only received one letter from him. Is that really the truth?"

"Yes, why should I lie about it?"

"Ma'am, I'll be as open with you as I can. Robert wrote a letter, addressed to his son and also, partly, to you. We found the last, incomplete, page next to the body. The letter was still in the typewriter. The rest is gone. We have no idea where it could be. But we have good reason to suspect that Robert was killed because of the content of that letter. According to a theory, and the FBI in New York agrees, he probably kept accurate records over the last twenty years about the people who hired him. Probably as a sort of insurance. The Mafia will do anything to get their hands on that letter and we don't even know for sure that it contains the information. They want it and they want to destroy it. If you haven't told us the truth, if you have been in regular contact with Robert, then it's my duty to warn you that you and your son are in serious danger from the people who want to lay their hands on that letter. They can find you as easily as we can. I'm sorry to have to tell you this, but I want to make sure you're aware of the danger."

"Sergeant, I'll swear by anything that I've spoken the truth. I have never received any other letter, or whatever, from Robert. I've never spoken to him, and he's never been back."

"He didn't call you on the phone, either?"

"Never."

"I believe you."

"You said there was an incomplete letter of his. May I read it?"

86

"I made a copy and before we leave, I'll give it to you. But you must promise me that you'll be extra alert. Report every suspicious telephone call to us. Make sure you're not followed. I don't want to worry you, but we're going to keep an eye on you, strictly for your own safety."

"It's all just too terrible for words."

"Listen, Ms. Lucas, I'm sorry that I'm the one to bring you this news. I probably destroyed a lot of beautiful memories for you and I have taken away any hope that you'll ever see Robert again, but let me give you this advice: Try to remember Robert as you knew him last, when you lived together. He loved you, I'm certain of that. That also shows from the letter I'll give you in a moment. He took responsibility for you and your son and has provided financial support. Possibly he had no other choice, at the time. He has killed people and he took payment for that. That's difficult to condone. But you may find some comfort in the fact that he didn't kill any particularly nice people. The people he killed under contract were all, without exception, the worst kind of criminals. Criminals who had run afoul of other criminals. As a policeman I shouldn't say it, but we're not exactly too unhappy about the one killing of which we are absolutely sure. Actually we're grateful to Robert for that."

* * *

When the two detectives had left the house, she read the letter from Serifos . . .

. . . I imagine that I will then tell her, every day, about a day of my life when we were apart. And she will be able to tell me about one of her days. Every day we shall have something new to talk about. It will take at least twenty years before we run out of things to talk about. I will be 76 and she will be only 60. But together we will have at least forty years of memories. Memories we can argue about, whenever we mix up the dates. Together, we will spoil our grandchildren and sneak them extra pocket money, despite your protestations. She will tell me not to whine about my little maladies and infirmities and I take her on short trips with the car. For the last time we shall travel to the places where our memories were formed and where we can recognize nothing. Once a week she will dress in her best clothes and I will proudly show her off in the best restaurants. The doctor will still allow us to eat anything. People will look at us and wish that they, too, could grow old as gracefully as we. She will scold me about the size of the tip and on the way home I take the wrong turn. I will hold her hand when we cross the street and I will have a little list, written in her own dear hand, when I go shopping. She makes sure that I wear a scarf when it is cold and I will squeeze fresh orange juice for her, when she is in bed with the flu. Daily we will tell each other that time flies and you will tell us not to be boring. She will decorate the house with fresh flowers from our garden and I polish the car once again. In Spring, I paint the picket fence and together with her I

From the kitchen table at which she was seated, she looked at the small hothouse with the exotic flowers and her thoughts were far away . . .

*17. Rome, Saturday, June 2, 1984

For the first time in human memory he was not at his regular spot on the Piazza Colonna. He was always there. Not because there were no other places in Rome to buy postcards, they could be bought on every street corner, in every shop. But the shoddy man, the seller of postcards, who seemed to have staked out the place only a few blocks from the terrace of *Tre Corone*, was not there. Nobody knew his real name, but everybody knew him by the name "l'Elastico", a name that was probably a hold-over from the time that he and his family still worked in the circus. On the Piazza Colonna that was visited by every tourist at least once, he was known to everybody. The waiters from the terraces used him to get small change and dates were made with as meeting place "l'Elastico". He was as much a part of the Piazza as the column of Marcus Aurelius that had stood there for two thousand years. But that day he was not there.

He lived in the basement of a narrow house in one of the Red Light Districts of Rome, in the neighborhood of the Via dei Parioli. A narrow street with bars, brothels, sex shops, massage parlors and peep shows. Where the ladies were called "ragazze" and the men were called "ragazzi". The sparse lighting of the street gave an impoverished impression and the casual tourist never suspected that millions of liras per day, and especially per night, were earned in the neglected street. Every sexual desire and perversion could be satisfied in those surroundings. Slovenly doormen tried to entice passers-by and the women whispered their prices. Late in the morning the street was always quiet and nearly deserted. The inhabitants were asleep, or recovering from the excesses of a busy night.

This morning it was different. The Rome police had blocked the alley from both sides with red and white colored tape and *Carabinieri* checked the identity of all who wanted to pass. In front of the basement entrance to where "l'Elastico" lived, a group of curious neighbors had gathered and tried to get a glimpse of what was going on inside. Chief Inspector Enzo Martella, of the Homicide Department of the *Questura Centrale* in Rome, looked at the corpse on the filthy bed.

"They really worked him over," he said.

"And a shot in the neck. Mafia," responded Inspector Enrico Tomasso.

"Found anything?"

"I haven't been here more than ten minutes, before you came."

"The rest is on the way?"

"They should be here any moment."

"Well, they finally got to 'l'Elastico.' Do you know his real name?"

"I had to look it up, before I came over. It's Carlo Pennisi, born January 13, 1918 at Naples."

"Oh, yes, I remember now. So, he was sixty six. He's managed to stretch it," said Martella.

"How's that?" asked Tomasso.

"He was a police informer and a letter-drop for the underworld. Sooner or later that had to go wrong. I warned him a number of times. I advised him to move, but he didn't want to discuss it. He didn't want to leave his street. Because he owns most of this street, you know."

"You mean, he actually was the *owner*?"

"Yes, I don't know exactly how many houses and businesses he owned, but it was more than me, because I don't own any. I don't even own the house I live in. But, what can you say, then I shouldn't have joined the police."

"The man owned this street and he lived in this filthy basement?"

"Yes, Enrico, it takes all kinds to make a world."

"So, he was rich?" Enrico Tomasso looked with wide-eyed amazement at the dead body on the filthy bed.

At that moment they heard the sirens of at least two patrol cars and a little later a number of men descended on the place. One was dressed in a white coat. Without a greeting he approached the corpse and remarked:

"Well, he's been permanently cured of his cold, Enzo."

"He had to study more than ten years to draw that conclusion," remarked Martella to Tomasso.

"Well, well, well. l'Elastico! Now where will I buy my postcards?" asked the police doctor with bitter humor.

"Why don't you take his place, Sergio, with your face they'll never notice the difference."

"Please, leave the jokes to the medical profession, ispettore, they've got a lot more brains."

"Oh, come on, Sergio, whether you're using your stethoscope, or the headphones of your Walkman, you'll never know the difference."

"All right already. Shall we be serious, now?"

"You can always try, but it doesn't become you," answered Martella.

Meanwhile, despite the light-hearted conversation, the procedure of the first, important investigation was being done by the book. After the police doctor had made notes of his preliminary examination, he gave permission to remove the corpse so that the other experts could start their work.

"Tell me something, Sergio," invited Martella while the doctor replaced the instruments in his bag.

"Tortured, professional. Mafia methods. Cigarettes, brass knuckles, you know the drill. A neck shot as gratuity."

"Close by?"

"Yes, a large caliber. Probably with silencer."

"You won't find much more in the lab, will you?"

"I'm afraid not. But you'll hear from me, later today. The body is on the way and I'll follow like the wind. We're like royalty. We never travel together in the same conveyance, isn't that weird?" The doctor disappeared up the stairs.

Chief Inspector Enzo Martella left matters to his inspector and departed for headquarters. A few hours later he received the first call from Tomasso. He ordered a car and returned to the decrepit alley.

"I'm sorry I asked you to come, but I thought it better if you were here. Before I have it wrapped up, I would like you to see this." He walked toward the small kitchen and pointed toward the

91

counter. It was covered with scores of gold and silver jewelry and watches. Rings with diamond settings and other precious stones. It would be difficult to estimate the value of what was displayed on the cracked granite of the counter, but it had to be several billions of liras.

"So, l'Elastico was also a fence."

"It seems that way," said Tomasso. "And what about this?" He pointed at several stacks of bank notes that had been found in different hiding places around the basement.

"Dio mio, he could have bought several more streets with that money. Has it been counted?"

"Not yet. That will take some time."

Martella looked at the stacks of American dollars, German marks and Swiss francs.

"He knew how to pick the right currencies for his piggy bank," he remarked.

"It's hard to believe. Everybody bought his postcards out of pity. He always looked so needy."

"Where was it hidden?" asked Martella.

"Everywhere! You can't imagine! In an inside pocket of an old coat, in a pair of shoes, behind a painting."

"In the mattress," added the Chief Inspector.

"Exactly."

"And nothing was stolen, or searched?"

"No, not as far as we've been able to determine. I don't understand it," answered Tomasso.

"I don't either. It *is* incomprehensible," began Martella. "First of all: they weren't looking for anything, but they wanted to know something. Secondly: they didn't know who he was, or what he did. If they *had* known that, they would have torn the place apart, let's face it. In other words: they weren't people from Rome. They were from outside. Possibly here for the first time. What about the gentlemen from the fingers department?"

"They left about thirty minutes ago."

"Has everything been searched?"

"We're still at it, but we're almost finished."

Martella spotted a stack of postcards.

"Don't forget to look through the cards?"

"What do you mean?"

"Look at every card individually."

"Every card?"

"Yes, one by one. Take them in your hands and look at them. He had a very specific way of communication."

"What about the money and all that other stuff?" asked Tomasso.

"Well, don't put it in your pocket. There's three of you here, right?"

"Yes, all from our department."

"You're armed?"

"Yes, of course."

"I'll send a car with two people and a safe. Put everything in it. Make sure that everybody is present when you do that. Everybody here signs for the transfer and the two with the safe sign a receipt. That way it will all be recorded and there will be no problem with it, later."

"I'll take care of it, sir."

For the second time Martella left the basement and twenty minutes later he was back at his desk. The phone almost immediately compelled his attention. He lifted the receiver and heard the voice of Tomasso.

"I found something, sir, and I wanted you to know at once."

"That's the way, Enrico."

"We found a postcard with some notes on it. Shall I read it to you?"

"Go ahead." Martella took a pen and a piece of paper.

"Salvatore Navonna and two numbers: 489297 and 315. That's all."

"Enrico, that's quite a lot. You've only recently arrived in Rome, so I won't hold it against you that you don't know all the names, yet. But Salvatore is really interesting. And I think the number is in Rome. Is there much left to do, over there?"

"No, almost finished. The money has been picked up, what a relief."

"All right, let the other two finish up and you come over here. There's work to be done."

"Yes, sir."

* * *

Forty five minutes later they were seated in the back of an unmarked car. The police driver managed to pilot it through the insane Rome traffic at breakneck speed without accidents, either without, or within the vehicle. They stopped in front of the Hotel Continental, to which the phone number on the postcard had been traced, and entered the lobby. They asked to speak to the Chef de Reception. After having identified themselves, Martella asked the man, who was dressed in striped pants and tails:

"Do you know this person?" He showed the photograph that had reached them via the fax from Athens.

The Chef studied the photo intently and then said:

"No, I do not. I have never seen this man, but I can ask my people at the desk. Do you have a name?"

"We have three names: Dupre, Dubour and Footman."

"When would the gentleman have stayed here?"

"About four weeks ago."

"Let me look that up for you." He sat down at a terminal and entered the three names one by one. He had to conclude that all three names were unknown to the computer.

"As you see, the names are unknown here. I instructed the computer to search the entire year."

"Alright, let's try it another way. How about any gentlemen that stayed here alone, during the same period. Would that be a lot?"

"We have, of course, a great number of business people at all times, you understand. I am not sure if I may reveal their names to you."

"Let's try something else. How many people work the front desk?"

"A total of eight."

"How many are now present?"

"At the moment there are three on duty."

"Can I speak to them?"

"But of course. Let me call them for you. You may use my office, that is more discreet."

The young woman who was called in second, looked at the photo and was very positive.

"He stayed here, sir."

"When?"

"Not too long ago."

"How long ago? Think hard!"

"Let's see . . . about a month ago."

"Do you remember the name?"

"No, you have to excuse me. We hear so many names. It was an English name."

"If you read the name, would you remember, would you recognize it?"

"Oh, yes, certainly. It was a common English name. I remember that very well."

"May I request," Martella asked the Chef formally, "to make a print-out of all single men who stayed here during the last four weeks. I promise you that we shall not use it in any way detrimental to the hotel. We're just looking for a single name."

The Chef sat down at his terminal, gave a number of commands and, by way of compromise, read off the names one by one. The girl from the reception shook her head as each name was called. Martella started to lose hope when the name Frank C. Johnson was called.

"That's it. I told you, it was a common English name. That's *him*. I'm certain, now."

"English passport?"

"Yes, English passport," she agreed.

"Signorina, you have helped us tremendously. Thank you very much."

After the young lady had left the office, the Chef de Reception asked:

"What are you going to do with that name? You do understand, they are all our guests and we have an obligation to protect their privacy."

"I will tell you," answered Martella. "We're going to contact Scotland Yard in London. Then that name will go into *their* computer. We will then find out if the man travelled on a false passport. If that's the case, we will, regretfully, have to ignore any rights to privacy. If everything checks out, then your guest will never hear of our visit. But in any case, you won't have to worry, because I have a strong suspicion as to his identity. We know him very well. If I'm right, the reputation of your hotel is the least of your worries, because the man has been dead for at least a week. So, he'll not be back in any case."

On the way back to the police station, Martella instructed Tomasso:

"As soon as we're back, have the photo copied. Send a courier with a copy to all TV stations and newspapers. I want to know what that character did, while in Rome."

"You'll be in your office?" asked Enrico.

"I can't be reached for a few hours, but I'll be back no later than four o'clock."

Everybody knew where Martella was those few hours in the afternoon. Visiting hours started at two in the afternoon. He usually did not stay longer than an hour. Three, sometimes four times a week, he visited her. When he then returned to his office, they tried to leave him alone for an hour, or so. That was an unspoken agreement, honored by everybody in the department. They knew his history and the sorrow that entailed. It was seldom discussed, not because they did not want to, but because they did not dare to do so. It sounded hard, but nobody was able to find the right words. Then, he was not the sort of man who would welcome pity. The only outward sign was a certain loneliness that seemed to emanate from him. Especially on the days that he had been visiting.

*18. Rome, the same evening

Despite his short, compact body, casino boss Salvatore Navonna was just able to peer over the steering wheel of his Mercedes 500 SEC. The car should not have been much bigger. He parked in a spot reserved for the handicapped, but that was one of the things he could care less about. His car was always parked there when he attended to business and the traffic cops knew who he was. They kept their mouths shut, smart of them. The salary that the Rome municipality paid them on a monthly basis was hardly enough to park a Fiat Panda, let alone own it. Salvatore liked that particular spot and was willing to pay for it. That is how he organized things in the neighborhood around his casino. Of course, it was not an official casino, but an illegal gambling joint with no holds barred and no limits. The business was in someone else's name, he had taken care of that. If there ever was a raid, he would be just one of the players. In addition, he had created a secret escape route from all of his businesses, known only to himself. Often, in the past, a new, young inspector would think that he had enough evidence to get casino boss Salvatore Navonna at least in front of a judge. But they had to let him go, time and time again. Lack of evidence. In the street behind the casino he operated a luxurious brothel.

That was primarily visited by respectable business people from the large concerns that had settled in and around Rome. They would regularly offer their clients an evening of "Sodom and Gomorrah", a specialty of the house that was not cheap. Salvatore's brothel only accepted Gold Credit Cards. The bills could always be written off as "recruiting" costs. Salvatore was part of the underworld, but he had class. He lived a long way from his field of operations in one of the most expensive neighborhoods of the city. None of his neighbors knew what he did for a living and those few that did know, perhaps because they recognized him from a visit to one of his establishments, avoided all contact with him in public and kept silent. His children attended private schools and he religiously attended all PTA meetings, although he preferred to keep his mouth shut during the debates.

He got out of the car and entered a narrow alley at the back of his casino, flanked by two small, impoverished shops. At the end of the alley was a steel door and only he had a key. It was eleven thirty at night and as usual, the alley was hardly lit. Because of that he saw the two men just a fraction of a second too late.

"Don't run away, Salvatore, we're friends," said one of them.

"Wadda you want from me?"

"Just a friendly little talk."

"Who sent you?"

"We don't get sent, Salvatore, we come of our own accord. We're small, independent business men, right, Claudio?"

"Si," said the other man. His only contribution to the conversation.

"We'll have a little drink with you in your nice, comfortable office."

"Wadda you want from me. You know I got protection."

"We know that, but we don't plan to damage you. We just want to have a little talk. Any problems?"

Salvatore tried to open the door, but was unable to do so.

"Here, let me help you, *paesano*. You're much too nervous, tonight."

The man took the key from Salvatore's powerless hands and opened the door. They walked through a short corridor that was closed off by another steel door at the end. Salvatore produced another key and they entered.

"Well, well, you *do* take care of yourself, Sally."

They were standing in a luxuriously appointed office with walls covered in red velours and decorated with expensive, black lacquered furniture. An inch thick, soft gray carpet covered the floor. A leather couch and a small bar were installed in one corner. The silent man walked over to the bar, took one of Salvatore's prize Tiffany glasses, filled it with ice, added a large shot of whiskey and drained it in one swallow. The other man checked the door that led to the casino, verified that it was locked and could not be opened from the other side.

"So, here we are. We can talk quietly and we won't be disturbed. That's nice," he said in a slimy tone of voice.

"I don't know you. Why should I want to talk to you?" asked Salvatore, who made a move to sit down behind the desk.

"Ah, ah, ah! You're not going to sit there, my friend. We watch James Bond movies too, you know. I bet you have a handy little buzzer there, or perhaps a small, teeny, weeny pistol in a hidden drawer? No, no, we won't play that game. I'll get you a chair and then you'll sit nicely in the middle of the room. We really *do* have to talk, you know." The man took the chair from behind the desk, placed it in the middle of the room and then sat down on the armrest of the couch. The silent one slowly pulled out a pair of brass knuckles and demonstratively put them on his hand.

"Listen, Salvatore, there's nothing the matter. My friend is just crazy about those things, but he doesn't mean anything by it. We just want to know something, that's all."

"Who's paying you?" asked Salvatore.

"Please calm down, my man, you don't even know us. We're really not as bad as you think. Listen, we just want to talk about a friend of yours. He lives in Greece on some sort of hole-in-the-wall island."

"I don't know anybody in Greece."

"Yes, you do, because 'l'Elastico' passed a phone number from him to you. By the way, he sends his warmest greetings. Things are not too good with him."

"But they don't bother him none," grinned the man with the brass knuckles.

"Shut up, Claudio, I'm talking. So, you have no friend in those asshole Greek islands, is that right, Salvatore?"

"I told you that."

"We know his name, we even have his picture. By the way, did you know he made the evening news, tonight?"

"Who?'

"Well, your friend from that asshole island. He didn't look too good."

"They forgot his make-up," laughed Claudio.

"What the hell are you talking about. Wadda you want from me?" Salvatore's voice squeaked at the end of the sentence.

"Listen, Salvatore," came the tormentingly slow reply, with long, irritating pauses after every word, "your - friend - has - been - damaged - a - little. . . . Apparently - he . . . eh, could - not - stand - the - heat, . . . so, . . ."

"Is he dead?" asked Salvatore.

"Oh, wait a minute! You know him, after all! That's not very nice of you, Salvatore. I asked you nicely if you knew him and you tell me you don't. And now you *do* know him, all of a sudden. That's not nice, my friend, you agree?"

"Well, if he's dead, what more do you want from him?"

"I'll show you something. A little snapshot. Made it with my own two little hands, in Palermo. Please ignore the quality, because, of course, I'm not a professional photographer . . . Now, what *did* I do with that damn picture?"

"I got it," contributed Claudio and handed it over.

"Yes, that's it all right. Look, your friend. Nice suite, eh? Looks like an Englishman, don't he? That's right, because he had an English passport on him. He pretended to be a treasure hunter on Sicily, some sort of archeologist, you now what I mean? He even carried a little shovel around. Of course, we figured him out right-a-way. We watched him. He had just come from Rome and that's when you talked to him. Oh yes, l'Elastico told us, may he rest in peace. But then we lost him and that's too bad."

"All right, cut out the bullshit! Wadda you want from me?"

"Calm, calm down! Everything in its proper time and place. It seems that your friend kept some sort of record and there are quite a few of us who aren't too happy about that."

"What sort of records?"

"Names and things, you know. And you see, a number of my friends would be very unhappy if that information wound up in the wrong hands. *Now*, do you understand?"

"I really don't know what you're talking about."

"List – en," started the other, again in slow motion.

"Jesus, don't piss around like that," said Salvatore.

"You seem a little nervous, tonight. Any particular reason?"

"Listen, I told you that I know that man, all right? But I don't know anything about any records."

"Well, Salvatore, that's really strange, you know. You're not convincing me."

"All right, I told you. I knew him, we were in the Army together. That's all. I don't even know what he did for a living."

"Well, finally a truthful answer. We don't know exactly what he did, either. But we have an idea. Listen, Salvatore, I'm losing my patience. I've *tried* to talk nicely with you, but you won't cooperate. You see, my friend, I've got a nice piece of ass waiting for me and I'm tired of wasting time with you. I'll ask you just one more time: What do you know about the records?"

"I know nothing about it."

"Go to hell, Salvatore. An old Army buddy! You talked to him, didn't you?" The man's voice became louder and he started to talk faster.

"Yes, I talked to him, but he never mentioned no list."

"Hey, Claudio, you hear that? It seems to be a list!"

The ex-boxer came closer and stroked the brass knuckles with his left hand as if he wanted to shine them.

101

"Goddammit, Salvatore, you're fucking with me, asshole! Tell me what you know about the list!"

With a wide, almost caressing gesture, the boxer stroked the left side of Salvatore's face with the brass knuckles. The small man's face tore open and four bloody lines formed from below his chin to his temple. He groaned, was momentarily stunned, but recovered quickly.

"That's enough, Claudio," ordered the first man. Then, turning to Salvatore, he said: "Claudio gets very emotional, at times, you know. And that's the wrong thing to be when you're a businessman, right, Salvatore?"

"Fucking bastards," hissed Salvatore. He felt his face tenderly. There was a lot of blood.

"You know what, Salvatore? You just sleep on it for a night. Tomorrow you'll remember a lot more, believe me. Come on, Claudio, we're leaving."

Claudio approached with the precious whiskey glass in one hand, threw it against a wall and watched it shatter in a thousand pieces. They left by the back door.

*19. Rome, Sunday, June 3, 1984

At eight o'clock in the morning, Inspector Enrico Tomasso, was waiting at the Leonardo da Vinci Airport in Rome. The case, which had started so innocuously with a corpse on an unimportant island in the Cyclades, was quickly becoming more widespread and everyone knew, almost instinctively, that this was but the tip of the iceberg. Yesterday after they had returned to the office, London had been requested to give further information about the man who had stayed at the Continental. The answer was back within two hours. The Brit, Frank C. Johnson, was born on May 3, 1934 in the village of Kenilworth. He died at the age of twenty one on February 14,

1956. They had worked until deep in the night. Telephonic contacts had been made, telexes had been transmitted and received and ultimately it was decided that the entire case was to be coordinated from Rome.

Extra space had been allocated and specially cleared technical personnel were engaged to install extra telex, telephone and fax lines. Additional material had been assigned, including fast cars, special weapons and telecommunications gear. The photo of the corpse from Serifos had appeared twice on all TV stations, last night and this morning. Depending on space and editorial vagaries, the newspapers would carry the information that had been released by a special news bulletin from the police. Of course, a tie-in had been provided with the Mafia wars that had continued after the mass arrests in the early part of April. The papers could be depended upon to embellish and elaborate on that, depending on what they thought their readers would, or could stomach.

Since that April 8th more than eighteen members of the various clans and families in Sicily, that fought each other for the ultimate supremacy, had been murdered, some were gunned down in the streets. But the innocent, too, had found death, bystanders who were hit by stray bullets. Another slaughter had taken place on the beautiful island and the end was not in sight. Sicily and Italy were slowly being torn apart from within, being destroyed by an ever more brazen, organized criminal element and it looked more and more like this cancer on society could no longer be isolated.

Enrico was waiting for two Special Agents, dispatched by the FBI in New York. They would leave the airport through a little used exit, reserved for personnel. It was important to avoid notice as much as possible when new faces were added to the team, that they should escape the attention of the throngs outside the airport. An unknown face was the best protection for covert operations. The luggage carousel started up and the first pieces of luggage appeared. The first passengers from flight 317 from New York stepped into the large receiving hall. Enrico had studied the photos of the men he expected and placed himself behind the passport checkpoint. Soon he noticed the faces of Special Agent Ferdinando Cotone and Special Agent Vittorio Scarfiotti. FBI people, born in the United States from Italian parents. Both were fluent in Italian and could even speak the dialect of the region in which their parents were born.

"Signori Scarfiotti e Cotone?" asked Enrico as the Special Agents stopped to have their passports checked.

"Si. Ispettore Enrico Tomasso?" asked one of the FBI men.

They showed each other their identity papers and walked in the direction of the luggage carrousels.

"You had a good trip?" asked Enrico.

"I feel lousy," answered Scarfiotti. "Jet lag. It's two o'clock in the morning for us. I should be in bed."

"Don't worry about it," joshed Cotone. "You're in Italy now, take a siesta in the afternoon and you'll soon be A-OK again."

"I should warn you, Enrico, my partner is sometimes so funny you'd cheerfully wring his neck. But he gets away with it, because he's a black belt in Karate."

They walked outside through the special exit. Half an hour later they were in the center of Rome and turned into the court yard of police headquarters. Soon they entered the office of Chief Inspector Enzo Martella who welcomed them heartily.

"And, how does it feel to be back in the old country?"

"Well, so far we've had only one short sight-seeing trip and it was a bummer, signore, the tour guide left a lot to be desired."

"Well, you get what you pay for, Cotone, you know that."

"Yes, I know, sir. My wife warned me about that, only yesterday, when I told her where I was going."

There was brief laughter, a few general remarks and then Martella became serious.

"You know what we're working on?"

"Yes, we read the report from Athens and we have some additional information."

"Excellent. We had some developments here as well, that you should know about. In order to save time, I propose the follow-

104

ing: The man from Sicily should be here in about an hour. I assembled a team and I'd like to begin with a meeting with all parties present. Let's say around eleven. Enrico will take you to your hotel, give you a chance to freshen up, unpack and so on."

When the FBI men had left his office, Chief Inspector Enzo Martella used the time to check on a few items for which he had issued instructions earlier. The special technical people were finishing up, desks, chairs and other furniture was being gathered from other parts of the building and the man from Sicily had to be picked up at the airport. One wall in the special office was covered with cork board to facilitate the pinning up of photographs and other information. People from Homicide and from Documentation had already provided photographs of the corpse in Serifos, Joe Bacelli and "l'Elastico". Every desk was provided with a list of internal and external phone numbers and a resume of the people who would be working on the special team, or where connected in some way.

At eleven the team gathered for the first time in one place and all had found a desk. Enzo Martella came in, greeted everybody and walked toward the end of the large room.

"People, let's start," he said from the lectern in front of the cork board wall. "The initial team assembled for this case, is complete. I have been made responsible for this case. I hope you will be satisfied with my leadership and you will not hesitate to voice any ideas, or suggestions. Needless to say, it's of the utmost importance that we always know what everybody is working on, and that we are able to reach each other at all times. We're all familiar with the methods of the opposition and the idea is for all of us to get through this in one piece. Just to make sure, allow me to introduce everybody."

He looked around the room, pointed at the FBI men and said:

"Two visitors from New York. Special Agents Vittorio Scarfiotti and Ferdinando Cotone from the FBI. They will operate in Italy, subject to our laws and will maintain liaison with the FBI. I have been able to obtain a number of special permits for them, including the right to carry a weapon. Let me emphasize that weapons should only be used in the direst emergency."

The FBI men nodded agreement.

"From Sicily," continued Martella, "we welcome Inspector Giorgio Bergarmi. He's normally attached to headquarters in Palermo and has thoroughly researched one aspect of the case. Finally, from our own office in Rome, Inspectors Enrico Tomasso and Franco Giovale. We will be able to draw upon additional personnel as needed and also the necessary administrative assistance has been put on stand-by. Everybody has received a complete report on this case and I assume that you all have had a chance to read it. Before we begin, however, I think it would be a good idea, to repeat a synopsis of the case from the beginning."

He looked around, took a deep breath and started:

"On the 27th of May a man was found on the Greek island of Serifos. The man had been killed. He had lived for ten years on the island and was known by the name of Robert Dubour, Belgian by birth. Interpol in Brussels checked the name and the fingerprints and discovered that the man's real name was Jean Louis Dupre. It's almost certain that Dubour and Dupre both served in the mercenary army of Jacques Schramme in the Congo. Dubour was never listed as missing, because his passport was regularly renewed, every five years. Under his own name, Dupre, the victim was incarcerated in South Africa for several years as a result of currency smuggling. When the people from Athens found the body, they also found the house had been searched and the victim had been tortured. The victim left an incomplete letter in his typewriter. Apparently he was working on that when he was attacked by his killers. According to the police doctor, collaborated by evidence from a neighbor, the man was killed on the 22nd, five days before he was discovered. The victim owned a sailboat, the *Christina*. The ship was registered as belonging to Neville James Footman. Interpol in London reports that Footman died as an infant, but that a recent passport was issued in that name. The photo in the passport matches the description of the victim on Serifos. With his sailboat, the *Christina*, the victim departed Serifos on May 14, accompanied by one Petros Theologitis. Their route is known and has been checked. They arrived on the 19th of May off the island of Favigna-na, near Sicily. We know that the victim mailed a fat envelope from Trapani, on Sicily. During the night between the 19th and the 20th of May the ship exploded. The sinking was investigated and divers have found the wreck. Two days after the explosion a fisherman 'found' a tender, originating with *Christina*, on the beach of the bay outside the harbor of Favignana. Therefore it's clear that at least one of the crew must have landed on Favignana and remained ashore. That same night, the night of the explosion, Joe Bacelli, as you know, a well-known family member, happened to die of a heart attack in the house of Alfonso Franchi, also well known."

He paused briefly. So far he had spoken without notes and the others watched him with rapt attention. Martella closed his eyes momentarily and then went on:

"Bacelli's death was a bit suspicious. The body has meanwhile been exhumed and examined by our own pathology department. The verdict was murder. A shot through the head with, presumably, a Winchester 125, equipped with silencer. Just to make it absolutely clear: this was a different weapon than the one used for the murder of Dubour. Another coincidence which seems to be connected with this case: On the 4th of May the body of a man was found in the toilet of a train originating in Palermo. The man had been strangled with a black, nylon cord. Further research revealed that two days earlier the man was on Favignana. He took the ferry to Trapani on the morning of the fourth and from there took the train to Rome where he was found by the cleaning crew. His name was Carlo Barinne. Well known, but also apparently immune to arrest because of lack of evidence. We do not know for which family he was working at the time. It's possible that he had something to do with the murder of Bacelli. Although there seems no connection at this time, we keep it in mind, because of his presence on Favignana. The Greeks went back to the house on Serifos for a second time. On their arrival they found that the house had again been searched by parties unknown. From the way the house was destroyed we can be certain that they were looking for something. Just like the first time. Logic demands that we assume that what they were looking for were names, dates, places. The second time the Greek police *did* find a piece of paper in one of the articles of clothing. There was a number on the piece of paper. It appeared to be a telephone number in New York City."

Again he paused briefly, as if to order his thoughts.

"As a result of this discovery," he continued, "the FBI checked the names of Dubour, Dupre and Footman. They discovered a house in Berkeley, California, in the name of Footman. The house is occupied by a Ms. Anita Lucas who, fourteen years ago, was the lover of Dubour, also known as Dupre. Ms. Lucas has a son and Dubour is the father. The letter found in Serifos was obviously meant for the son. It also seems that this letter was the latest in a series of letters. He must have written a long narrative and therein he must have mentioned the facts that have the Mafia so worried. Yesterday morning we found the corpse of Carlo Pennisi, nicknamed 'l'Elastico'. He was a police informer and also a go-between for the opposition. In addition to a large amount of cash, jewelry and other valuables, we found a postcard in his house with the name of Salvatore Navonna, casino boss and brothel owner in our fair city. The number, also on the card, was the telephone number of the Hotel Continental. As an aside: we have not yet interrogated Salvatore. We may assume that he is next in line for a visit from the killer, or killers, of l'Elastico. I have given orders to keep an eye on Salvatore. In any case, the receptionist at the hotel recognized the man from Serifos. He stayed there under the name of Frank C. Johnson. Last night London confirmed that also as a false name. That's what we have so far. Questions? Ideas?"

Ferdinando Cotone stood up and said:

"The FBI is convinced that the man in Serifos was a hired killer. Athens was the first to suggest that and it was a shrewd suggestion. If we assume that and add the fact that the various families

108

are extremely nervous and are looking for something, then it's only a logical step to decide that they are *aware* of some sort of records. He probably told them, either directly, or indirectly, because that was his life insurance. We believe he has been operating for years and knew too much. He was almost fifty years old and wanted to retire. That's also evident from the letter we found. He probably planned to obtain a completely new identity with the resources at his disposal and that wouldn't have been very difficult for him. We believe that his records will surface, in time. The man has been able to be invisible for more than twenty years. To us and also to the Mafia. The fact that he lived quietly on that small island only confirms that supposition. That list, or whatever it is, is safely deposited with some lawyer, with instructions to make it public if he dies an unnatural death. We don't know, of course, the identity of that lawyer. Nor do we know how that lawyer is supposed to know when the man dies, or died, rather. We further believe that it was never the intention to kill him. Whoever visited the island were either beginners, or stupid. In any case, it went too far. The big boys *know* that they should have kept him alive. His death is more dangerous than his knowledge."

"That would mean that we have to do nothing at all and just wait until some lawyer wakes up?" asked Tomasso.

"Well, at least we could ask the people at the Post Office in Trapani a few questions," opined someone else. "Perhaps they remember something about the address on the letter."

"That hasn't been done, yet?" asked Cotone.

"I don't think so."

"That should have been the first thing you guys should have done."

"Just a moment," said Giorgio Bergarmi, who felt slighted. "I talked to Trapani. There are three mail boxes in front of the Post Office. One for the island, one for Italy and one for foreign mail. The mail for abroad goes into the bag without sorting. It's then sent directly to Rome."

"Who guarantees that lawyer is outside Italy?" asked the FBI man.

"They don't have all that much mail in Trapani and nobody could remember a fat envelope for Italy," said the man from Sicily.

"Just a moment," said Martella, "the man sent a fat envelope abroad, not registered, or insured. There's quite a bit of theft in the mails these day, especially mail for abroad and especially mail that looks different from the norm, we know that. That man was no fool, he must have figured on that. Therefore he must have kept a copy."

"But who can guarantee us, Chief, that the letter mailed from Trapani was the list with names?" asked Enrico. "Perhaps it was just a narrative, in the same style as the letter we found. When he sent the actual list, he probably *did* send it registered, perhaps from Athens, where it would get lost in the large volume of mail."

"Let me first respond to something Enrico said earlier," said Vittorio. "Of course, we cannot wait for some lawyer. But I do believe that we must give the mob the impression that we're looking for the same thing. We could even 'leak' that through a reliable channel. The more nervous they get, the more it's likely that they'll make a mistake."

A man entered who handed an envelope to Martella. He looked at the contents. After a moment's pause he said:

"People, this is a report from the forensic lab. No fingerprints were found in the basement of 'l'Elastico', but the same weapon was used as on Serifos. We're dealing with the same guys."

"They're not too smart, they left their visiting card," remarked Enrico.

"As I said, probably beginners," agreed Ferdinando.

"It's possible," said Martella. "In any case, it probably means that they didn't use their own people, but outsiders. They want to avoid the chance that the trail leads back to the families. I propose that we keep that in mind. We have to know who they are, or he is, as the case may be. Let's start with a sweep in the street where l'Elastico lived."

110

"Yes, they're all people that talk easily," said Franco Giovale ironically.

"It won't be easy, Franco, I grant you that. But, nevertheless, I propose that you and Enrico start there. I would also like to ask Salvatore a few questions, but as I said, we'd better leave him alone for a while. It's always possible that l'Elastico talked and then we can be certain that Navonna will be next. Therefore, keep him in sight. Vittorio and Ferdinando can do that. You two are unknown here and I'd like to keep it that way, for a while. So, take no action, leave that to us. I will remain in the office and I'll put some people on checking the reactions, if any, we received from the newspaper articles and from the TV."

* * *

When everybody had left, two technicians came in. They installed a tape recorder on a special phone line that, via the exchange, could tape all the conversations on all of Salvatore Navonna's phone lines. The electric clock showed eight minutes past twelve.

*20. Rome, Monday, June 4, 1984

The daily morning ritual was in full swing in a large, luxurious apartment in one of the more expensive, exclusive neighborhoods of the city. The live-in maid had risen at seven, washed and dressed. Her first stop was the rooms where the children slept and she woke them. Pietro and Angelo got out of bed with the usual protests and went to their respective bathrooms. Meanwhile the maid selected the clothes they were to wear that day and placed them in neat stacks on the beds. Then she went to the lower level of the large apartment, started water to boil and set the table in the center of the enormous kitchen. The walls of the kitchen were covered with the most expensive marble available in Italy and the latest developments and gadgets in kitchen equipment were built into the walls and concealed in the specially designed kitchen furniture. The large space bordered the living room at one side and was connected to the library at the other side. The library doubled as TV and rec room. All rooms were large because each floor of the apartment covered almost two thousand square feet. The decorations were rich, but gaudy and flashy. The enormous dining room was dominated by a table with eight chairs. The surface of the table was supported by a single leg in the shape of a bunch of grapes, that were painted in natural colors. The grapes were just a little too blue and the leaves were the wrong color green. The carved backs of the chairs depicted a variety of fruits in diverse colors and looked uncomfortable. The walls were covered by paintings from fashionable masters and everybody knew the prices of the individual works. Their claim to fame as painters was created by a number of representatives of down-at-the-heel nobility, often quoted in the tabloids and elaborately praised by the usual coterie that seemed to feed on itself. The rooms were filled with the most expensive "kitsch" that money could buy.

The lady and the gentleman of the house were still asleep and would not breakfast before eleven. The maid was used to that. The children entered the kitchen and sat down at the table for their breakfast. The bell rang twice at a quarter past eight, which meant that the driver was waiting to take the children to school. The maid urged the two boys on, took their short jackets from the hall closet and finished dressing them. They took their schoolbags and walked to the elevator that took them downstairs, where the doorman greeted them.

"Buongiorno Pietro e Angelo, back to the studies, eh?" said the easy-going man with the friendly face.

"Si, signor Ungari," was the reply.

The chauffeur, in spotless dark blue uniform, opened the glass front door and led them to the shiny, black Jaguar. As they drove off, the maid waved at them.

The English private school was a half hour's drive from the apartment. The school was located in a building that was more than four hundred years old and had been the monastery of an order that had long ceased to exist. It was completely restored and was operated by an owner who had never received a fraction of the education that was the staple of his establishment. The plaster work had been painted yellow and the windows were accentuated by wide, white borders. The building was surrounded by a wall made out of rough-hewn blocks of local rock and just outside was a large parking lot that afforded ample space to the Alfas, Lancias and the occasional Ferrari of the older students in the upper classes. Next to the parking lot was the sports field, a meeting place for the students between classes and during breaks.

The black BMW with two men was waiting when the Jaguar turned into the parking lot of the school. The two men followed the Jaguar with their eyes and watched the two boys get out of the car. There was a constant traffic of cars with parents, or drivers, who dropped off their children, or the children of their employers. When the traffic subsided and all students, in obedience to the ancient clock which still functioned in the old tower, had entered the building, one of the men started the BMW and drove off. Five minutes before the morning break, at a quarter to eleven, they were back and parked the car in front of the entrance to the sports field. The man next to the driver lowered the visor and checked his moustache in the mirror. The glue was holding. He donned a pair of glasses with plain glass and got out of the car. The first children came cheering in the direction of the sports field.

* * *

Around noon the phone rang in the apartment. Casino boss Salvatore Navonna stood up and walked to the instrument. The left side of his face was discolored with iodine and the wounds, which had required a number of stitches, were covered with gauze and tape. He had told his wife that it was the result of an accident in the alley

113

behind the casino. He had elaborated on a set of unlikely circumstances, but his wife had hardly listened. He picked up the phone and identified himself. While he listened to the voice at the other end of the line, his hands began to shake and his face paled.

"One moment," he said, "I'll pick it up at another phone."

He left the room into the direction of the library. His wife called: "Who is it?"

Without answering he went into the library, took the phone off the desk and snarled: "Goddamit, are you crazy? Where are they?"

"Don't worry, Salvatore, my partner is playing a game with them. They're having a good time, just don't worry about it. Didn't you enjoy playing hookie, once in a while, when you were young?" It was the same slow, irritating voice.

"Wadda you want?"

"How's the face, Salvatore? A bit tender, is it? I thought that was pretty nasty of Claudio. Believe me, the boss was really upset with him. But that's no help to you, that doesn't make it go away."

"You just listen to me, I don't know who you are, but I'll find out. I've enough contacts who can find you."

"Don't you remember what we asked you? Or have you forgotten already?" answered the man.

"I told you, I don't know nothing about a list."

"I never mentioned a list, you started that yourself. If you hadn't said anything about it, we would never have known the difference. But, you see, now that we *do* know, it's your problem."

"Where are my children. I want to talk to them. Right now!"

"They are here. They're staying with Claudio. He loves children so. Just don't worry about your heirs. Just try to remember something we can use, something about your friend Dubour from that asshole Greek island. Jesus Christ, Salvatore, what a fucking hole-in-the-wall island that is! I've been there twice, now, and I hope to never see it again."

"I told you I want to talk to my children," whispered Salvatore desperately.

114

"Listen, tell you what we'll do. We call you tonight, because your kids want to spend the night here. I'm sure you know somebody who will want to help you. Just ask around, here and there, find out what we want to know and we'll all have a happy ending." The connection was broken.

Salvatore sank back in his chair, devastated. They had finally reached him. Everybody in the country, sooner or later, would get their turn. For more than twenty years he had been able to operate outside the Mafia. He paid his *pizzo** for the business, but he had never known, or wanted to know who his "protectors" were. Of course, they must have been among the regular visitors, from time to time, that was almost a certainty. He sometimes thought he recognized them, imagined that he could smell them. If he was not sure, one of his personnel would usually confirm his suspicions. Those types of guests were as much as possible ignored, they were given bad service, wrong drinks, unresponsive girls, things like that and generally they would not come back. That way he had been able to keep his business "clean". But now they had penetrated into his family, had taken his children. The bastards!

He had indeed spoken with Robert Dubour toward the end of April. They had dinner together and he had passed some information to Robert. A small service, because he heard enough. They had been friends for years. Robert had told him that he wanted to retire and that he had made a list. But that was all he knew. Just that there was a list with names. Robert had not said anymore about it and he had not wanted to know. They had been buddies in the mercenary army of Schramme to the greater glory of that bastard Tsjombe. A black politician who wanted to have his own kingdom. One of many at that time. He had filled his pockets with the development money provided by Belgium and then, when things got too hot, he had fled to Franco's Spain, a refuge for many a criminal. Later he had heard that Tsjombe had gone to Mallorca and had started a nightclub with a French sounding name. He and

---

* Protection money

115

his accomplices ran the club for a while. One night, his own pilot, bribed by the opposition, had flown him to Algeria in his own plane. There he had wound up in prison and had died a convenient, early and, of course, natural death. Nobody disputed the facts. That was all a long time ago.

He stood up, looked at his watch, noted the time as seven minutes past twelve and left the room.

*21. Rome, the same day

A plain clothes policeman entered the office of Chief Inspector Enzo Martella.

"We've followed up on every call we received as a result of the TV pictures and the newspaper stories and we haven't found much useful."

"The usual crazies and wise asses?"

"Yes, sir, a lot of them. But we have *one* lead we should follow up. The owner of a second hand store. He recognized our man and was extremely positive about it."

Martella read the address and said:

"Keep me informed of any other possible leads."

"Of course, sir." The detective left.

Martella picked up the phone and had Enrico paged. He and Franco were trying the get some additional leads in the street of the postcard seller. When he reached them he asked:

"How's it going?"

"You know how it is, Chief. Most people won't talk and those that do, don't know a thing."

"Yes, it was to be expected. How far have you got?"

"People to the left, right, across the street . . . about forty people so far. But all *niente*! If you've something else, we'd probably be more productive, there."

116

"I have the name and address from somebody who called in response to the TV picture."

"Positive?"

"Yes, according to the one who took the call. Get on it, all right? Let the street wait, for the moment."

He passed on the name and address and returned to his own work.

* * *

Inspector Enrico Tomasso, accompanied by his partner, Inspector Franco Giovale, entered the store that smelled of mothballs.

"Good afternoon, sir, are you the owner?" asked Enrico, addressing the man behind the counter.

"Si, signore."

"We're from police headquarters, you called us." Tomasso identified himself.

"Yes, yes, I saw the picture in the newspaper, this morning. I'd seen him on the TV also, I recognized him at once. But, you know, the TV is so fast, don't you know? But when I saw the same picture in the paper, I looked at him for a while, don't you know? And now I'm sure. That man was here, about four weeks ago."

"You're certain?"

"Oh, yes. I even remember exactly what he bought, don't you know."

"That's very good."

"Yes, well, usually you forget, don't you know. But this customer was special, so to speak. He bought all kinds of stuff I had planned to throw away for some time. But I don't easily throw something out, don't you know."

"Yes, I understand," agreed Enrico.

"He came in about two o'clock."

"Do you remember the date?"

"Yes, well, what a question. It was about a month ago, don't you know."

"Would you try to remember? Think hard!"

"Is it that important?" asked the shop keeper.

"It could be very important."

"Well, yes, what a question. A month ago, what sort of day could it have been? . . . well, well, . . . that's not easy, don't you know."

"Let me help you. Easter was on the 15th and 16th.* Was it *before*, or after Easter?"

"Oh, I know for certain, now. It was *after* Easter."

"Do you remember what sort of day it was?"

"Well, it was in the beginning of the week, don't you know. Wait a minute, it was a Monday. Yes, I'm sure. Yes, I'd just cleared the counter of a delivery from one of my suppliers." The word "suppliers" was pronounced as if he represented one of the famous fashion houses.

"Yes, he always comes on Monday, because he's on the road during the week, don't you know. Then he comes here on Monday and I go through his offerings."

"So, a Monday after Easter, let's see." Enrico took out his notebook. "That would have been either the 23rd, or the 30th. The next day was May 1, Labor Day."

"Give me a break, sir, Labor Day. That's one holiday I don't celebrate. Shopkeepers work every day, don't you know, just to make ends meet. Anyway, the 23rd, or the 30th, I really wouldn't know."

"Well, let it go for the moment. What did the man buy?"

"Oh, well, that's different. First of all a pair of knickerbockers, *plus-fours*, I should say. You know what I mean? You've got to wear those long stocking with it, don't you know, and clasps below the knee."

"What color?"

"Green corduroy and it looked a mess. It was real old stuff,

* In Italy, as in most of Europe, Easter is a two-day celebration.

118

don't you know. When I saw it on the counter, in the light of day, so to speak, I wondered why I hadn't thrown it out long ago."

"What else?"

"A jacket. A sort of English jacket, but really old-fashioned. Hunters wear a coat like that, sometimes."

"What color?"

"Light beige, with leather patches on the elbows."

"What else?"

"Yes, a couple of shirts, but I don't remember that very well, don't you know. But I remember the trousers very well, also that jacket."

"Anything else particular about the man?"

"Not that I noticed."

"You've helped us a lot. Here's my card. If you remember anything else, please give us a call. If I'm not there, just leave your number and I'll be in touch with you."

"No problem, ispettore. By the way, if you don't mind my asking, what has he done?"

"To tell you the truth, we don't know, we're trying to find that out."

"You guys must have a rotten job, don't you know?"

"Yes, sometimes," laughed Enrico, "but we're stuck. We never had enough schooling."

"Well, I'd be careful, if I were you. There's a lot of scum around, these days."

"I've got my big brother with me," answered Enrico, pointing at Franco.

"Yes, make jokes, but it isn't funny, don't you know."

They left the shop and walked in the direction of the car. They were perhaps a hundred feet away when they heard the voice behind them.

"Gentlemen, Gentlemen!"

It was the shopkeeper and he came running.

"I remember now, it was the 30th, because my brother stopped by that evening. He's got a similar shop, don't you know,

119

and we talked. That's when I told him about the green pants I managed to sell. We laughed about it. He couldn't figure out what sort of pants they could have been, so I put the ends of *my* pants in my socks. Yes, I remember now, because the next day he went to Milan, to our oldest sister. I can ask him, if you want, but I'm certain, now."

"You're fantastic. I want to thank you most sincerely for your trouble."

"No problem. Would you let me know when you've solved the case? It's a nice idea to have helped, don't you know."

"I promise."

"Well, good bye, gentlemen. Good luck. I better get back to the store, before they steal me blind."

*22. Rome, the same day

Two detectives of the *Questura Centrale* had relieved the two FBI men from the surveillance of casino boss Salvatore Navonna. At six o'clock the complete, original team was assembled. Inspector Enrico Tomasso glanced at his notes and began:

"As was to be expected, we didn't find out anything from the neighbors of 'l'Elastico'. Nobody heard, or saw anything. *Niente!* Even the neighbors directly above don't know a thing. It's hard to believe, because they must have made a lot of noise and the sound insulation in those houses is hardly from this century. But nothing. They didn't hear anything, saw anything, or noticed anything. The apartment just above the basement is occupied by a family of eight. We talked to them all. But, as we know, in cases like this, Italians are all deaf. Therefore I propose, Chief, we don't waste anymore time on that aspect. We next visited a second hand shop. The owner was very positive. Our man was there on the 30th of April and we know what he bought. In my opinion it was a disguise. A pair of green, corduroy *plus fours*, knickerbockers, don't you know . . ." Franco smiled briefly, but Enrico continued: ". . . and an old-fashioned, beige hunting jacket with leather patches on the elbows."

"At least we have a reasonable description," remarked Enzo Martella.

"Yes, as you say, but they're not exactly clothes that help you hide in the crowd. If you were to wear those in Rome, the whole town would be talking about it."

"But that's really cunning," said Special Agent Vittorio. "Exactly by dressing so outlandishly, nobody will suspect you of anything. Somebody who wants to hide in the crowd, for whatever reason, dresses differently. You make sure you don't get noticed if people are looking for you. Everybody knows that. He does the opposite, he makes himself look like a clown. Also that sort of outfit suits him to a tee. Somebody by the name of Frank C. Johnson from Kenilworth. You can't *get* more English than that."

"Or Neville James Footman," said Ferdinando. "Don't forget, he's got *two* English names."

"You're right, that's another possibility."

"But why," asked Enzo Martella. "We haven't a clue that he has done anything in particular while in town, other that the fact that he knows Salvatore and that he stayed at the Continental."

"*Momento, signore*," interrupted Ferdinando. "We should tell you something before you go any further. At around three o'clock, our friend Salvatore got into his car and went to his club. He was there for about twenty minutes and then went home again. Nothing unusual, except for the fact that our friend was badly damaged. He is covered in bandages and I don't think he cut himself shaving."

"Anything else?"

"I thought it important, Chief."

"What are you suggesting?"

"I propose we have a little talk with him and ask what sort of razor he's been using, lately."

"I think he's had visitors," said Martella.

"I think the same, but perhaps it was only his mother-in-law."

"He could be the next one to be knocked off."

"I don't think so, it would already have happened, otherwise. They have kept him alive because he knows something."

"Enrico, pull Navonna in for an interrogation," ordered Martella.

"Now, at once?"

"Yes, I want him here. If he knows something, and that's not impossible, we have a good chance that he'll be killed at any time."

"May I add something about the disguise, Chief?" asked Enrico.

"Go ahead."

"Let's assume that the man kept some sort of records that are extremely dangerous for a number of people in the opposite camp and we further assume that he deposited that information with a lawyer. Name, address unknown. Via l'Elastico he contacted Salvatore. At that time he stayed at the Continental. Nice suit, nice clothes. So, not the knickerbockers. If that had been the case, the people at the hotel would have told us. Then he bought those ridiculous clothes. We don't know why. But we can safely assume that they were meant as some sort of disguise. Who knows, perhaps that lawyer is here in Rome. The lawyer knows him as 'that crazy Englishman'. You see, let's assume that you deposit a number of papers with a lawyer with strict orders for secrecy. You can do that. But a lawyer isn't crazy. If a distinguished gentleman enters his office with a number of papers for safekeeping and the request not to open them, except in the case of a violent, an unnatural death, then what does a lawyer think, especially an Italian lawyer?"

"That it's Mafia related," added Martella.

"Exactly and an Italian lawyer won't touch it with a ten-foot pole. But if, instead, some crazy Englishman hands him a bunch of papers and talks about a scientific discovery, or something, then the lawyer won't be at all suspicious. What I mean is this: With what we have so far, we should question all lawyers in Rome. It's possible that what we're looking for is right here, in the city. Because, other than that, what could have been his purpose in Rome?"

"Anybody object to overtime?" asked Martella resolutely.

There was a bit of a murmur and Special Agent Ferdinando Cotone of the FBI remarked: "As long as I can be home at ten o'clock."

"All right, then let's carry on. Enrico's theory is not impossible, but . . . the opposition may have come to the same conclusion. If that's so, there's a lawyer in danger. Enrico and Franco go and pick up Salvatore. Giorgio, go to Documentation and get a list of lawyers. We'll start calling, perhaps soon we'll know more."

✳23. Rome, the same evening

"Listen to me! I don't know what you want from me, but I'm *telling* you, it was just an accident. That should be enough, even for you. I know you've been after my ass, all my life, but let's talk as normal people, shall we? So, I happen to have a bandage on my face and right-a-way I'm picked up with a paddy wagon." While he talked, casino boss Salvatore Navonna raised his hands in a theatrical gesture. Martella was sitting behind the desk and Enrico leaned against the wall, his arms crossed.

"But you don't think we wanted you just because of that little scratch, now did you, Salvatore? You want to talk like normal people. All right, let's do that. We know what you do for a living and we know it's against the law. But, we won't talk about that. That's not my business. That's a matter for Vice. Let me show you something, pal."

Martella showed the postcard that had been found in the basement of the murdered postcard seller.

"You see? There's your name and the number of a hotel."

Salvatore looked at the card, read what was written and placed it back on the desk with an expression of disgust.

"So, what?"

"Do you know where we found the card?" asked Martella.

"No idea and I couldn't care less."

"In the basement of l'Elastico. You know he's dead?"

"I heard that, yes."

"How did you know? It wasn't in the papers."

"Ah, well, you hear something, now and then."

"You know Salvatore, I'm starting to dislike you. You think we're all stupid and that all we do is twiddle our thumbs at the tax-payer's expense. But look here, my friend, I've been hired to make sure that there are as few unexplained deaths in this city as possible. That's what they pay me for. Now, some corpses have my deepest sympathy, I don't mind telling you, but others, well, I couldn't care less. So, Salvatore, don't get the idea that I'll be at your funeral. We asked you to stop by, because we think you may be able to help us with an ongoing case. It's just a bonus for you if it means that your wife won't be an untimely widow and your kids won't have to miss their papa. You know what I mean? Look, the case in question, we know more about it than you. You can believe me, or not, but we're dealing with a more important type of characters than the pimps you usually deal with, there in the Via Veneto. Therefore, I'd advise you urgently: don't try to bluff us, don't be the big man, but cooperate with us. You see, without your help we'll get there as well. Perhaps it will take a little longer, but that won't be your concern anymore. You'll be long gone, dead, cold and with a label attached to your big toe. You get me? So, do as you like. I, for one, would just as soon go home, right now, because I've been here since early this morning."

It remained silent in the office. Salvatore looked in front of him as if he was trying to weigh every word Martella had spoken. Finally he said:

"Wadda you want to know?"

"Do you know Robert Dubour?"

124

"Yes, I do."

"You know he's dead?"

"No, I didn't."

Martella noticed the slight hesitation and knew the man was lying. He pretended not to notice and went on.

"Dubour was killed on the Greek island of Serifos, where he lived. We've reason to believe that it was the work of a well-known organization."

"Yes, I figured as much," said Salvatore, defeated.

"Why did you figure that?"

"I *did* talk to him. l'Elastico gave me the number of his hotel."

"When was that?"

"End of April."

"Did you know him?"

"For more than twenty years. We were in the Congo together. We were army buddies."

"What do you know about him?"

"Little. We saw each other once in a while. But I've no idea what he did."

"Never thought about it?"

"Oh, yes. I thought he did the dirty work for a couple of big guys."

"Did he ever talk about it?"

"No, he never talked about it. Except the last time, I started that myself."

"How did he react?"

"That it would be the last time. That he wanted to retire. I warned him."

"What for?"

"Come on, I don't have to tell you. The whole fucking country has gone to hell. I'm not exactly an upstanding citizen, nobody knows that better than me, but at least I've never had anything to do with the mob."

"Was Dubour one of them?"

"The mob? No way!"

"How can you be so sure?"

"He was much too smart for that. He was a loner. Roberto was in business for himself."

"What did he want from you?"

"Information."

"What sort of information?"

"Joe Bacelli."

"Aha, Bacelli. What did you know about him?"

"Little. I just asked around."

"Where?"

"Ispettore, let's not make it more difficult than it is, already. I just asked around and gave the information to Roberto."

"Such as?"

"That Bacelli was staying with a friend, I don't know who, and that was enough for Roberto. Money will get you all you want to know in Sicily. Especially when it's about somebody who's no longer among the favorites. But, after I told him that Joe was staying in Sicily, he could narrow it down."

"That was all?"

"Yes, I offered to go with him."

"Why?"

"Because I hate the scum as much as you do, that's why. Nowadays they even send children into the streets to shoot anybody they want. The whole fucking country has gone to hell, I tell you."

"Let me tell you something, Salvatore. The people who killed l'Elastico, are the same that did it to Dubour."

"I didn't know that."

"You know what that means, Salvatore? You're next!"

"My ass! What could they want with me?"

The man was getting more nervous and it did not escape Martella. Ruthlessly he used the opportunity. He leaned forward and after a long pause he whispered: "How did you get hurt, signor Salvatore Navonna?"

"I told you, a small accident at home."

126

"Go to hell, man. But, OK, it's your funeral. You're old and wise enough to know what you're doing. Just one more question: Did Dubour ever tell you anything that might be important to us?"

"I told you everything. You can't ask more than that."

Martella took another long pause that gave the entire conversation an extra dramatic meaning. Enrico felt the tension in the room and knew that the man in the chair was getting uncomfortable and was on the verge of collapse. When the tension in the room had become almost unbearable, Martella sighed deeply, rubbed both eyes as if he had just woken up from a deep sleep, looked Navonna deep in the eyes and said: "I'll ask you just one more time. How did you get hurt?"

Salvatore began to shake, tears filled his eyes and with clenched teeth he uttered: "Because they have my kids!"

"What!?"

"Si, ispettore, the bastards took my kids, Pietro and Angelo, that's what's the matter, signor Martella, they've been kidnapped! That's your Italia! And I beg you in the name of all Saints, keep them out of it. Don't mess with it!"

"It's too late, Salvatore, we're in it, up to our necks."

"The bastards have kidnapped my children! They called me this afternoon."

"Who did?"

"The two sons-of-bitches that beat me up, last night."

"Wait a moment, wait a moment, Salvatore, calm down," said Martella soothingly. "This is something entirely different. Let's talk about it." He gestured.

"Shall I get something to drink, Chief," Enrico asked, interpreting the gesture correctly, feeling something had to be done to diffuse the situation.

"A good idea, get something," said Martella wanly.

While Enrico left the room, the two sat silently opposite each other, both occupied with their own thoughts. It was true, the tactics of the Mafia were getting more merciless all the time. The situation deteriorated every year and was almost catastrophic. The

Mafia was the uncrowned king in at least three large provinces of Italy. The areas they controlled were being transformed into underdeveloped regions. In Mezzogiorno at least twenty thousand Mafiosi, all with a police record, were registered. At least five hundred criminal organizations operated openly in Italy, leaving poverty and misery in their wake. Wherever the Mafia had the upper hand, the economic development lagged behind. In the early days it was only capable people who removed their "clean" capital from regions like *Mezzogiorno* and moved North. Nowadays, even cities like Milan were practically dominated by the Mafia. Indeed, as Salvatore had remarked, a new phenomenon, that of the "gangster youth" had sprung up and terrorized entire cities. Children took advantage of the fact that, as juveniles, they would get a lighter sentence and at the same time they received practical training in criminality. In the old days the Mafia would execute pick-pockets and purse-snatchers when they became a nuisance. Today they encouraged such petty crimes. That is how they created their own "training schools". The best, or rather, the most merciless, were then later selected for full membership in one of the families. The criminal organizations did not fear the harshest actions of the State. They had seen that such actions made no real difference. Two hundred and fifty thousand people worked for the various judicial and police organizations. That seemed like a lot for a population of less than sixty million Italians. But most of them were occupied with paper work, the endless red tape: immigration, issuing permits, checking the postal services, passport offices, driver's licenses and so on. An endless parade of tasks that had nothing to do with maintaining Law and Order in its most basic form.

In the old days, the Mafia had been primarily an Italian concern, but now it spread through all of Europe and the world. The Neapolitan *camorra* owned a network that was primarily aimed at South America, The Calabrian *andrangheta* was firmly established in Canada, Australia and France. The Sicilian *mafia* was almost all-pervasive in the United States of America and had their tentacles in England and Germany. And you never knew who they were, who were your friends and who could not be trusted. This power system maintained the needless waste which depleted entire regions of Italy and left millions in poverty and want.

Enrico had returned with some soft drinks and poured them in the plastic cups.

"Start at the beginning," said Martella.

"I told you about Dubour, I talked about him."

"Have you told me everything?"

"No, to be honest, but I need you, you understand? As I said, I gathered some information for him. From a couple of customers. Small fry, not worth your trouble. That's how I found out that Bacelli was hiding in Favignana. I spent an evening talking with Roberto. Over the years he told me things, from time to time, but I never really knew what he was up to, although I had a good idea. In any case, he *never* mentioned names. Look, signor Martella, what did we learn when we were young? We learned how to shoot and how to suppress the natives. That's all. I still know all of them from that time. None has become a priest. But Roberto was always the smartest. He could have been big, I mean *really* big, no matter what he had started, business, or whatever. But . . . he was from the wrong side of the track. He spoke better Italian than me, knew more than me. I don't know exactly, but I bet he spoke at least eight languages fluently . . ."

He paused, took a sip, seemed to prepare himself.

" . . . but I did understand," he continued, after a brief silence, "that he only concentrated on really difficult jobs for the really big guys. Political, too, I think. The last time we talked he assured me that nothing could happen to him. He had, let's see, how *did* he say that? Oh, yes: 'I've recorded twenty years of history and carefully documented it,' he said. 'If something ever happens to me, they'll grab another five hundred,' that's what he said. Then I asked him: 'Do they know that?' and he answered: 'They do, if they're smart.' He was convinced that he was safe. Maybe you think I'm crazy if I tell you, but Roberto was a sensitive and above all, a civilized man. I'm convinced he didn't kill innocent people, respectable family men with kids to care for. No, no, the scum he took care of had it coming. *That* he did tell me, once."

"How was he approached for a contract?"

"No idea. I've thought about it, sometimes. One way or the other, he must have been reachable, but nevertheless, he's been able to remain the invisible man, all those years."

"And that's all you discussed with him?"

"Yes, during the first meeting. A few days later he called again."

"When was that?"

"Maybe a week later."

"What did he want?"

"Information again. He told me that a guy had been strangled in the train from Palermo to Rome, somewhere in the beginning of May. Apparently he had heard that. He wanted me to find out who it was."

"And did you find oút?"

"Oh, yes. It was in the paper. Well, of course, only the initials. But it wasn't too difficult to figure out."

"Carlo Barinne?" asked Martella.

"Exactly, that's who it was."

"What did you find about him?"

"Little. You know probably as much as I do. A soldier of the Lovallo family, just a punk."

"We didn't know that."

"Well, maybe it'll help you."

"I hope so, Barinne was well connected."

"That scum is everywhere, ispettore."

"You're right, Salvatore, the good old days, when all we had to worry about was an illegal gambling house, are gone for good."

Salvatore laughed.

"You should see it more as a sport, a sport that pays off, sometimes."

"Sometimes? Really? Never mind. Now, what about the kidnapping. From the beginning, please."

"Last night two armed guys caught me at the back door of my casino. They went inside with me, I had no choice. They were riff-raff, there's no other word for it. I'm not exactly an altar boy myself, but this, this was scum of the lowest order. They wanted to know if I knew Roberto. I finally admitted that. They were talking about 'records' that Roberto kept and they wanted to know what I knew about *that*. Well, as I told you already, I didn't know anything about it. But they insisted that I knew where the stuff was. Then one of them hit me with brass knuckles and they left. This morning, at about eleven thirty, they called me to tell me they had my children."

"In exchange for the records?"

"Exactly. And you can believe me, or not, but if I had any idea where I could find those records, I would have picked them up already and I wouldn't be sitting here."

"I understand."

"So, then I called the boys' school. Apparently they had already started a search for the kids. They were just about to call me. That's it, signore, that's all I know."

"You're sure that the man on the phone was the same that came last night?"

"Absolutely. The son-of-a-bitch speaks real slow, pestering, you know what I mean? I'll never forget that voice, it was the same bastard, I'm sure."

"They mention any names?"

"One of them was called Claudio."

"You ever seen them before, in your . . . eh, establishments, or wherever?"

"No, never."

"Did you see what they looked like?"

"I could draw you a picture."

"We'll do that in a moment. What did they tell you?"

"They told me that Roberto was dead. So, I *did* know that. I just lied to you. Mi scusi."

"Never mind, go on."

131

"They even had a picture of him. He looked like an eccentric Englishman. Knee pants, or something, a strange cap, a pipe in his mouth, mustache, a back pack. But you could clearly see it was Roberto. They told me they took the picture in Palermo."

"Anything else?"

"Yes, they said he was pretending to be a treasure hunter, an . . . eh, an archeologist. They'd spotted him in Rome, at first. They also knew I had talked to him. l'Elastico had talked, they said."

"So, he talked before they killed him?"

"Yes, I think so. But the only thing they were interested in, was the records of Roberto. That's all they asked about. I've no idea how they found out. Roberto was much too smart to let that leak."

"You're wrong there, Salvatore. Roberto was smart enough to let it leak on purpose. That was his insurance policy. That's why he could carry on as long as he did."

"But this time they killed him anyway, I don't understand that."

"Well, it's a mystery to me as well," said Martella. "There's no way to reconcile it with the regular way the families operate. It was a very dumb mistake."

"Yeah, I thought so too, but that's what makes them so dangerous. There's no talking with the scum."

"Salvatore, I'll tell you honestly, it's an extremely dangerous situation. If I had known sooner, what I know now, I wouldn't have had you picked up. There's a chance they know where you are. And that's dangerous for the children. But, who knows, maybe we'll get lucky. In any case, let's make sure. You're going home and you *stay* home. We'll call you a cab, that's less noticeable. Is there another entrance to your apartment building?"

"There's a fire escape, at the back."

"We'll tap your phone and we'll assign some guards. We'll come in over the fire escape. We'll supply you with our mug shots and you take your time over them. Perhaps your visitors are included. But above all, we must make sure that they don't get the idea we're involved. That's just for the children's sake, nothing

132

else. I know about it and so does my colleague. There will be no report about it, at least for now, so there will be no leak from this end. As you said yourself, you can't trust anybody, anymore. But we'll minimize the risk as much as possible. If you have to negotiate for your children, we'll not interfere. We don't need any heroes and we'll keep it out of the papers. You agree?"

"Grazie, grazie, ispettore. I trust you."

"You have no choice, Salvatore, because you have no one else."

The man left the office after emotionally shaking Martella's hands and thanking him profusely.

*24. Rome, the same evening

While Salvatore Navonna was being questioned in one of the offices of the *Questura Centrale*, in another part of Rome, in one of the expensive suburbs, *padrino* Giovanni Lovallo threw the telephone back on the hook and swore loudly. Only four days ago he had talked to Riccardo Mannucci in New York. That same evening, his cousin Mario had been found in an alley in New York, riddled with bullet holes. Joe Bacelli had taken a bullet through the head in Favignana. Both Mario and Joe had fallen from grace as the result of a few enormous blunders. Carlo Barinne who had worked for him for years, had been found dead in a train in Rome. If the current case kept on track, it would not be hard to figure who would be next. And now, in a mood of sheer arrogance, those two bumbling fools had kidnapped two children.

They were only supposed to have asked questions of Salvatore. They knew that Salvatore had spoken with the man they had spotted in Sicily. They *knew* that the man had kept extensive records, with names, places and circumstances that could cause them all to wind up in jail if that information fell in the wrong hands. But to kidnap two children for that? No, dammit, that was too much. And besides, there was too much risk involved. Anyway, the casino boss was an unimportant link. The corpse in Serifos, the purpose for it all, would have been too cunning to share his information with anybody. He most certainly would *not* have shared it with Salvatore Navonna. He shivered at the thought that he had to inform the man in New York. The little bit of respect that he had left with the Cosa Nostra would then be a thing of the past.

In addition, he would be in danger himself. He decided not to call. He had to find those two bastards *before* he called New York to keep them informed. The kidnapping had to stop. The list had to be recovered, no matter what. Riccardo had been right about that. If they had just let the man live, nothing would have happened, nobody would have been any wiser. The stupidity of killing him, would cost them all their necks. He had used those two bastards on the advice of his own people. Had it been a honest mistake, or was it a set-up, to make him look bad? That's the usual way power was eventually transferred within the organization. In the eyes of his closest lieutenants he was already an old man. He was fifty-six and that was the end of the line to an ambitious young punk of thirty-five who, whatever the cost, wanted to get the power. How cunning was he? What were the plans to unseat him? And, above all, who was it? Most probably one who did not have to worry about the list from the man on Serifos. His name would not appear on the list.

And was it not an ideal way to neutralize a number of families? That would clear the way. If a person was aware of the importance of the list, if he knew that the compiler of the list, in order to save his own neck, had built a "safety" in the system in case he died under suspicious circumstances, then his killer would only have to wait. What a simple way to take care of all who stood in the way of his own rise to power! He would be untouchable. It was almost too simple. You just kill the right man and within a certain amount of time a document surfaces that will put at least five hundred competitors behind bars, or worse. But who would do such a thing? Who, of all his people, had both the intelligence and the will to set such a trap? They were all *family*, after all. There were no strangers in his immediate circle. That had always been one of his most important rules. But he also knew the story of Cain and Able.

Was it possible that under his very own eyes, without him noticing, within his own immediate family, there festered a disease, a swelling that was about to burst? A plot that was about to hatch? He went over the names in his mind and tried to remember incidents that, afterward, had seemed suspicious. How had he achieved power himself? How many had he killed, or ordered to be killed, in order to sit in this chair? Was he any better? No, of course not. So, how could he be so naive as to think that history would not repeat itself? He was already obliged to dance to the tunes played by Riccardo Mannucci in New York. That one had gathered more and more power lately. He, Giovanni Lovallo, was these days hardly more than a branch manager for headquarters in the United States. Cosa Nostra boss Riccardo Mannucci had his tentacles in chemical waste, public works, everything. Anybody in the know, knew that drugs had become less and less important as a source of income. It had gradually diminished in importance over the last three years. Of course, there were still healthy profits, but the increase in the use of narcotics just didn't go fast enough. More and more bribery and public works, so-called "clean" enterprises, including garbage collection, returned a higher profit, many times higher, than dealing in drugs. And those high profit enterprises were all under the ultimate control of Riccardo Mannucci.

Did Mannucci's name appear on the list from the dead man in Serifos? It was the first time the thought crossed his mind. What did Riccardo know? Was he behind it all? It was hard to imagine. The phone conversation, only four days ago, did not point that way. Riccardo had been furious about the handling of the case. He had even said that "we" would all wind up in jail if the list fell into the wrong hands. That "we" had clearly included himself. But, of course, it could be a trick, a trap. The two families had always gotten along well. There had been marriages between the families. They were connected in a thousand ways, but that could change overnight, especially if it was a question of business, of money. Despite all the embraces, the greetings and the kisses, during meetings, farewells, weddings and other festive occasions, a healthy suspicion and a certain amount of distrust, remained the best assurance for a long life.

There were plenty of examples for that in the past of most families. The agreements not to cross into each other's territories and to respect each other's business interests were old and of long standing. Agreements made by people from an earlier generation. And for a young, cunning, calculating *padrino* like Riccardo Mannucci, that was ancient history.

He decided to discuss the matter with the few people of whom he knew for sure they could be trusted. Nobody else would be involved, for the moment. Not even Riccardo Mannucci. Especially not him! The contact with the two punks who had kidnapped those two kids had been made by his own organization. New York did not even know who they were. Mario had been the only one and he had been found dead in an alley, hidden under a heap of garbage.

He stood up from behind his desk, opened the door and called a name. A man entered. It was obvious from his clothes and his appearance that he paid daily visits to the barber. His clothes must have cost a small fortune. He had an arrogant demeanor and there was no feeling in his steel blue eyes. He looked like the typical Italian macho who thought highly of himself.

"Ruggero, they fucked it up," started Giovanni. "Those two assholes kidnapped Salvatore's kids."

"Well, that don't make it no easier."

"Ruggero, it's a catastrophe! Don't you realize that?"

"*Ascolta, padre mio,* I've been kept outside this business from the start. You only told me to call Mario and tell him to fix it," said the son in a bored tone of voice and he looked demonstratively at his vulgar gold Rolex, decorated with diamonds.

"I did that for your own good. I want you to stay clean."

"Go to hell with that fucking excuse about what is and what ain't good for me and how I have to stay so fucking clean."

"You can get angry all you want, I don't give a damn. Just take it as a warning. If you've got to go fuck some broad again, go ahead. But I'm telling you, we're in trouble, deep trouble. And if you can do no better than give me a big mouth, to talk back to me, then I couldn't care less. But let me warn you: you, your brother and me, we better pull together, or otherwise you too, will look at thirty years behind bars. And the only piece of ass you'll see in those thirty years may be the nurse in the hospital."

"*Mi scusi, mi scusi*, I'll shut up."

"Yeah, I've heard that before, *le scuse*, but what does it get me? We're in a heap of trouble, you, me, the whole family! I don't know who betrayed us, but there's *one* fucker among us who's forgotten his oath!"

"Tell me about it," said Ruggero.

"They took those two kids of Salvatore. If you want to get the whole fucking police force of Italy on your ass, that's the best fucking way to do it. Somebody is trying to set us up, that's what I say."

"How?"

"That son-of-a-bitch on that Greek island had a list with names. My name is on it, you can be fucking sure of that."

"So far, nobody's got that list."

"Not yet! But that list will show up, you can bet your ass on that! We've been betrayed, Ruggero."

"Who done that?"

"I wish I knew."

"Well, that makes it fucking easy," answered the son carelessly.

"Goddamn you, no fucking jokes, you asshole!"

"What else you want me to say? You want I should tell you who betrayed us and how? So, what's the use of that if the *Carabinieri* get the list anyhow? They'll be on it too, right?"

137

"Not all of them, Ruggero. There are a few who never used the man. And what could be better for them than that all the names are nicely delivered to the *Questura Centrale*, eh? Then they can take over here, just like that. It's war, Ruggero! You can see that in Sicily. Whole fucking tribes behind bars since April. More than eighteen have been killed, just to divvy up the spoils. Everybody knows that we, the Lovallo family, are a nice little gold mine. How many, do you think, can't just fucking *wait* to take over?"

"So, where's it coming from, you think?"

"It can come from anywhere. They should never have killed that fucker on Serifos. Everybody fucking *knew* that! Mario knew that! Nobody should have been stupid enough to open *that* can of worms. But it fucking happened! Now it's being said that those two exceeded their orders! My ass, Ruggero. They had their orders and they followed them. Just like Carlo Barinne. His orders were to follow him, no more, no less. But somebody figured different. Somebody said: kill the son-of-a-bitch, *up* comes the fucking list, *poof* goes the competition and the business is fucking ripe for the taking!"

"Yes, but if it was orders, why do they go on? The asshole on Serifos is dead, they got what they want. What else do they want?"

"To draw attention, my boy, to draw attention. *Ascoltami*, somewhere in the world a lawyer is waiting to hear that his client is no more. How does that lawyer find that out, eh? There were no invitations to the funeral. Maybe there was a notice in some fucking Greek newspaper, but what American, or English, or whatever lawyer, reads Greek newspapers? *Nessuno*, nobody! Of course, if he doesn't hear from his client for a while, it's possible that he reads the fucking list and sends it to the local constable. But when does that happen, eh? Lawyers are like snails, that can take years. So, how can you speed it up? Publicity, my boy, get it in *all* the fucking papers. A simple murder is no longer interesting, the news hounds ignore them, most of the time. But what about a kidnapping of two little children, eh? Nice pictures and all! *That's* news! They want a piece of that! And that's what the bastards are after.

138

They want to make sure that this lawyer finds out that his client has gone to hell. The sooner that happens, the sooner they can sit back and watch the big clean-up. Now do you fucking understand?"

"But who would wanna do that to us, *padre*?"

"I wish I knew."

"What can we do?"

"Do you know those two fuck-ups?"

"Vaguely."

"How vaguely. Do you know their names?"

"One only. I know what broad he goes to."

"Thanks be to Christ. All that fucking around you do is good for something, after all. Go after it."

"Alone?"

"Take two of the boys, but don't tell them what's it all about. I want you to talk to that broad, do it alone. Don't take any risks. Don't fuck it up, be nice, pay her."

*25. Rome, the same evening

When Chief Inspector Enzo Martella stepped into his car at ten thirty that night, he suddenly realized that it was his birthday. He was now forty-seven years old. He had not given it a thought and no one had reminded him. He had almost no family and it was difficult to make friends in his job. He was a child from a small family, unusual in Italy. His only sister lived in the United States and his parents had passed away. He drove home at a sedate pace, thinking about the current case. He liked to mull over things in the anonymity of his car. His thoughts wandered. As happened more often, his thought returned to that catastrophic day in October, now three and half years ago. He would have to accept the fact that Giulietta could not be cured, although he resisted that thought with all his might. The doctors who treated her were very careful in their diagnosis and offered little hope. Silvo had been just seven years old at the time of the accident. Two days later he died as a result of his injuries. They had been shopping together, Giulietta and Silvo. A normal weekday. Suddenly he had pulled lose from his mother's hand and had run across the street. To this day nobody knew why. Something must have caught his attention, attracted him irresistibly.

The driver of the car had been a gentle, amiable man of about sixty. He drove slowly, but could not avoid the child that suddenly appeared in front of the hood of his car. A violent turn of the wheel, an impulsive, hopeless attempt to avoid the child, had caused him to hit a telephone pole. His head had shattered the windshield. His name was Giuseppe Ansaloni. When Giuseppe was released from the hospital, three weeks later, he appeared on Enzo's doorstep. Despite the fact that everyone agreed that he was blameless, Giuseppe was deeply affected and had changed.

The consequences to Giulietta became clearer, more unbearable, as the weeks went by. She became more and more silent, withdrew within herself, started to lose all interest in her surroundings. Finally she just sat and stared. For days on end she would look out of the window with empty eyes, as if in a trance, completely absorbed by daydreams and phantasies. All connection with reality, with life, seemed to have been completely severed.

Doctors spoke about a severe form of autism. Shortly thereafter she was placed in a clinic and she had been there for more than three years. But the driver of the car, Giuseppe Ansaloni, had shared Enzo's grief. The two men had become friends as a result of the terrible catastrophe. From one day to the next they had been faced with a sad reality, a reality with which both would have to learn to live.

When Enzo parked his car in one of the few remaining spots, he saw the light was on in his apartment. As he got out of the elevator, Giuseppe waited for him in the door of his apartment.

"I knew it was your birthday and I knew you hadn't eaten yet," he said simply. "Therefore I fixed us both something."

"It's good to see you," answered Enzo.

Giuseppe took his hands, embraced him and said: "Happy Birthday."

"Thank you, Giuseppe, I had forgotten all about it."

"Busy day?"

"A bit."

"But surely you'll want to eat something."

"I'm starving."

"Well, that's a good thing, because I took a lot of trouble."

Giuseppe had been Chef in some of Rome's best restaurants and cooking remained his passion. He did not work regularly since his wife had passed away, but concentrated on private parties for people who appreciated his artistry in the kitchen and could afford to pay for it. After Giuseppe had poured the wine and served the *antipasto*, they sat down at the table and ate in silence. Giuseppe was the first to speak.

"Are you going to see her tomorrow?"

"Yes, I planned to go."

"How is she?"

"The same, no improvement."

"You want me to go with you?"

"Thank you, I'd rather go alone."

"I understand. I don't want to force myself on you, you know that."

"Well, you really pulled out all the stops, Giuseppe," said Enzo, to give the conversation a different direction.

"Do you like it?"

"Like is hardly the word. Man, you're an artist. I don't know what I'm eating, but it's fantastic."

"*Mousse de truite a la Giuseppe*, that's all I'll tell you."

After an hour, two bottles of wine and three culinary highlights, they sat down in the living room. Giuseppe started a story about his latest client, a well-known, rich family in Rome. About the forced formality, the self-conscious arrogance and the snobbish attitude, which he shamelessly exploited.

"It's a matter of selling yourself, Enzo," he laughed. "I can make them eat anything, no matter what. It's just the way you present it."

"And they pay you dearly for it."

"Oh, boy, you should see me sometimes. What an act! And it's always expensive. The more expensive the better! I wear all my medals and lots of colored ribbons. The other day I found an old medal I'd won in fifth grade, for running. I put it around my neck, too. Nobody noticed. That's *my* joke. Especially if they're *nouveau riche*. Fat, ostentatious Rolex watches, dresses of two million liras from a 'boutique' where they've also learned the trick of soaking the rich. And the moment they open their mouths, you know exactly from which part of the slums they came. And you just *know* what sort of business is generating all the cash. That's the way it is, these days. But, what the hell, I cook for them and they pay me well. But, to tell you the truth, sometimes I have the urge to mix a little rat poison in the food. But, as you know, that's against the law."

"Indeed, Giuseppe, that's against the law. You'll have me to deal with, then."

"Oh, come on, you'll give me a break, won't you?" he asked, laughing. "I was counting on that, you see."

"Well, I might even pay for the rat poison myself."

"Exactly. That's what I call fair. You don't want me to incur unnecessary costs. Tomorrow I have a 'special assignment' for the Lovallo family. Scum, you know, Enzo. I've been there before. My, my, the faces you meet and all with a bulge under their coat."

Despite the fact that the alcohol had lulled him into a nebulous lethargy, the name Giuseppe mentioned was able to wake his policeman's instinct.

"Do you always know the guest list in advance?"

"Of course I do. After all, I'm also responsible for the placement at the table. You see, one of the women gives me a little sketch of the table and I deliver calligraphed place cards. That's all they do. Then I take care of the service, as well as the food. I supervise the setting of the table. In short, I organize the entire dinner party."

"So, you see the names."

"Yes, of course. And sometimes I hear things. You see, that's one of the peculiarities of people with a lot of servants and who are used to have somebody take care of their slightest whims. Servants are just slaves to them, or worse, just things. They won't even look at you. They only notice you when you make a mistake. Among themselves they talk about anything that comes in their heads. Well you see, if you've been brought up with the idea that servants are just things, you just naturally assume that they're also deaf. Things don't have ears, Enzo, no heart, no eyes, no nothing. Things are just like furniture: things!"

"Lovallo belongs to the Mannucci family, isn't that right?"

"Hey, you old cop, you're much too alert for my liking. I think I'll get you another cognac."

"Does the name Bacelli mean anything to you?" asked Enzo as he accepted the cognac that Giuseppe had poured for him.

"Of course it means something to me. Signora Eleonora Bacelli e Signor Joe Bacelli! The last time I saw them was about six weeks ago. There was a loud quarrel at the time."

"Tell me about it."

"Listen, you have to understand, the Mafia *never* discusses business when there are ladies present, you know that. Only the old money does that. When there are ladies present, the mobsters are almost civilized people. But actually women are second-class citizens as far as they're concerned. They're only good for bed and children. That's the way it was in the old days and it's still that way. They can't imagine that the first horny waiter can have those women, anytime he wants. That scum is so full of themselves that they simply won't believe that their women could even think about another man. So, while they're at the table together, it's all wine and roses. Sometimes you can tell from the mood at the table who's the favorite of the moment and who is not. But that's all. Business waits until the scum leave for the 'smoking room' for their after-dinner drinks. Well, that's when there was such a row about Bacelli, or because of Bacelli. I don't know the details because I don't do any of the serving myself, but one of my waitresses told me about it."

"I believe Bacelli is a cousin of Mannucci, is that right?"

"Aha, Riccardo Mannucci, the slippery man from New York! Famous star of radio, television and court room. He looks so trustworthy, you'd even buy a used car from him. Yes, I know him. He's often there. Yes, he and Bacelli could be cousins, but I don't know for sure."

"Well, I can look that up. But you don't know what they talked about?"

"Listen, Sherlock Holmes, I'm not a private eye. No, I can't tell you that."

"Giuseppe, can you keep a secret?"

"If you want me to, you can depend on it."

"I'm going to tell you something in the strictest confidence. The case we're working on at the moment . . ." Enzo gave a brief resume of the investigation as a result of the corpse on Serifos.

When he finished talking, Giuseppe asked: "What would you like me to do?"

"Names. I want to know who's going to be there, who's visiting Lovallo tomorrow. But, please, Giuseppe, be careful. Don't write anything down, but try to remember. I rather you forget some of them than that they catch you making notes. You can't trust the servants either, remember that."

"You can count on me."

They had another drink together and at one o'clock Enzo called for a cab. When the driver rang the doorbell, they walked down together. At the door Giuseppe embraced him again and said: "Take care of yourself."

It still sounded like an apology.

The Transfer

*26. Rome, Tuesday, June 5, 1984

"These are the two faces that the police artist has made from the descriptions of Salvatore Navonna," said Martella and showed the pictures around. "Unfortunately they don't appear in our rogue's gallery."

It was nine thirty in the morning and everybody was seated behind their first plastic cup of coffee.

"Did he have anything else to say?" asked Vittorio Scarfiotti.

"How's his little scratch? He didn't have an accident, I hope?" added Ferdinando.

"Calm, gentlemen, calm. It gets better. We had a long conversation with Signor Navonna, last night. Before I update you, I want one thing clearly understood. What we found out last night, must not go any further than the people in this room. Nobody outside this room with the exception of the Commissioner, of course, must know about it. There will be no reports for the moment. Keep notes to yourselves and memorize the rest."

"My colleague will have trouble with that," remarked Ferdinando.

"We've interrogated him thoroughly," continued Enzo, ignoring the remark. "And finally we got the whole story. I believe he spoke the truth. Night before last he had a visit from two characters that worked him over with brass knuckles. They knew that Salvatore had been in contact with Dubour and that they had met in the Portofino Restaurant. They asked him for a list. From that we can definitely conclude that some sort of important records exist. We had assumed it, but there was no proof, just suppositions. Now we're sure. Yesterday morning, at about eleven thirty, Salvatore received a phone call from the two heavies. The message was that they've kidnapped Salvatore's children. We haven't a clue as to the children's whereabouts. Of course, they're after the list. During the beginning of our conversation Navonna wasn't all that cooperative. Easy to understand, in retrospect. He's scared stiff that those two will find out that we're involved. That too, is realistic. But because his two children have been kidnapped, I'm sure he has told us the truth. He has no way out and he's desperate. I'm also sure that he has no idea about the location of the list. But he did mention that Dubour made a reference to the list and I quote him, according to Salvatore: 'I've recorded twenty years of history and carefully documented it. If something ever happens to me (he meant Dubour), they'll grab another five hundred.' So, it's obvious what the families are after."

"Does he have any idea as to who those two are working for?"

"No, they're strangers to him, as well." Martella paused to let that sink in. "Now, as to the secrecy. I promised him that we would not report anything, for the time being, would not inform anybody and would do nothing to endanger the children. This is a large building with a lot of people. I cannot guarantee the trustworthiness of everybody. After all, we live in Italy. That's why I must ask you not to discuss this with anybody outside this room. Needless to say, those children are in real danger, because the demands that are being made, cannot be met. Salvatore doesn't have the information, doesn't know where to look for it and the problem is that they don't believe him. We already know that those two are capable of anything. Salvatore is being protected at the moment and his phones are tapped. All we can do now, is wait."

"At least we can assume that this is *not* an action of Kidnap Incorporated?" asked Giorgio Bergarmi. "I mean that gang that specializes in kidnapping?" In Palermo he had often run across that particular form of crime.

"Yes we can. This is not an organization. Kidnap, Inc. is only interested in money. Also, they wouldn't have shown their faces in advance, but these two guys did. Salvatore had a good look at them. This is a private operation by two criminals with a superiority complex. And that's what makes it so dangerous."

"Signor Martella, I'd like to propose something."

"Go ahead, Vittorio."

"Ferdinando and I are unknown here. Nobody can tell we're not Italians. What about letting us hit the streets and have a little talk, here and there? You can tell us the bars and other establishments where we're most likely to run into that scum. We could take a look. You never know."

"Yes, you're right, you never know. We don't have much else to go on."

"Can't we produce a list with names and pretend it's the real one?" asked Enrico.

"For what purpose?"

"Well, I assume that somebody sent those two. Therefore, they won't know about the content. The guy who's behind it all, also has never seen the list. Nobody knows what names *are* on the list. Neither do we, so every name we put on it, is a good one. We could go through the archives and compile a list of all the unsolved murders with the names of the suspects who, for one reason or another, have never been convicted. That would help to make it believable."

"Don't you find it a little too obvious that Salvatore can produce the list all of a sudden? They're not *that* stupid," Martella said.

"Then I would propose to pass on a name of a so-called contact person," said Franco Giovale.

Ferdinando answered: "The family who ordered the search is also aware that a cunning fox like Dubour would never have given the list to somebody else."

"Then I propose something else," said Vittorio. "My partner and I dive into the scene tonight and *we* pretend to be the contact people."

"Wait a moment, that gives me an idea. It's an excellent suggestion, but let's do it right. You'll only have today to rehearse yourselves in the role of those two creeps."

149

"My partner won't have to act," remarked Ferdinando and everybody laughed.

"Keep the jokes to yourself, Ferdo. Listen, we're on the right track. We make a false list. Vittorio and Ferdinando will be the so-called contact people. But it would be too obvious, if there was a real contact person, that the information would be that readily available. Even if he knew that there were two children in danger. A character like that *knows* the value of his merchandise and will never give it up because of some baby-blues. They're not related to Mother Theresa. The kidnappers know that as well. In other words, they'll suspect something. So, if we're going to create a contact person, we have to demand money. Salvatore can pay the ransom. That's to say, he'll offer to pay it. Thus, he'll have to go to the bank with one of the kidnappers and get the money that our so-called contact man demands."

"Then we can follow them."

"Too dangerous as long as we don't know the location of the children," said Ferdinando. "Also, we still don't know what their connections are. We can assume, judging by past performances, that we're dealing with a couple of punks, not too smart, purse snatchers that reached above themselves, probably exceeded their instructions, but it's too great a risk for the children to bank on that. Therefore, Salvatore pays them and is out the money if we can't find them back after the children have been released."

"Let's recapitulate," said Martella. "If they call back, Salvatore tells them that he knows where the list is, but that it will cost them. He mentions an acceptable amount for such a transaction. He proves that he cooperates by offering to pay the money himself. He'll give them the money, plus an address, or a phone number."

"I would like to say something," observed Enrico. "I would propose that we divide it into two operations. Salvatore pays the money, but doesn't reveal any address, or phone number. The fact that he's willing to hand over the money to pay the contact man, should be enough evidence of good will to achieve the freedom of the children. Therefore he tells them that he will give them the additional information, *after* the children have been returned. That should be the condition and that would be considered normal, especially among thieves. I'm afraid that if Salvatore does *not* demand that, they'll smell a rat. That would be too easy. If I put myself in the place of the kidnappers, I wouldn't believe it either. He pays for the contact man and that's evidence of his cooperation. They know that Salvatore couldn't care less about the list itself. He doesn't belong to any family and has no interests in that direction. Whoever sent those two creeps after the list, knows that as well. Salvatore is an unimportant link and if they can secretly undo the kidnapping, it will be to their advantage. They know that we place a priority on the kidnapping of children and this sort of thing can only be bad for business. If Salvatore, after the children have been released, reneges on the agreement, they can always find him again."

"But then we have another problem," said Martella. "If Vittorio and Ferdinando contact the two, I would just love to arrest them on the spot. But then they would know at once that it was a trap. And that Salvatore helped set the trap. After that, I give him three days, at most."

"That means we have to let them go?"

"It looks that way."

"So, what does that get us?" asked Vittorio. "They could start all over again."

"Wait, it gets worse," said Martella. "Now they have a false list. The families will know that within twenty four hours, you can bet on that. And when they find that out, Salvatore gets it also, because he's betrayed them."

"I'm glad I'm not in Navonna's shoes," said the FBI man.

"No matter how we do it, Salvatore is going to be the fall-guy," said the other. "Whether we pick those two up, or let them go, Navonna is in it up to his neck."

"There's just one solution, Chief. The Navonna family will have to move their cash to a bank in who knows where, sell out, buy new identities and disappear on an island in the Pacific."

"And all that because he had a nice little chat with an old army buddy," said Martella.

*27. Rome, the same day

"Well, those are some lousy prospects for us," concluded casino boss Salvatore Navonna, after he had listened to Enzo Martella.

"It's for the sake of the children, Salvatore. I don't want those kids on my conscience. There's no way for you to comply with their demands and you can take it from me that they won't believe you. You have no bargaining position. Of course, I can mobilize the entire Italian police force to find the kids, but I can't keep that a secret. They'll know within hours and we can't risk that. I see no other possibility to break the deadlock. We hand over the list with names to those two. Their bosses will know almost at once that it's a worthless piece of paper. You and your family are then no longer safe. I can't protect you under those circumstances. I wouldn't even want the responsibility. You know how they work."

"All right, then, let's assume that I make it to, let's say, Spain, with my family. How can you guarantee they won't find me there?"

"I can't guarantee that, Salvatore. I can only promise you that this case will not be officially reported. Nothing will be put on paper. The only people who know are the Commissioner, myself and the members of my immediate team. Nobody else. You don't have to tell us where you'll go. We'll make sure you get new passports with fictitious names. That's all I can do."

"What a fucking mess."

"You can say that again."

"I got nothing to do with it all!"

"You're right."

"What time is it now?"

"Half past twelve."

152

"They haven't called yet, it makes me sick."

"They'll call. Have you got your story straight?"

"Yes, yes, I tell them that I know the contact man for that damn list, an American. I paid for him to come here. Only, he wants to be paid, too . . . and I'll do that. I give them the money to pay to the contact man, on the condition that they first give me my kids. After I have my children, I give them the address of the American and they're on their own."

"That's it," said Martella, he walked to the door and opened it.

"Come in, Antonio."

A heavy-set, middle aged man entered the room. He was dressed in jeans with a tee-shirt that bulged over his belt. Over the shirt he wore a shoulder holster.

"I leave you two alone. I'll be out of town for a few hours, but I'll be back at four. Call me if you need me."

"OK, Chief, understood."

Martella left the room and descended to his car via the fire escape at the back of the building. He worked his way through the insane traffic for about half an hour and left the city via the Strada Pontina. About eight miles outside the city, just before the village of Pomesia, he turned off onto a side road and saw in the distance the gray building to which his wife had been banished. It was not just the reason for his visit that depressed him, the building itself seemed to offer no hope. He parked his car and went inside. The place smelled of disinfectant and peppermint. Nobody ever lit a cigar here, just for the smell. Nobody ever swore from the bottom of his heart, nobody even farted. Everything was serene, white and cool and permeated with a religious servility that set one's teeth on edge. The plump nuns in the starched uniforms and white caps that hid three quarters of their pale faces, shuffled silently from one room to another. They spoke in whispers and their love for mankind was endless, but distant. With every visit Martella was torn between revulsion and sympathy. In these surroundings the separating line between hypocrisy and spirituality had been so watered down and so cunningly obfuscated, that every normal human reaction had become an impossibility. If this was a gateway to heaven, he would prefer hell.

He climbed the wide marble stairs to the third floor and announced himself at the ward where Giulietta was being nursed.

"Good afternoon, Sister Josefina," he told the nun on duty and heard himself whisper.

"How do you do, Signor Martella. Your wife is waiting for you," she answered.

Just the mere fact of her saying so, made him mad, although he realized how unreasonable that was. How could she say that his wife was waiting for him? Both knew that Giulietta did not expect anybody, ever again. The optimism without foundation, the hospital cliches, he hated it all.

"How's she doing?"

"She's very happy, Signor Martella, and few people can say that."

"No reactions?" He asked it every time, although he knew the answer.

"No, she lives in a world of her own. She seems to prefer it over ours."

"Thank you, sister," he said curtly and left the room.

He entered Giulietta's room and saw her sitting in front of the window. As ever. For three years she had stared out of the window. Always in the same direction, the same angle. Only interrupted by daily needs such as eating, sleeping, bathing.

He kissed her forehead and called her by name.

"How are you?" he asked.

"Very well," was the automatic response, as if studied.

"Did you take a walk this week?"

"Did you take a walk, very well," she said. Her eyes continued to stare into emptiness.

He put his arms around her and stroked the side of her face. He felt the warmth of her body, as before. She remained seated, never turning her eyes from the point in the distance that seemed

154

to absorb her. He uttered an endearment from time to time, but did not receive an answer. It was the same for three long years, three, four times a week. She accepted his caresses and endearments without any outward sign, but he believed she needed it and that it might be the only way to eventually reach her, to ever get her back.

"Very well."

Perhaps the nun was right.

✻28. Rome, the same afternoon

Salvatore Navonna and the detective were seated opposite each other at the kitchen table. Both had a can of beer in front of them. Everything that could be said, had been said and they looked at each other silently. The cop had read the morning paper from the first to the last page. Salvatore stood up and started to pace. It was an unbearable situation. It was more than twenty four hours since the kidnappers had contacted him and the delay did nothing to reassure him. From time to time he walked over to the phone and lifted the receiver to make sure there was a dial tone. A few people had called and he had barked them off the line in short order. The tranquilizers he had taken, had no effect on him. His wife was upstairs, in bed, being cared for by her mother. Every five minutes the old lady came down the stairs to inquire if there was any news. She would disappear again after a short: "I'll let you know," from Salvatore. For the first time in his life he was afraid. An all-consuming fear. A feeling that was unknown to him. He had never been afraid.

He had not been afraid in the jungles of the Congo, nor as a mercenary. He had never been afraid in his business, although that had its own dangers. Many times he had been threatened, many times he had almost been killed. After all, it was part of the way business was being done in his part of the world. He had seen it all, jealous competitors from the underworld, pimps who demanded their share, vengeful employees, gambling addicts who wanted to take it out on him, all of it, but he had never been afraid. He was not afraid of the police, either, yet they were always watching him for a chance to do him in, to arrest him, to put him in jail, put him out of business. Never had he known fear. But now he did!

Now he knew fear. This time he was powerless in a situation without a satisfactory solution. He had always been able to take care of anything with money. Everyone can be bought, he maintained, it was just a matter of price. But suddenly that did not work any longer. The most terrible crime in the world had struck him, his family, his children. He wondered how the children were being treated. He had visions of a dark, cold room, perhaps they were tied up and perhaps they were being beaten because they cried. Had they been fed? Did somebody care? Were they still alive? The questions chased each other in his mind.

The kids were old enough to provide an accurate description when they were freed. The kidnappers knew that as well. Would they run the risk, or would they opt for certainty and kill the two tiny witnesses. If they let the children go they could almost bank on it that no place in the world would be safe for them. They would be hunted down. Not just by the police, but also by the families who did not condone such tactics because they were bad for business. If they killed the children, they would get off scot-free and it would be almost impossible to find them. Logically, objectively, the children did not have a chance. And there was no reason to suspect any kind of pity, or feeling where those types of criminals were concerned. A life meant nothing to them and the age of the victim was of no concern. During his time as a mercenary he had seen and experienced the depths of human depravity and it had left him with no illusions. He felt fear, an uncontrollable, unbridled, encompassing fear, that caused tears to form in his eyes, that caused his body to shake and tremble. He felt like a spring that was wound too tight and his heart throbbed in his throat.

Again he lifted the phone to check the dial tone. His mother-in-law entered the room, just when the phone started to ring. The cop jumped up, walked over to the tape recorder and pushed a button. Salvatore picked up the receiver and heard the well-known voice at the other end of the line. The slimy, slow, irritating voice of his tormenter.

"How are you, Sally, shit in your pants yet?"

"Goddamnit, cut that out. How are my children?"

"But I promised, man, don't worry about your offspring. My buddy is crazy about kids. He plays ever so nicely with them."

"Listen, I don't feel like a lot of pissing around. I have a proposition for you."

"Hey, paesano, you've got me curious."

"I don't have the list, I told you that. But I did check around and I know where the list is."

"So, progress at last. When do we get it?"

"That's not so easy. I found out that Dubour gave the list to a lawyer in the States. Also an old army buddy from the Congo. I called him."

"I knew you had connections, Sally. When do we get it?"

"Just hold on a minute. The lawyer doesn't want to let go of it. That was his deal with Dubour. Well, he's not exactly a lawyer that deals in divorces and things like that. He's a cunning bastard. He knows what he has and he knows it's worth something. So I told him what scum you are and that you kidnapped my kids. That's why he wants to deal."

"He wants money?"

"Two million dollars."

"Well, you have that, Sally."

"Listen, I took care of getting you the list. Now you want me to pay for it, too?"

"One million per kid, Sally. It's a bargain."

"Where do you think I can get two million dollars, just like that?"

157

Salvatore played the game as he and Martella had rehearsed. They had agreed that he would object about paying. It would be too suspicious if he just offered to pay the money.

"That's your worry, Sally. I'm sure you got the bread. If I were you, I'd call my banker and take care of it, right now. Also, my buddy, the children's friend, is getting a bit impatient, you know. He's starting to get bored with all those fucking kid's games."

"Jesus Christ, you bastards! I take care of the list, you have my kids and now you want money, too! So, what do you want, the list or the money?"

"The list, of course, you know that. That it happens to cost a bit, isn't our fault."

"What guarantees me I get my children back? Before you know it, I've got a list I could care less about, I'll be out two million bucks and I still don't know where my kids are."

"So wadda you want, Sally, you've no choice, do you?"

"Listen, I want nothing to do with that fucking list you keep talking about. I don't even want to *see* the thing. I don't even want to know about it. I know where to get it and I'll pay for it. Now, are you satisfied? But I'll be goddamned if I do anything, until I'm sure about my kids."

"You can be sure about them."

"How?"

"Because I'm telling you."

"Go to hell! You don't believe that yourself."

"So, what's your solution, Sally?"

"I give you the money, but *no* address. First I want my kids back and *then* I give you the address."

"What if you don't give us the address."

"Oh, I know you bastards well enough to know that I won't have another week, in that case. You can be sure to get the address and I hope it makes you happy. For me it's the only way to be left alone and you know that just as well as I. Shit, I'm even giving you an extra two million and that ain't hay."

"Let's assume we do it your way, Sally. How can we be sure there are no copies of the list?"

"Shit, is there no end to this? How would I know how many copies Dubour made? For all I know he had a book printed!"

"I'll think about it. Call you back in five minutes."

Salvatore replaced the receiver and wiped the sweat off his brow.

"Goddamn, what a job."

"But I think they're biting," said the detective, stopping the tape recorder.

"It's scum, Antonio."

"You're right. But you'll be out of it, soon. I've got another fifteen years to go before my pension."

∗29. Rome, the same evening

It was planned as a small, intimate party for just the closest family members, with children and grandchildren. The occasion was the name day of the youngest grandchild, Francesco, the son of Ruggero and destined to become the third *padrino* of the Lovallo family. Master Chef Giuseppe Ansaloni, Martella's friend, was in the kitchen with an assistant for the easier tasks and a Turkish man, who hardly spoke a word of Italian, for the dishes. Signora Lovallo had left clear instructions regarding her wishes and Giuseppe was here to execute them. He gave instructions to the two girls, who were part of the permanent staff, for the setting of the table. Twenty five people would be seated. The cheering of children could be heard from the game room and the laughter of adults sounded in the enormous sitting room. The warmth and conviviality of an Italian family, gathered to honor the name day of a grandchild, is boundless. Nothing is more important than such a day. The whole family gets together and celebrates.

159

"Listen," cried Antonio Lovallo, when the laughter subsided a little. "Let me start at the beginning. Violetta had bought the lamp on approval, but she didn't like it, after all. So, she called the store and got to talk to Signor Valdarno himself. He offered to come and get the lamp, but he never did."

"How long ago was that?" asked somebody.

"About a year ago. A few months ago there was a guy from a collection agency at the door. He had the bill and it included a large penalty for late payment. We were asked to pay."

"Where is the lamp?"

"In my study."

"Still in the box?"

"No, of course not, on my desk."

"Is it a nice lamp?"

"I think so. Violetta is the only one who doesn't like it."

"Antonio Lovallo, you're lying through your teeth," said his wife, wiping tears of laughter, careful not to smear her make-up. "You also think it's an ugly thing."

"Well, at first, yes, but now I'm used to it."

"Never mind, go on, you had the guy from the collection agency at the door," said Marco, the youngest of the three Lovallo sons.

"Well, of course, she ... ," he pointed at his wife, "... wouldn't let me pay. So, I tell the guy we had the lamp on approval and had never really bought it."

"Did you receive him in your study?"

"Are you crazy, then he would have seen it in use."

"So, you use it?"

"Yes, of course, I couldn't do without it, anymore," he exclaimed and everybody burst out laughing. "Anyway," he continued, "the man leaves and a few weeks later we're ordered to appear in court. Paolo Valdarno versus Signora Lovallo for refusal to pay for one lamp. So, I used office stationary to explain the situation. I got an answer from some lawyer who wasn't going to give in and insisted on getting Violetta in front of a judge."

160

"So, we got a lawyer too," shrieked Violetta.

"Did you find a good one?"

"Oh, yes, I sleep with him every night."

"Indeed, the following week, Antonio Lovallo, Esquire, counsel for signora Violetta Lovallo, appeared in court."

"How much was that lamp?"

"Ninety thousand liras."

"Perhaps we should ask how much it's *going* to cost."

"Anyway, to make a long story short, the decision was against signor Valdarno, his lawyer looked stupid and the judge decided that he had to collect the lamp *and* pay the court costs."

"That's going to cost him another three lamps."

"But he hasn't picked it up, yet," laughed Violetta.

"Well, tell you the truth, I'd miss it, you know," laughed Antonio. "If he doesn't show up, make sure to buy new bulbs from him, when we need them."

"Yes, and be sure to tell him for which lamp you need them."

"No, no, you should go there and say: Signor Valdarno, can you tell me what sort of bulbs fit in the lamp we have on approval?" said the third son.

"No, better yet, go there and say: Signor Valdarno, the bulbs don't last too long in that lamp. I think there's something wrong with it. Would you mind stopping by to repair it?" This was the contribution of one of the women.

"Ask him about the warranty."

The laughter was so loud that it could be heard in the dining room where Giuseppe looked carefully around for a place to hide the small transmitter. He had purchased it only this morning. It transmitted in the FM range and could be received on most radios. He had also bought a small transistor radio that fitted in his breast pocket. A small cord ran from there to an earplug. As far as anyone could determine, he was hard of hearing and wore a hearing aid. The transmitter and radio were tuned to the right frequency, he had tested the set-up and it worked. The range was not great, but enough for his purposes. With two-sided tape he attached the tiny

161

transmitter inside the marble fireplace. He fumbled a little, but it was, after all, the first time he did anything like it. Otherwise he would have known that all rooms were equipped with a hidden camera, connected to a set of monitors in the old porter's cottage, near the main gate with the automatic locks.

Moments later, dressed in a sparkling white chef's uniform with a large gold medal attached to a colored ribbon, he entered the sitting room and announced:

"Signore e signori, dinner is served."

"I'll call the children," said Violetta. She walked up the wide, marble staircase and returned shortly after that, followed by the children.

"Francesco has to sit in the center," said Appolonia, Ruggero's wife.

"I'll sit next to him," said Giovanni Lovallo

"No, papa, *prego*, you'll sit at the head of the table."

"Today I'll sit next to Francesco. Let Ruggero sit at the head of the table, it will be good practice for him. Today I must discuss important matters with my grandson." He winked at the boy.

The meal was bountiful and took a long time. There was a lot of laughter and talking and children were hugged and caressed. They stayed at the table a long time after dessert had been served. The little ones had fallen asleep in the arms of mothers and grandmothers and the bigger children played in a corner of the room. A chaotic mess of left-overs, cutlery and plates covered the table. Spots of spilled wine stained the damask table cloth and wrinkled napkins were everywhere. Giovanni prohibited the personnel from clearing the table. He liked it this way. After a good meal, the evidence of the past feast should be visible.

This was no formal dinner with business relations where everything had to be just so. This was a family dinner, relaxed, without frills. That is the way it used to be in the large house in Sicily where he grew up. The house of his father. Those were good memories and he wanted to keep them. He did not really like Rome, he much preferred the island. There he felt safest, surrounded by family and friends. Everybody there knew him and respected him. Here, in Rome, he was lost in the masses. There was no gazebo with this house and his father's chair, the one he liked the best, was in Sicily.

It had been a wonderful evening, the normal evening of an Italian family that celebrated the name day of its youngest grandchild. At first glance no different from thousands of other families who celebrated the day of Saint Franciscus. Families who were just as cheerful and jovial and who loved each other. Families that had violent discussions during the meal so that an outsider would fear the worst, but that belonged to the customs and folklore of the country, where everybody spoke much too loud and where everything had to be repeated several times. It happened everywhere with the same gusto, in the same way. No matter if your name was Lovallo and you lived in an expensive villa in the suburbs, or if your name was something else and you lived in one of Rome's slums. It was all Italy!

But around the Lovallo table they knew better. They knew different. All who sat around the messy table in the expensive suburb knew how things were. They belonged to one of the thirty-six Mafia families in Italy. The women, too, who so lovingly cradled the sleeping children, they too belonged. They knew their men were gangsters and criminals of the worst kind. They knew the money came from crime, they knew very well. They just did not know how, they did not *want* to know.

They lived comfortably, knew what was going on, but had learned not to ask questions. They could not worry about the thousands who, because of their husbands, or sons, would never again celebrate a name day. That was too bad, but the Church forgave all sins. That is, as far as they still knew the meaning of the word. They knew that their men, the men who shared their beds, the men they caressed, the fathers of their children, they knew that these men killed. But they never asked the number of corpses. They had been reduced to a slavish obedience to their own laws and those of the family clans. Their eyes were closed to the misery they caused. But, at first glance, they looked like just any other close-knit, normal, cheerful Italian family.

Only the children were still innocent, but they would learn in time.

* * *

It was two thirty when Master Chef Giuseppe Ansaloni was about to step into his car. He had walked from the house, along the long driveway, to the gate with the automatic locks. The hired help was not allowed to park within the fence. His car was parked to the right, under the trees, just outside the gate.

At six o'clock in the morning he was found by a passer-by. He was still alive when they delivered him to the hospital. Before the surgeon started the operation, the nurse removed the gold medal with the colored ribbon from the damaged body. Then she carefully undressed him.

*30. Rome, Wednesday, June 6, 1984

When Martella entered the Commissioner's office at nine thirty in the morning, he immediately noticed the list on the old fashioned desk. Inspectors Enrico Tomasso and Franco Giovale had worked on it all night. They had ransacked archives, read newspaper articles and researched old reports. They had compiled a list of forty-two names of people who had been killed in the last twenty years. Unsolved crimes. The list contained the names of messengers, murderers, Mafia wheels, but also politicians and judges in Italy, the United Sates and a number of European countries. The names of those who were presumed to have given the orders had been distilled from the various documents. The result was a believable piece of fiction.

The inclusion of a certain number of cases that had been dismissed over the years, dismissed for lack of evidence, judicial hair splitting, or other spurious reasons, but cases from which any reasonable person knew that something had been covered up, helped to give the list a certain authenticity. And there were a lot of those. A saddening cooperation between bureaucracy, fear and intimidation was the reason that so few arrests actually resulted in prison terms. The chronic shortage of judiciary personnel in Italy made an ideal playground for the criminal elements of society. There were empty offices in the court houses and entire floors lacked basic requirements such as typewriters and other office supplies because of an opaque system of forms and permits. A number of big bosses who appeared on the list, had already left this earth permanently. It was remarkable how few had died a natural death.

"I went through it," said Commissioner Carsini, after greeting Martella, "and I believe we should go ahead with it as written."

"I have been thinking about it, sir," said Martella. "I keep hoping there's another solution." He sounded worried.

"I don't think we have much choice. It's possible that, as soon as we have the children, the town will look like Dodge City for a while, but we'll have to deal with that as it comes."

"The case stinks from all sides, Commissioner, I just don't know where the stink originates."

"I read the report of Navonna's telephone call. Any follow-up?"

"Nothing yet. But he has the money ready."

"He had that handy, just like that?"

"Not exactly, he had to mortgage the apartment."

"There's been no talk about the purpose of the money?"

"I wasn't there, I didn't think that was wise. But I have to assume that Navonna knows what he's doing. I told him emphatically that nobody, apart from us, was to know about the kidnapping. Also, I believe he may have had some loose change stashed away. Anyway, that's the least of my worries."

"Just to make sure, Martella, who are involved in the case, at the moment?"

"Still the same, the two Americans, Scarfiotti and Cotone."

"They can be trusted?"

"I've no reason to doubt it, they're FBI!"

"I take it they know what they're doing?"

"Yes, sir. Then we have my right hand, Tomasso and Giovale, also from our department. And the man from Palermo, Giorgio Bergarmi."

"Yes, the man from Palermo. That worries me. It's almost impossible to be a policeman in Palermo without being tainted. Palermo is infected, you know that?"

"I thought about it."

"It's almost too much to expect that man to be on our side, almost inhuman. He has to go back there, after a while. We stay here, but he doesn't."

"You're right."

"Let's say we bring this affair to a satisfactory conclusion. That will mean that we'll have to arrest whole tribes of people. And he will have helped with that. Then, back in Palermo, his life wouldn't be worth a plugged nickel. He'll be an outcast."

"What can we do? He's already into it up to his neck."

"I'd talk to him. Point out the dangers. Does he have any children?"

"No, he's a bachelor."

"That makes it a little easier. But, still, talk to him Martella. Emphasize the dangers and let him make his own choice. Who else do we have?"

"Just the man who is looking after Navonna, Antonio Alberti. And then, of course, the parents of the children."

"Are Navonna's other family members informed?"

"Only his wife's mother. She lives with them. All contact with other family, friends and relations has been broken off."

"What about the school, do they suspect anything?"

"Enrico talked to them. He told them that a relative in Milan was in a traffic accident and the children went there for a few days. That's why they were picked up from school so suddenly."

"So, there's been no further investigation around the school. Did we check with other children?"

"No, I'm not too happy about that, but if we had done anything in that direction, all the wise guys would have known at once. So I called it off."

"I agree."

"We have to wait for a phone call to tell us where to bring the money. They have accepted the deal, so all we can do is wait. As long as they have the children, our hands are tied."

"Let's say we solve that problem. Then we have to deliver the list. How are you planning to do that?"

"Yes, well, the easiest way would be to arrest them during the transfer. But we'll only wind up with a middle man, a messenger. We want the big guys who have ordered this action. So they're worth their weight in gold as bait. They're the only ones who can lead us to the prize."

"You could lose them."

"Of course, that's the frustrating part. Then we have two creeps running around, guilty of at least two murders and a kidnapping and they won't have a thing to worry about."

"We can always circulate a description."

"Yes, we can, but you know yourself, Commissioner, Italians talk a lot, but they're always silent at the wrong moment."

"The Judge-Advocate called me early this morning and he wants reports," said the Commissioner dejectedly.

"Yes, I expected that. But for the moment I advise against letting any paperwork circulate in this building. I hope to solve the business with the children today and after that, it's a different matter."

"Well, I'll invent some sort of tale to keep him calm. Leave that to me."

"If you don't mind my advice, please don't tell him everything. He's one of those bureaucrats that makes notes of everything and then has them typed up by a talkative lady in the typing pool."

"I'll be careful."

Martella stood up and walked in the direction of the door.

"I'll keep you informed, sir," he said.

"Please do," answered the Commissioner. Just before Martella left the room, he asked: "How's your wife?"

"The same, no improvement," Martella made a hopeless gesture.

"I feel for you. You know, if there's anything I can do, if I can help you, please let me know, Enzo." It was one of the few times that the Commissioner used Martella's first name.

When Martella had gone, the Commissioner picked up the telephone and dialed a number. He mentioned a name and spoke a few moments with the man on the other end of the line. Five minutes later there was a knock on the door and the commander of the *Carabinieri* entered.

"Here I am. Fast enough for you?" He approached the Commissioner and they embraced like old friends.

"There's some urgency," said Carsini while they sat down.

"Just tell me, Commissioner, what can I do for you?"

"We're involved in a case and it's hard to predict what the consequences will be. I'm certain that a number of families are involved. We just haven't been able to identify them, yet. I won't bother you with the details, they wouldn't interest you anyway, but I need your help."

"Mine *and* the *Carabinieri*?"

"Exactly. It's only a small team that's involved and we'd like to keep it that way. I don't want a lot of sabre rattling, but I *do* want some protection for my people."

"And for you?"

"I think so. As you know, I keep in the background, I'm not exactly on the firing line, but it's known that I'm in charge of the case. Soon that will be more widely known. I would feel a lot better if you could take care of a permanent escort."

"Four man?"

"That should be enough. The same for Chief Inspector Enzo Martella. He moves around without protection at the moment and that bothers me. I want you to cover him at all times. He'll protest, but I'll take care of that. Then there's a list here of some other people who are involved. Protect their families and watch them as well, but from a distance."

"As far as their families are concerned, you want visible presence?"

"I think that can be very preventive. Perhaps you can post some guys with machine guns, it can do no harm."

"I understand and I don't have to ask you how soon you want it done."

*31. Rome, the same day

While Enzo Martella visited Commissioner Carsini, an impatient Giovanni Lovallo was seated in his study. Nervously he drummed his fingers on the top of the enormous, mahogany desk. The room was large and impressive. The most expensive, exotic wood had been used for the trim along the ceiling and the panelling of the wainscotting and doors. The furniture consisted of antique masterpieces and the marble floor was covered by a carpet worth a fortune. In a specially built niche stood a twenty five hundred year old bust of an ancient Roman. Few such pieces were still in private hands and its value was incalculable. The walls were covered with plaques and framed certificates, extolling the virtue and wisdom of the man in the room. Filled crystal carafes stood on a silver tray on a table on one side, flanked by two vases filled with red and white carnations. The fresh flowers were placed there every morning, every day of the year.

When the phone rang, he opened the drawer of his desk that contained the instrument. It was a direct line with a secret number, known only to a few.

"Aha, finally. Can you talk?" he asked.

"Yes, I'm alone," answered the other, arrogant voice.

"What have you found out?"

"No more than I already told you."

"Do you have the reports?"

"Not yet."

"Fabrizio, that ain't no fucking help!" Lovallo was angry.

"I can't force matters, Giovanni."

"Well, you can get after their ass, can't you?"

"You overestimate me. I haven't that much influence. Everything here is according to the rules, by the book, you name it. I can't do as I'd like. That would be too noticeable."

"Well, you just have to make a better effort, Fabrizio, you're in it up to your ass. We have enough people at the *Questura Centrale* on our payroll, right? Don't they know something?"

"Carsini and Martella are dealing with the case. I don't have any pull, there. I've got to watch myself."

"So, they ain't the only ones."

"Yes, I know the names, but forget it."

"Reports, reports! You can demand reports!"

"It's a closed team and they don't leak to the outside. I'm almost sure they agreed not to make any reports, for the time being. Nothing has been written down."

"Well, have you found out anything about the kidnappers?"

"No, but you told me Ruggero had a contact."

"Yes, a fucking contact and I *mean* fucking contact. Just put *that* out of your mind, Fabrizio. He went after it, but no results. The chick he was talking about has disappeared and there's nothing I can do about that."

170

"Listen, Giovanni, let things rest for a while. I want those two children returned, healthy and in one piece. That's for our own benefit. If something goes wrong, there, all hell will break loose and you can forget about all contacts from this side, no matter how much you pay them. And God help you if anything happens to those children, because heads will roll and we'll have a revolution on our hands. No good for us, at all. Commissioner Carsini and Chief Inspector Martella are two of the best they have and they have a small, but qualified team. They have a plan, but nobody knows anything about it. But I'm sure they're concentrating on the kidnapping. Let them take care of that, first."

"Listen well, Fabrizio, if I have the least suspicion that I'm gonna get fucked in this deal, I'll hold you responsible. I can make it hot for you and I will, count on it! You'll be ruined. Pedophiles aren't very popular anywhere and especially not in Italy, what with the Pope in the backyard and all. Besides you have a few bank accounts the tax people would be very interested in. I *know* that we can all hang because of that son-of-a-bitch from Serifos, but now you're the only one who can prevent it. That's what you're getting paid for! But if we hang, you hang right with us, Fabrizio Vitelli. I'd try harder if I were you!"

"But of course, Giovanni, I'll do my best, I promise." He hung up without greeting.

"The cocksucker," growled Giovanni while he threw the receiver angrily back on the hook. Then he closed the drawer. He pushed a switch on the intercom. A woman's voice answered.

"I want Ruggero, now, at once!"

"*Scusi*, Signor Lovallo, you son isn't here."

"Where is he?"

"He didn't say, signore."

"When is he coming back?"

"I couldn't say, Signor Lovallo."

"Never mind."

*32. Rome, the same day

Casino boss Salvatore Navonna sat down in one of the rattan chairs on the terrace, close to the curb. That was the agreement. He placed the briefcase with the money on a chair next to him. He did not feel very secure about it. The city was overrun with all sorts of thieves and other scum who operated from Vespa scooters and had developed a remarkable agility for stealing loose items. They always worked in pairs. The man on the buddy seat was the quick fingered expert. Salvatore shivered at the thought that two million American dollars would wind up in the wrong hands. But this was the only place that had been acceptable as a rendez-vous. It was the usual system of organized crime. Always have the meeting in a place with a lot of people. That way they could be sure that there would be no unexpected surprises. Navonna had no idea how they intended to contact him. Just to be sure, he had proposed a password. The man would identify himself with the word "Serifos". He had not been asked to assure that police would not be involved. As long as they had the children they had all the trumps and would not have to fear any stupidity from their victim.

The waiter stopped by and he ordered a cappuccino. The table next to him was occupied by two gentlemen, he looked suspiciously at them, but put the thought away. Impossible. It was too obvious. He was nervous and placed his left hand on the briefcase. His eyes roamed the street and he looked intently at everyone who passed. It could be anybody. Cars were parked across the street, but he had seen no movement. No cars had left, as long as he had been sitting here, and no cars had arrived. Again he looked at the row of cars, but could not detect anything suspicious. Certainly not the rust colored Ford Taunus with the black, vinyl roof. The waiter arrived with his order and placed it on the table. At that instant a scooter zoomed onto the sidewalk. The driver wore a closed helmet, his face was a black piece of plexiglass. It was obvious that he only braked when he saw the waiter next to the table. He stopped and searched around the engine compartment of the scooter.

After Salvatore had paid the check and the waiter had gone back inside, the man with the closed helmet placed the scooter on the stand and approached the table. Without removing his helmet, he said: "Messenger service, sir, for Serifos."

Despite the fact that the helmet, which reached below the chin, distorted the voice, Salvatore recognized it immediately. It was the man with the slimy voice.

"Oh, yes, for Serifos. You'll need this." He handed him the briefcase.

The man undid the snaps, opened the lid about an inch, looked inside and nodded approval. He closed the briefcase again and said: "Thanks, so long." Then he walked calmly back to his scooter.

He placed the briefcase on the running board below the saddle and commenced, with exasperating slowness, to secure the case. He was fully aware of the power he had over the other. Navonna was so irritated that he stood up and left the terrace without drinking his coffee. Therefore he missed seeing the friendly wave from the man on the scooter and did not notice that another man suddenly rose from behind the wheel of the rust colored Ford Taunus. The man started the car and drove off. Two children in school uniforms stood at the edge of the pavement and cried. An older couple approached and asked what was the matter.

If Salvatore had waited just a little longer, he would have had his children back, then and there. But he was not expecting them that soon and was already around the corner, on the way to his car.

*33. Rome, the same evening

Martella entered the stark white hospital room to which Giuseppe Ansaloni had been taken. On the night table were a small transistor radio and a gold medal with colored ribbon. When he saw his visitor, he groaned and lifted his right arm, the only part of his body that was not bandaged, in a semblance of a greeting. Martella sat down next to the bed and looked at the ravaged face.

"I screwed up, Enzo," The sound barely passed the swollen lips.

"What happened?" asked Martella.

"I wanted to help you."

"Giuseppe, you could have been killed."

"Don't make me laugh, it hurts," he groaned.

"Who did this?"

"I don't know, they were so fast, I didn't see any faces."

"What did you do, Giuseppe?"

"Nothing, just a little transmitter."

"What!? A transmitter? What sort of transmitter?"

"Listen, Enzo, I know I screwed up. Let it rest."

"Giuseppe, you don't know what you're talking about. I have to know what you did. You mean to tell me you placed a transmitter in Lovallo's house?"

Giuseppe nodded his head with difficulty.

"Oh, no. I warned you!"

"Some private eye, eh, ispettore?" His faced twisted into a painful grimace, it was meant to be an apologetic smile.

"Just relax, stay calm. You're indeed the prize idiot of the western hemisphere. But it's really my fault. I should have kept my mouth shut."

"Enzo, I just wanted to help you. Surely, I'm allowed to help you? You know, it's the . . . least . . . you . . . eh, understand? What else could I do?"

"Just calm down. I understand." He took Giuseppe's hand in his own. Both remained silent for a long time. The silence in the room became tangible.

"Are you able to tell me anything at all?" asked Martella.

"Yes, I think so."

"I'll listen, but take it easy. If you're too tired we'll stop and pick it up another time."

"No, I'll manage," said Giuseppe laboriously. "It just hurts a little. I think I busted some ribs, that's all."

"You were lucky. It could have been a lot worse. Tell me what sort of stupid stunt did you pull?"

"Yesterday I bought two small transmitters in one of those stores, you know, where they sell that sort of stuff."

"Sure, you got the address from the classifieds, right? Spy and surveillance equipment for every need, or something like that," concluded Martella.

"Yes, ridiculous, isn't it?"

"I won't contradict you."

"Well, I put one under the clock in the sitting room and the other I attached inside the fireplace in the dining room."

"We're talking about the Lovallo family, right?"

"Yes, you knew that."

"I just want to make sure."

"Well, I also bought a small radio with a tiny tape player built in. That way I could receive and record. I'm sure nobody saw me when I hid those things. Maybe I screwed up, but I was really careful, Enzo."

"Yes, but you didn't know that it's almost a sure bet there was a hidden camera in every room."

"Really?" Giuseppe was astonished.

"Yes, really! They figured you out from the first moment, James Bond. But never mind, what else can you remember?"

"Little. My car was outside the gate. I remember walking there."

"What time was that?"

"About a quarter after two, two-thirty, maybe."

"Did you see anybody at all?"

"No, nobody. When I came to, I was here."

"Well, that doesn't help us much."

"Yes, but you know what's crazy about it, Enzo? I did record almost all evening and they let me keep the tape. Look, there it is. You would think, wouldn't you, that they would have taken it?"

"Yes, *you* would, but they didn't," answered Martella. He picked up the small instrument and looked at it. Then he said: "But it's not all that mysterious, Sherlock Holmes. You see, they knew from the beginning that you had planted a bug. They informed the boss and the family just didn't discuss business. They're well disciplined, you know. I'll bet there's nothing important on your tape. That's why they let you keep it. Besides, if they *had* taken the tape, the one that did you in, would have left a certain indication that they'd been sent by Lovallo. Because the tape was recorded at Lovallo, the connection would have been obvious. The way they handled it, it could have been pure coincidence. Just another mugging, nothing to do with the Lovallo family. I don't believe it, but that's no proof. Lovallo knows that."

* * *

On the way to the office, Martella placed Giuseppe's tape in the tape deck of his car. He heard voices and a lot of laughter from a convivial group that seemed to have a lot of fun with a story about some lamp.

*34. Rome, the same evening

Vittorio Scarfiotti and Ferdinando Cotone had taken two rooms in the *Pensione Villa Giulia* in a side street, just off the Piazza Navona. Yesterday they had arrived by taxi from the airport. While paying the driver they had made a lot of noise about the price, causing the owner of the *pensione* to come out into the street and offer his help. They had hoped for that. There should be no doubt in the mind of the owner that they had come from the airport. They had not left the room since they arrived. They read a bit, played some poker, but mostly they were poised for a telephone call.

176

At three in the afternoon the phone finally rang. They had been told where the exchange would be made. The voice at the other end of the line was the same voice they had heard on the tape recording from Salvatore's house. A slimy, slow talking man.

"You got the bread?" asked Vittorio.

"Of course, I got it. One million bucks," tried the man.

"Just a moment, my friend. Either you have a speech impediment, or there's something wrong with my ears. *How* much did you say?"

"Two million, of course, it was only a joke," said the man.

"We don't like jokes, friend, especially not tonight."

"All right already. Eleven-thirty in the industrial park, behind the building of *Vasallo*." The line was disconnected.

As a result of that call, Inspectors Tomasso and Giovale had driven a delivery van to the indicated area, had parked it just behind the building and had locked themselves into the cargo space. Through small, one-way windows they had a perfect view of their surroundings. The antenna looked like a regular radio antenna, but in reality supported a transmitter and a telephone. They were armed with two automatic pistols, two cold pizzas and a six-pack of beer.

Near the entrance to the terrain, people from the Municipal Works Department had started to dig a hole in the ground. First they placed red and white painted barricades around the work area, next they set up a tent over the hole and then they disappeared inside. These men were also armed with automatic weapons, hidden under their yellow coveralls.

It was about fifteen minutes before eleven when the two FBI men put on their shoulder holsters and left the hostelry. The car that had been left by Enrico was parked about three hundred feet from the entrance. Vittorio slid behind the wheel and Ferdinando sat down in the passenger's seat. The Fiat felt heavy from the extra armor that had been installed and the engine too, sounded a lot more powerful than was usual for a Fiat.

"You know how to drive this? It's a straight stick, you know."

"So?"

"Well, you're so used to your Pimp-Mobile with automatic transmission and stuff."

"Well, just because you drive that rusty old Japanese rice bowl, doesn't mean you're the only one who knows how to drive a straight stick."

"Hey, hey, don't insult my car, it's got more than 170,000 miles."

"Must have belonged to a little old lady from Dubuque, right?"

"Yes, indeed, with grandchildren in Tokyo."

Joking to relieve the tension, they navigated through the insane Rome traffic, so different from the relatively orderly traffic flows in their native country.

"I'll be go to hell, they're *all* crazy here!"

"You just figured that out? And you have an Italian family."

"Yeah, but I never let them drive."

"You hear about the lawyer at the Pearly Gates?" asked Ferdinando.

"No."

"Well, he told Peter there had to be a mistake, he was only thirty-six. And Peter answered: 'Maybe, but according to the hours you charged, you must be at least eighty nine.'."

"That's an old one."

"So, why are you laughing?"

"That way you won't miss your wife as much."

"You were in Germany, while you were in the service, right?"

"Yeah, why?"

"You must have picked up their sense of humor, is all."

At twenty minutes past eleven they drove through the gate of the industrial area. Sweat beaded Vittorio's forehead. The area itself consisted of a series of low buildings, most of them covered by galvanized steel roofs. There was a scattering of buildings that seemed to have been designed with some attempt at taste, but the majority looked gray, dirty and neglected. The trash had been piled in heaps behind the buildings. The streets were laid out at right angles to each other and did not have names, but numbers.

"It's almost like being back in the Bronx," said Ferdinando. "I feel at home here. Look, thirty-third street, I've got a cousin there."

"All right, we'll stop by, afterwards. Maybe he's home."

"No, we can't, they've taken his floor off the building."

"Probably didn't pay the rent. Family trait?"

They spotted the *Vasallo* building, drove around it and found the rear loading area. The delivery van was still parked in the same place and it was dark inside the temporary shelter of Municipal Works. They parked the car and looked at the surroundings. They had seen photos of the area and had been thoroughly briefed on the plan. They were aware that there could be shooting, after the exchange had taken place. Therefore they had been instructed to stay in the car, unless they absolutely had to get out. There was no other traffic on the terrain. The parking spots were empty and most of the lights were off. A few "security" lights were lit in some of the buildings. After about ten minutes a black BMW turned around the corner. They could not read the license tags on the front of the car. Italian license tags are small.

"Gimme a microscope and I'll read the number," whispered Ferdinando.

"He's alone."

"Great, my insurance premiums won't be increased."

"But, isn't that weird?"

"Not really, he's just a messenger. His boss couldn't care less, he's got thousands more where that one came from."

The BMW stopped and the driver looked around. Vittorio flashed his headlights and the other crept closer. When he was parked next to the Fiat, the window opened a crack and the man called: "Serifos!"

Vittorio lowered his bullet proof window a fraction and answered: "Serifos."

"Where's the money?" asked Vittorio while Ferdinando looked at the surroundings with hawk's eyes.

"Right here," said the man and pointed at the seat next to him.

"Bring it over," said Vittorio and closed the window.

The man maneuvered his BMW until the rear end of his car touched the two left doors of the Fiat.

"What the hell is he up to?"

"Nothing, he just wants to make sure we don't take off."

The man left the BMW with a large briefcase in one hand and a heavy caliber revolver in the other. The FBI men showed their own weapons. Vittorio again opened the window a few inches and said:

"Let me look in the briefcase."

The man opened the briefcase and Vittorio nodded his satisfaction when he saw the content. Then he showed the envelope with the impressive seals and asked:

"Satisfied?"

"Tell your buddy to come outside. I don't trust you."

"Well, that's a relief."

Ferdinando stepped out of the Fiat and walked toward the man. When they were opposite each other, they exchanged properties. The man took the large envelope and Ferdinando took charge of the briefcase. The man walked quickly back to his BMW, started the engine and drove off. Franco Giovale, who had seen everything from the cargo compartment of the van, crawled into the driver's seat and started his engine when the BMW was less than fifty yards away. He followed the BMW to the edge of the city, another unmarked police car took over the chase.

The driver of the BMW made it as difficult as possible for his pursuers. He drove fast, but it was not certain if he suspected that he was being followed. It was obvious, from the way he drove, that he considered the possibility. He utilized every opportunity the traffic offered him and suddenly, on the Corso, near the Santi

Apostoli, he disappeared. Enrico Tomasso's voice could be heard over the radio.

"I've lost him." It sounded disgusted. "I don't see him anywhere."

"Where did you see him last?"

"Just past the Sabini. He was right in front of me, waiting for the red light to change. I was only two cars behind."

"Spread out between the Sabini and the Apostoli." It was the voice of Martella. "Call all cars, pass the number, but DO NOT, repeat, DO NOT apprehend. Locate and report!"

"OK, ispettore," came the voice from the Central Dispatching Office. Despite the rapid Italian, Vittorio, who listened in on the radio in the Fiat, was surprised not to hear the familiar "10-4".

The search lasted until the next morning. Then everybody went home to sleep. The only positive result of that night was a computer print-out that reported the BMW as having been stolen fourteen days earlier. The owner was an accountant from Pisa.

*35. Rome, Thursday, June 7, 1984

Every reporter could write the report without thinking. The only thing left to do, would be to fill in the place of the crime and the name of the victim. That would be enough. The report showed up so frequently in the newspapers, that it could almost be termed a standard text.

(NAME OF CITY) Dateline—Assassins today killed (name of victim) in (name of city). The body was riddled with bullets and a final shot was fired into the back of the head, from a short distance. The identity of the assailants is unknown. A short distance from the scene of the crime the *Carabinieri* found the burned out wreck of a (brand of car) which had been stolen from (name of city) and which was used during the attack. The police have no clues,

181

but a spokesman said that the (name of Mafia family) was probably responsible for the killing.

The black BMW, which would later that day be mentioned in the familiar newspaper article, had been found in a different district of Rome. The driver was found with his head on the backrest of the seat. His mouth was open and his eyes were closed. He had not closed the black, leather jacket and his shirt collar was loose. The hands were folded in his lap and his feet rested on the pedals of the car. The gray interior of the car was drenched in blood and glass splinters covered the body and the area around the car. Exactly fifty three bullet holes were found in the body of the car. Some in a straight line, like perfect perforations.

As soon as Martella read the message on the police telex, he ordered Giovale to pick up Salvatore Navonna to identify the corpse. Franco left the *Questura Centrale* to do as he was ordered. Within half an hour Martella received a phone call that confirmed his suspicions. The corpse was that of the man with the slow, irritating voice. So, one of the kidnappers was dead. But where was the other one? The manner of killing had not been the work of a single assassin. It had been done by an execution squad. The list had not been found. That meant that the dead man had become dangerous, superfluous. He did not belong to any of the families. But who was the other one? He had to still be alive, unless he had been drowned, or made part of the concrete foundations in one of the buildings of a Mafia-controlled construction project. Who was behind it all and what was the meaning of it all? The list would already have been delivered to whoever gave the orders and within forty-eight hours they would know that it was false. Vittorio and Ferdinando entered. Martella called them over.

"They found a corpse in a black BMW. I give you one guess."

"The lazy talker?" asked Ferdinando with an exaggerated New York accent.

"Yes, it's him. Franco took Salvatore to identify the body and there's no doubt. He definitely identified him as the man that visited him."

"What about the list?"

"Gone, disappeared."

"Well, we'll hear about that, soon."

"Yes, you can bet on that. Meanwhile, I want Salvatore and his entire family to disappear. He's got his two million back?"

"Oh, yes, all taken care of," answered Ferdinando. "Minus, of course, ten percent for our usual commission." He laughed. Sometimes Martella had trouble deciding whether or not Ferdinando was joking. The FBI man had such a *strange* sense of humor.

"Well, I want you to escort him across the border and put him on a plane."

"Where to?"

"Switzerland, for the time being. The Swiss hate the mob with a passion and their police are very efficient. The families have almost no influence in Switzerland and he'll be safe there, for a while. Tell him, that if he doesn't go of his own free will, I'll have a deportation order for him within the hour. He has two hours to pack, no more. Take an armored bus and some help. Now disappear."

"Do we have time to fix a box-lunch, Chief?" Ferdinando could not resist asking.

"Go to hell!" laughed Martella.

*36. Rome, the same afternoon

The cab driver was obviously ill at ease as he approached the counter in the *Questura Centrale*. First they had searched his car from top to bottom, before they even allowed him to drive into the parking lot, then two *Carabinieri* had searched his person before allowing him into the building. The cop behind the bulletproof barrier was abrupt and obviously not in the mood for long conversations. He was very conscious of the importance of his function, and his uniform.

"Go ahead," he said curtly.

"I have a parcel for a certain Signor Martella," answered the driver.

The cop looked at him contemptuously and asked:

"Did they check it at the entrance?"

"Yes, they even X-rayed it, put it through a machine."

"So why didn't you hand it over, there?" asked the cop.

"I have to deliver it personally."

"Don't you trust us?"

"That has nothing to do with it. They paid me for the trip and I was told specifically to deliver it personally to Signor Martella."

He was one of the few Roman cab drivers who still did exactly as the client asked. Most of them would have just thrown the parcel in front of the door, if they had not already thrown it in the trash on the way home.

"What's your name?"

"Antonio Clemca."

"One moment," answered the cop. He picked up a telephone and dialed a number. After a short conversation he replaced the receiver and told the driver: "He's coming." He then turned his back on the man.

Martella came into the lobby, saw the man and introduced himself with a friendly smile.

"Ah, Signor Martella, I'm sorry to disturb you, but I'd promised the customer I would hand it over personally. But if I'd known in advance the trouble I'd have to go through, I wouldn't have taken the job. He paid me well, it isn't that, and then you don't mind a little extra work. But, hell, what a business, just to get this far."

"Let's sit down, a moment," said Martella.

"I don't want to keep you, Signor Martella, but you understand . . ."

"No problem. Would you like something to drink, Signor . . . eh?"

184

"Clemca, sorry, I should have introduced myself."

"Unfortunately, we only have a machine . . ."

"Doesn't matter, Signor Martella. I'll take *un succo di frutta*. It's a bit warm today and I've had hardly any time to drink anything."

They drank their fruit juice in companionable silence and then Martella said:

"Tell me, Signor Clemca, who gave you the parcel?"

"A man in the street. Elegant man, nice suit. Not unusual, you know, Signor Martella, it happens a lot. Don't think that this is the first time I've had to deliver a parcel. About a year ago I drove all the way to Venice, just for a letter. Well, I ask you! A letter, imagine! Just between me and you, it's nice work, it pays well. A parcel can't read the meter."

"I understand. Where did you pick it up?"

"At the corner of the Regina Margherita and the Via Bon Compagnie."

"What did the man look like?"

"Not too big, about thirty five, small moustache and he wore sun glasses."

"Did he say anything?"

"No, just that I had to deliver to the *Questura Centrale* and to deliver to you personally. That's all."

"Signor Clemca, if you saw a photo of the man, would you recognize him?"

"I think so."

"Would you mind looking through a few of our books? It wouldn't take long, maybe fifteen minutes. Can you spare the time?"

"With pleasure, this was my last trip for the day."

Martella stood up and led the way to Documentation. He asked for a number of photo albums and went patiently over the pages with the driver, page after page. The driver was a nice guy, who wanted to cooperate. Almost unique in this day and age. Most people refused to see anything, hear anything, or say anything. The few who did, immediately won Martella's sympathy. The strange thing was, he mused, that it usually were the older people who still cooperated with the police. Exactly the group that suffered most from petty crimes, still had the courage to speak out. The younger generations were too wrapped up in themselves and did not want to be bothered.

When Martella led the driver to the exit after twenty minutes, he suddenly realized that he still had not opened the package that had been delivered. He went back to his office, picked up a knife and opened the package. The first thing he saw was the sealed envelope, containing the forty seven pages for which Franco and Enrico had sacrificed their sleep. Then he saw the letter. A typed letter. He opened a drawer of his desk and took a pair of silk gloves out of it, put them on and unfolded the letter. He read:

Chief Inspector Martella:

Enclosed you will find a document we obtained through our contacts. It concerns the complete documentation regarding the activities, over the last twenty years, of some well-known Mafia families. The document has been prepared by a Belgian, lately from the Greek island of Serifos.

A member of the Anti-Mafia movement.

Martella placed the letter in front of him and wiped the sweat off his forehead with a shirt sleeve. He picked up the envelope with the forty seven pages and noticed that the seals had not been broken.

✳37. Rome, the same afternoon

"It's an incomprehensible case, sir," said Martella. They were in Carsini's office. The sealed envelope was on the desk between them.

"And you think there's no possibility they have seen through the ruse?"

"I've tried to figure every angle, but I just can't see where we could have made a mistake . . . if we made a mistake, or if there's a leak . . . but I can't come up with anything."

"They didn't open the envelope?"

"Out of the question. The lab was very positive. They've looked at it, that's almost certain, but they didn't touch it. What can it mean? First they try anything to get the list in their hands and when they finally have it, it seems all the trouble was just to make us a present of it."

"Let's see if we can think this through," said Carsini. "Let's start with the corpse on Serifos. He knew something and some people found out that he had made a record. That made a lot of people unhappy. We assumed the record, or list is somewhere and will eventually surface. We knew that, but the opposition didn't, because we know it from Salvatore. Meanwhile they tried everything to get their hands on the list: they searched the house in Serifos twice, they tortured and killed Dubour, they tortured and killed l'Elastico, they threatened Salvatore and kidnapped his kids to put more pressure on him."

He paused briefly, as if to gather his thoughts. Then he continued: "Because of the kidnapping, we manufacture a list, purporting to come from Serifos. We use our American friends, because they're unknown here, to make the transfer, incidentally financed by two million American dollars, contributed by Salvatore Navonna. Fine, the kids are freed, Salvatore has his money back and they have, they think, the list. Next thing we know: the creep that participated in the kidnapping and made the exchange of the money, is killed. Definitely a Mafia killing. But why? Supposedly he followed orders all along. Both of them were no more than messengers. One reason could be that their boss discovered the contents of the envelope was worthless and he took it out on him. A clear case of 'kill the messenger that brings you the bad news'. But that isn't so, because the envelope hasn't even been opened. They sent it to us!"

He sighed, looked at Martella who listened attentively, and then went on: "If they'd known the envelope came from us, they would either not have kept the appointment, or they would simply have kept the money, it's no chicken feed, after all. So, they *were* interested in the information and they got it. Then they make us a present of it. Because we can forget about the so-called 'Anti-Mafia Movement'. Those type of organizations are mainly political, they're not involved in terrorism. There's only one conclusion: They need us! They want to use us for their big clean-up. They know, or suspect, that the man from Serifos gathered enough evidence to take a lot of them out of circulation and they were afraid that a competitor would get the information first. Let's assume, for a moment, that this was the genuine list and that, with the help of that list, we were able to achieve mass arrests, like last April? What then?"

"The remainder could take over the business."

"Exactly!"

"So, somebody's waiting for that," said Martella.

"Yes, indeed, this so-called member of the fictitious Anti-Mafia League, or whatever, is poised for a considerable expansion of his business. As you saw, in April, more than eighty had to leave their interests behind and immediately there was a war for the spoils, between the remaining family members. And this time again, but now the stakes are higher, because the list is presumably longer. That's what this is about, Martella."

"But nothing is going to happen, because there *is* no list."

"You're right and we keep it that way. We just sit back and see. Perhaps some of them will jump the gun, get nervous. I'd like that."

"No reports?"

"No, nothing, I take full responsibility. You and your team take some time off, you earned it."

✳38. Rome, the same afternoon

As soon as Martella had left the office, Carsini called the Judge-Advocate. Within moments he heard the pretentious, supercilious voice.

"I hope you have something to tell me, Carsini," said the voice without greeting.

"Yes, sir, I have."

"When will I see the reports?"

"We're working on that, sir, rest assured."

"What's the status?"

"The kidnapping has been solved satisfactorily, the children have been freed."

"How did you manage that?"

Reluctantly Carsini related the events, including the falsification of the list, the transfer of the money and the role of the two FBI people. He finished with the corpse found in the black BMW and the envelope which had been returned to Martella. It remained silent on the line when he finished speaking.

"So, the real information they were looking for, has not yet been found?"

"No, sir. But I think we just have to wait for that. Sooner or later the genuine list will surface."

"How so?"

"The man from Serifos has deposited that somewhere. Nobody knows where, but it will surface after a specified length of time. I'm convinced of that."

"Who was that man you found this morning?"

"No idea. We're investigating. He has no record with us."

"What are your plans?"

"Nothing, sir. We wait."

"Where's Navonna?"

"No idea, sir. Somewhere abroad."

"Any idea about the second kidnapper?"

"No, we've only a sketch, based on descriptions, that's all."

"Well, that isn't much. Send me a copy of the sketch and the list. Send it now, by courier. I'll expect it within the half hour. Are you keeping the team together?"

"Yes, for the moment, sir." Carsini's tone of voice clearly indicated that he considered the conversation closed and shortly thereafter it was.

Carsini did not like the man. Or, rather, he did not trust him. He had never been able to prove it, but he felt it instinctively. He would not be the first, nor the last, with connections to the Mafia. Almost a common thing in Italy. Organized crime had penetrated everywhere. He, Carsini, fought a war on two fronts. On the outside and on the inside. It was disheartening. Italy had just about ceased to be a democracy. The country did not really fit in with the rest of the European Community. The insolent, merciless Mafia machine committed murder with the regularity of a clock, even in broad daylight. It proved, so thought Carsini, that the real power was in invisible hands.

The very word "democracy" had become a joke and an insult. The various Governments that followed each other with intervals of a few months, had lost all semblance of trust, of believability. Always composed of the same corrupt fossils, but in different categories, with different labels. Even if you belonged to a strong party in Italy, you could be weak. It did not make much difference. You were a victim of the musical chairs game in parliament. That is why Italian politicians were eternal, self-perpetuating. Only death put an end to their careers, not elections. They had either given up the battle against the Mafia, or had closed their eyes to the entire problem.

The barrenness, loneliness and hopelessness in regions such as Calabria, Campania, all of Southern Italy, was an affront to the judicial system of the country. Roman Law, which had once been the basis of most judicial systems in the world, which used to shine as a beacon of enlightened jurisprudence, was despised and ignored in the country of its origin, trampled in blood. Schools, courts and hospitals functioned partially, or not at all. Local politicians were assassinated, or blackmailed. Judges and lawyers who actively fought against the Mafia were subject to execution. The bitter necessity of a strong and unified attack against the terror of organized crime was obvious to all who truly loved Italy.

But the restrictions were countless and protests against the firmly established, ossified christian-democratic mentality could be dangerous. Countless faceless people used their political protection to resist change. The rot permeated into the highest regions of government. Because the Mafia was intertwined with the politicians, was connected to all political parties and exploited their connections shamelessly. Politics and Mafia were *not* abstract concepts. They could be connected to the names of men and women. Common names that could be found on the mailboxes of any house. Real, living and breathing people. This was not fiction, created for a TV series, or a movie, with actors playing roles.

The people who listened to names like Badalementi, Gioia, Greco, Mannucci, Vernengo and more, were not actors. They existed somewhere. They issued orders to their private armies of murderers, thieves, pimps, politicians. They bought the right people, blackmailed others and corrupted the rest. Every Mafia boss and under-boss, in every city, in every district, had sworn fealty to his *padrino* and followed him with slavish obedience to his criminal edicts. That's how they kept their connections to weapon smuggling, to the drug trade and other criminal activities that were so very, very profitable. Because that is what held them together. Money! Money was power. And they had the power.

An authoritarian regime held Italy in its grip. Political crimes remained unpunished for years. Nobody knew for sure how much

191

of the actual power was in the hands of parliament and how much was controlled by the Mafia. World War III had already started for Italy. The new Mussolini's had the upper hand and there were enough Hitler's left in the world to share in the enormous profits.

Carsini swept the papers off his desk, placed them in a drawer and locked it. He put on his jacket and left the room. His Lancia was parked outside. The Captain of the *Carabinieri* saw him get into the car, there were some commands, four motorcycles started up. Accompanied by his escort, Carsini swept through the gate en route to his heavily guarded house. Life in a democracy, he thought bitterly.

*39. Rome, the same evening

Padrino Giovanni Lovallo looked at the sketch of a suspect in front of him. Next to the sketch were the forty seven pages compiled by Franco Giovale and Enrico Tomasso, a few nights ago. On a separate sheet were the notes that the source of the information had added with a certain malicious pleasure:

```
May 22: Man killed on Serifos
May 30: House in Serifos ransacked for second
        time
June 1: l'Elastico killed
June 2: Two men visit Salvatore Navonna
June 4: Salvatore's children kidnapped
June 6: Children released
June 6: (11:30 PM) transaction for papers
June 7: One of the kidnappers killed.
```

Fabrizio Vitelli, Esquire, Judge-Advocate, had personally delivered the papers. That was unusual. He never came out in the open, all was done from a distance. He could still hear the supercilious, nasal voice: "I'd check the data myself, Giovanni." The voice had been mocking and had been accompanied with a grin of malicious delight, almost gloating. He was such an asshole! They all were. He, Lovallo, had made him what he was. The former, unimportant, stupid little lawyer from Reggio, with a penchant for small boys and child's pornography. But he was not above accepting his share from the Lovallo table. He had been paid billions of liras, he had become a rich man. The revolting, supercilious, arrogant manners had come with time. Lovallo had always had the little twit in his power. He could make or break Judge-Advocate Fabrizio Vitelli. He could ruin him, end his career, with the snap of a finger. At this moment he was tempted to do just that. But what was the use? Especially now. The chance that he would talk, would do irreparable damage to the reputation of the Lovallo family, was a possibility, a real possibility. He had to choose between two evils. He could maintain the little bastard and keep using him to protect his influence within the *Questura Centrale*, or he could fire him, which meant he had to kill him. He had become a pustule, the little, perverted lawyer, an arrogant piece of shit!

But now, he, Lovallo, was the loser. The information delivered by the Judge-Advocate, the information now in front of him, had made him, once one of the most powerful and most influential bosses in the Mafia, one of the biggest losers of all time. The situation had changed one hundred and eighty degrees! He could still see the self-satisfied, puffy face in front of him when he received the proof from the pale, clammy hands. The drawing on his desk was incontrovertible and the dates checked. He had double checked his calendar and there was no doubt. He *knew* the second man, the one who had arranged it all. It had been reported that the man was called Claudio. That is how Salvatore had identified him. That was right, it was the second name, that was never used within the family. Of course, Claudio could not have predicted that the information he had obtained, that he had delivered to the *Questura Centrale*, was worthless. The bastard had never realized that the opposition could be smarter than he thought. He had simply underestimated the police. But what was the cause? Why had it happened at all? Was he to blame? Had he failed as a parent? They had all had the best possible education, the best schools, the most expensive wives. They could afford anything. They lived like crown princes and princesses.

He heard the voice of one of the servants speaking to somebody in the hall. A little later the door opened wider and Ruggero entered. He walked toward Giovanni, embraced him and dropped into a chair.

"How are they hanging, pa?"

"I better ask you how you are, I haven't seen you for days."

"Business, papa, a lot of work."

"Yes, I know. One of your businesses, a piece of your work, is right here in front of me." He picked up the falsified list and handed it to his son.

"Take a look at that, Ruggero."

The son looked at the papers for a few moments and paled.

"You probably haven't read them, because the seals were unbroken when the package was delivered to the *Questura*," said Lovallo.

"Wadda you mean, papa? What's it got to do with me?"

Giovanni walked back to his desk and picked up the sketch and the notes provided by Vitelli. He handed both to his son.

"Now clear?" he asked.

Ruggero's hands shook while he looked at the sketch and read the notes. His voice trembled when he stuttered: "W-what does it mean? It ain't my business."

"Why are you shaking, Ruggero?"

"What's happening here?" demanded the son.

"I would like to hear that from your own mouth, my boy," said Giovanni.

"What do you want me to say?"

"Nothing, my son, nothing. I understand. Just do me one

favor. Tell me this is your own idea. Don't tell me you've been bought by another family."

"I've got nothing to do with it!"

"Little man, or should I call you Claudio, you're full of shit! Don't you understand? The list there, it's false! Two smart cops at the *Questura Centrale* put that together. This has *nothing* to do with the man from Serifos, the man you and your buddy killed! For nothing! You've been fucked, Ruggero! Ruggero Claudio Lovallo, the son and heir of *padrino* Giovanni Lovallo!! Fucked!!! By the way, that job last night, your buddy in the BMW, did you do that by yourself, or did you hire some torpedoes?"

"Wadda you mean?"

"Don't give me that shit, Ruggero, don't lie to me. You've insulted me enough already, you little fucking bastard. From the very start you fucked it up deliberately! You and Mario! Did you make a deal, eh? Were you going to split the business of the Lovallo and Mannucci families between you, eh? Oh, you were so eager to take care of things for your papa, at the time, remember? You were gonna hire two outsiders, right? But one of them was YOU! You, from the very start! You knew very well that the man in Serifos was *NOT* to be killed, didn't you!? You knew that the kidnapping of those two kids was *not* in our best interest, didn't you? You *knew* fucking well that would bring them ALL down on us, didn't you!? Including the *Carabinieri*!! Now I know why Barinne never came back from Favignana. Was he in the plot, too, eh? He had been with me for more than fifteen years, he had *sworn* his loyalty to ME! He respected me! How long did it take you to convince him, eh? What did you promise him? Too bad for you they found his fucking corpse in the crapper on the train, eh? You'd already planned to kill the man from Serifos at that time, didn't you!?"

Giovanni paused for breath. His face was red. He had never been so angry. He glared at his son, daring him to interrupt.

"Four weeks ago, already," he continued in the same loud voice. "You would have liked to sit in this chair more than four weeks ago, already! Right, you little sneak? But you made a mistake. Barinne was never one of the smartest. You should have known that, stupid! He had a drink somewhere, said too much and that was curtains for him! You should have known you could not trust him to keep his mouth shut, stupid! He was just a soldier. Give him an order, let him execute it. DON'T ask him to think! I don't know why he wound up with a rope around his neck in the crapper of that train. I could care less! Maybe you did it yourself, asshole! Perhaps you thought he had the documents from Greece, eh? Then you could have sent them to the *Questura* four weeks sooner, right!? But you were too stupid to think it through! But what can you expect, if you spend too much time with whores, your brain turns to mush. How could you be so stupid as to think that the man from Serifos would walk around with the papers in his pocket? That's your biggest trouble, you know that!? You're so fucking full of yourself that you think everybody else is just stupid! That's what you thought about me, too, didn't you? The old bastard won't notice a thing! He's gone soft in the head! Were you really in all that much of a hurry, eh? Wasn't I dying fast enough to suit you? Were you *that* impatient to get the strings in your filthy little hands? Is that why you betrayed me? Betrayed the family? Who *are* you Ruggero Claudio? Where the hell *did* you come from?"

He sank back in his chair, nearly exhausted.

"I tried to help you, papa."

"Don't lie to me anymore, Ruggero," said Giovanni tiredly. "It's no use. Just one more favor, that's all I ask. Keep your mother out of this. I don't want her to know that she had a son who betrayed the family. You *owe* her that. With the last little bit of honor that's left you, show her your respect. Go home, Ruggero, go to your wife and my grandchild, never come back."

Mafia boss Giovanni Lovallo opened the door of his study and waited until his son had left the room. Dejectedly he walked back to his desk. His heart throbbed in his throat and he felt a terrific headache starting behind his eyes. At his desk he looked around, a bit dazed and undecided. He remained seated for several

196

minutes, staring at nothing at all. He mulled over the situation again and again. He could not make a decision.

The Sicilian tradition allowed no pardon of traitors. Nobody escaped the *omerta*. Once one belonged to a family, had sworn fealty to a *padrino*, it was for life. The holy alliance could not be broken. Certainly betrayal could not remain unpunished. Even if it was your own flesh and blood. When he finally had made the inevitable decision, he picked up the phone and dialed an internal number.

A few minutes later a man knocked on the door and entered. His attitude was servile. He waited near the door. His face was pock marked and his nose had been broken, once, maybe several times. The narrow lips were closed and had never smiled. Two cool, unemotional eyes that saw nothing, stared in the distance.

"Take two men and go to Ruggero's house. Wait for him to leave the house and make him disappear."

"Si, Signor Lovallo."

"No fucking around. Quick and painless."

"Understood, Signor Lovallo," answered the man tonelessly, without any excitement, without questioning the orders. He left the room.

"If the man from Serifos had been alive, *he* would have had this job," thought Giovanni Lovallo bitterly.

✳40.

When the corpses of a prostitute and Ruggero Claudio Lovallo had been found in a luxurious sex-club near the center of Rome, there was only a perfunctory investigation for the perpetrators. Salvatore Navonna identified the man as the second of the kidnappers. Both kidnappers were now dead and there was no clue about their killers. There were plenty of suggestions and theories. But all those who had been involved with the Serifos case from the beginning, knew that a full-scale clan war was in progress. While the wars between the families raged, a smart policeman kept to the sidelines, unless he was suicidal. It was a well-known pattern, almost cyclical. About every ten years, or so, a new power structure would be created within the families. This was always accompanied by executions and internal punishments. No policeman was going to risk his life for that. Of course, reports were prepared, a search was made for the guilty, but it was more an administrative requirement, a placebo. No policeman felt involved, or had sleepless nights over it. If anything, there was a sense of relief that the wise guys were systematically wiping each other out. Every murder of a member of one of the families, was one less headache to worry about. As far as the police was concerned, it could go on forever.

Sometimes the murders led to unexpected discoveries. A week after the death of Lovallo's son, the corpses of the Vitelli couple were found. The car, carrying the Judge-Advocate and his wife, had fallen into a ravine, about five miles from the Brenner Pass. The car had not caught fire, so the coroner was able to establish that the couple must have been dead before they had been pushed off the road. The perpetrators had not taken the trouble to destroy the evidence, which would have been a simple thing to do. They had not thought it necessary, strengthened by their knowledge of immunity from prosecution, provided by influential relations and friends. Contemptuous of the laws of a country that had no means to fight back, that was powerless to keep its own house in order.

The documents, which had started it all, could not be found and the secret was buried in a simple grave on the island of Serifos. They knew the names he had used, they had his fingerprints, but that was all. The Belgian police had tried to investigate the Dupre family in Brugge. The father refused to talk, was hardly aware he had a son by the name of Jean Louis. A brother, Paul, was an out-of-work miner, under doctor's care for Black Lung Disease. Nevertheless his only complaint was that the mines had been closed. Jean Louis Dupre remained invisible. Any images were from long ago. The short period in San Francisco. The information from the Belgian Department of Defense, conversations with the inhabitants of Serifos. That was it. He had been around for forty nine years and nobody really knew him. In a time when practically everything was known about everybody, when almost everybody was classified, identified, registered, stored and kept in electronic vaults, Jean Louis Dupre, alias Robert Dubour, also known as Neville James Footman, or Frank C. Johnson, remained an enigma. It was as if the man had never lived, as if he was no more than a story, a legend.

After a few weeks the team was disbanded. The manure heap uncovered by the death of Judge-Advocate Vitelli was still pending investigation. As a result of that, a number of high ranking functionaries and politicians were arrested, interrogated and eventually, after several weeks, honorably dismissed from their offices with a high pension, leaving dejection and frustration in their wake. Vittorio Scarfiotti and Ferdinando Cotone returned to New York. Giorgio Bergarmi went back to Palermo. Chief Inspector Enzo Martella and Inspector Enrico Tomasso were assigned to cases dealing with purse snatching and domestic violence. The aftermath was always a disappointment, a let down.

Giulietta Martella died during the third week of August. Heart attack, said the doctors. Martella knew better. She had died of sorrow, a disease unknown in the medical text books.

*41. Dublin, Friday, August 31, 1984

The law firm of Adams & Gerrard, Solicitors, was located on the fifth floor of a large gray building on Saint Stephens Green in Dublin.

As usual, James Adams, senior partner, arrived at ten o'clock in the morning precisely. He greeted his assistant. Together they entered the cluttered office of the lawyer and he seated himself in a chair next to the semi-circular desk.

"Anything special today, Howard?"

"A few appointments, sir. I made a list for you."

"Right," said Adams, reading the list, "a nice, uncomplicated list for such a beautiful day, don't you agree?"

"Yes, sir. There's also a note regarding Monsieur Jean Louis Dupre."

"Have you heard from him?"

"That's just it, sir. The latest contact was on the second of May."

"Second of May? That's more than three months ago!"

"Almost four months, sir."

"Thank you for mentioning it. I'll contact the bank myself."

The assistant left the room and Adams picked up the telephone. He dialed the bank and made an appointment for that afternoon.

MASS ARRESTS
OF MAFIA MEMBERS

ROME (October 1, 1984)—Tomasso Buscetta, 56, Capo di Mafia, decided to cooperate with police, presumably as an act of vengeance for the murder of his family members and in retaliation for being at the top of a "Hit List", compiled by his former colleagues. The police in Rome were also assisted by information contained in a document received via Interpol, Dublin. This document was prepared by a hired killer of Belgian origin, who had compiled the information during the last twenty years. The documentation provided proof of a variety of serious offenses committed by organized crime. An avalanche of arrests was the result. During the week-end of September 29 and 30, the Judge-Advocate in Palermo issued 366 arrest warrants that were executed by more than 3,000 police officers.

MORE MAFIA MEMBERS ARRESTED

NEW YORK (October 19, 1984)—Twenty eight Mafia members in the United States were arrested yesterday. The action was an indirect result of the mass arrests of 366 Mafia members in Rome and Sicily, earlier this month. More than 3,000 police officers were used during the action in Italy. The direct cause for the arrests in the United States was a list compiled by a hired killer from Belgium. The list contains names and secret information about the Mafia and had been deposited with a law firm in Dublin, Ireland. Copies of the list were provided to the New York Police Department and the FBI. Because of the arrests, at least eight of the incarcerated Mafia members in Italy have offered to provide additional information to the police in exchange for reduced sentences, or new identities. The arrests have intensified the internecine warfare between the gangs in Italy. In Sicily alone, 14 people have been killed during one week in October.

Mafia Financiers Arrested

PALERMO (November 13, 1984)—Two of the richest and most powerful financiers have been arrested in Sicily. They are suspected of having connections with the Mafia. Last week the former mayor of Palermo was arrested on the same charge. With the latest arrests the police have finally arrived at the so-called "Third Level", a term used to describe the political and financial elements of the Mafia.

These arrests, also, were made possible by secret information delivered to Rome police on behalf of a heretofore unknown man. Toward the end of August the police was provided with a document that enabled them to arrest more than 400 Mafia members.

The affair was initiated by the murder of a man of Belgian nationality, who lived on the island of Serifos, in Greece. Apparently the victim was a hired killer with connections and business contacts in the Mafia and organized crime. He maintained detailed records during his lifetime, including the names of the victims and the people who hired him to do the killings. The murdered Belgian hired killer had managed to "ply his trade" for more than twenty years, unnoticed by the police. With the exception of a white collar crime in South Africa, he had never been arrested and had a clean record.

The Confession

Serifos, Friday, April 20, 1984

During the next few months I will write a letter to my son, Jon-Jon Lucas, born on November 30, 1970 in Berkeley, California. His current address is 2859 Shattuck Avenue in Berkeley and he lives with his mother, Anita Lucas, born on May 25, 1949 in New York City. She knew me as Robert Dubour.

This letter will be mailed in sections via Registered Mail. Each section will be sequentially numbered and addressed care of my attorneys, Adams & Gerrard in Dublin, Ireland. In addition I will be sending a special red envelope marked with the number zero. My lawyers have all the necessary powers-of-attorney and are instructed to place the envelopes, as they are received, in a Safety Deposit Box at a bank. The envelopes may only be opened on the dates indicated, or in the case of certain circumstances:

1. On the 30th November, 1991, the numbered envelopes, with the exception of the red envelope (numbered zero) must be handed over to my son, Jon-Jon Lucas. The red envelope, unopened, must be handed over to the Dublin Police.

2. If I die a natural death, the conditions above will remain in force.

Every three months, starting on April 1, 1984 and ending on November 30, 1991, I will contact Mr. James Adams, Esquire, senior partner of the Law Firm of Adams & Gerrard in Dublin. If I fail to contact Mr. Adams, or his designated representative, by telephone within any three month period, he will be authorized to act on my behalf and will be requested and required to perform the following:

a. Deliver ALL numbered envelopes, including the red envelope (numbered zero), unopened to the Dublin Police.

b. On the 30th November, 1991, the contents of the numbered envelopes, with the exception of

the contents of the red (numbered zero) envelope, must be delivered to my son, Jon-Jon Lucas.

Hereby executed, attested and signed on the
20th April, 1984, on the island of Serifos:

[Jean Louis Dupre]

Serifos, Saturday, April 21, 1984

For Jon-Jon:
Today is Saturday, the 21st of April, 1984
and it will be dark in half an hour. I will now
start to write what I have postponed for too
long. A letter for you. I do not know how long I
will keep it up. But I am determined to tell you
everything. At least, everything I still remember and find important. As you can read from the
date of this letter, the place where I am typing
this on my old, portable Remington, is on the
Greek island of Serifos. From my window in the
rear of the house, near the top of the mountain,
I can just see a small light in the distance, on
the quay below where the fishing boats are
docked and of course, my old beloved "Christina", a wooden, two-masted ketch from 1929, designed by Colin Archer. The wind, that has given
us no rest since the middle of March, seems to
abate in strength and I really think that this
night I will not hear the constant howling of
the wind around the bare rocks on which the
chora, the Greek village, has been built. I hear
the bus stop, near the top of the village. People are getting out and their voices resound in
the narrow streets. They will be home in a few
minutes and then nothing will happen in this
remote village, home to madmen, refugees and old
people, who have lived here all their lives.
And, of course, your father. The village is near

the top of the island. The island itself is little more than a rock in the sea of approximately 30 square miles, where nothing grows. 1,133 people lived here until yesterday. Today there are only 1,132, because an old fisherman died at three thirty this afternoon. Heart attack, they said in the village on the mountain. They called for a doctor, but the phone was out of order. It made no difference. Even if the phone had worked, the doctor would have been too late. And if the doctor had been on time, it still would not have made any difference, because he had been at the ouzo since early in the morning and at four o'clock in the afternoon he would have been unable to tell the difference between a heart attack and the common cold. And even if the old fisherman had been stricken early in the morning, before the doctor could get his first ouzo down, it still would not have made any difference, because the doctor is incapable of telling the difference between a heart attack and the common cold under any circumstances. On this mountain you are either healthy, or dead. There is no in-between. Athens is 73 nautical miles away and it takes the ferry more than four hours, too long to save a life.

This is the village in which I live, with just one friend, Petros Theologitis. That is all I have and all I want. I bought the house ten years ago for the equivalent of three hamburgers and I probably paid too much. But, as far as a man can be happy, I am happy here. Here one does not notice the rest of the world. I do not want to know. I am not curious about anything and have few lusts left. That is well. Nobody on the island knows who I am, or what I have done and I would like to keep it that way. Of course, they look at me strangely, even after all these years. But nobody asks questions. I pay the butcher, the baker, the candle stick maker, I make a small donation to the church, each year

207

and give a modest tip to the bar keeper. As long as you do that, nobody will ask who you are, or where you come from. It is the best character trait of these folks. They leave you alone. They do not ask where you were if you stay at home for a few days. Nobody worries about you. You could be dead for weeks, before someone will notice you are gone. A place for people who have given up everything that makes life worthwhile. That is what I am.

What else can a man need, but a bed to sleep in, a stove to cook on and a table to eat from? I would not wish for anybody to share this life with me. I am impossible, I know it. Sometimes I have already had too much to drink at four in the morning and want to sleep it off until noon, in a bed I do not have to share with anybody. I am not an alcoholic, at least I hope not. If I have a contract, I will not touch a drop, for weeks on end. Because in my job, alcohol is the worst enemy. I eat regularly and take care not to become too slovenly in my habits. I shave every morning, take a shower every day and make sure I have clean clothes. That is my way to survive and I am still alive. A gift from a higher power in which I do not believe. You just happen to appear in the world, it happens on a certain day and then you die, finished. The hypocrisy about souls and heaven and the hereafter are fairy tales for those who need an explanation for their presence on earth. I do not believe in the Last Judgement, either. It is an artificial world, tenuously held together with laws and regulations that will cost you money, or your freedom, if you ignore them. But it is all imitation and you cannot trust imitation.

The church threatens with hell and damnation, in itself a good business, because, in my opinion, there is no power on earth that is better acquainted, from bitter experience, with the depravity of man, and what he is capable of.

Because the leaders of the cathedrals, mosques, synagogues and the like are themselves power hungry egocentrics who play the game and are fully aware of the power and attraction of evil. Do not believe they believe. They are interested in the means. That is why they fold their hands, bend their knees, or face East and murmur their prayers. Moses, Jesus, Mohammed were probably people who, so very naively, wanted what was best for mankind. When they gradually gathered a following, it included the vultures, the tricksters, the politicians. They took over the means that could work for their benefit, whereby they could exercise power over the ignorant masses. They learned the gestures, the language and the rituals, they took the books and the writings and exploited them for their own glory. But believe? Truly believe? That is for the ignorant, the kind and those that are dependent on them for their daily bread. I have no belief. I only believe that man is the only animal in the world, stupid enough to destroy itself.

Your father is not a cheerful man, that is the first thing you should know. Never have been. Sometimes, usually in a bar, I can act different and if it involves a contract I can assume almost any personality, even carefree, but I am no longer cheerful. I do not want to pretend it is otherwise. I write as I feel. That is, in my opinion, the best way to let you know what sort of man I am. If I had been there during the past years, while you grew up, you would have known my peculiarities. You would then accept my personality and way of thinking as something normal, something you were used to. Now I must try to close this twenty year gap with mere words. A letter from a stranger.

Therefore I write as I feel and will not embellish things, or present them in a better light than what they are. The older I get, the more difficult it becomes to even just act

cheerfully. Nowadays I can only do it when I am
working on a contract. But that is a necessity
in my kind of work. To be able to perform. I
play the part required. I am a master of my
trade like no other in the world. I am unique
and I know it. My rates are figured accordingly.
It is a good thing to know your own worth. That
is important. Nobody else can put a value on
your services. You must do that yourself. That
is the first lesson I would like to share with
you. Perhaps there will be more lessons in these
letters, but that was not the purpose. I do not
want to be your teacher, but I would like to
tell you about my experiences and enable you to
draw your own conclusions. I think that is what
fathers are supposed to do.

But other fathers have had more time, than
I. I write this letter in an attempt to make up
for lost time. Because you are my son. I have
never seen you and will probably never meet you.
That is not my wish, but I know it is better so.
Your life must be different from mine. I must
not stand in your way. I was the son of a
dirt-poor miner in Belgium and you are the son
of a very rich hired killer. It is only a small
step higher on the social ladder, but perhaps it
is just enough to enable you to reach your
goals. Something I was unable to do.

Your mother and I met at 1:14 PM in a deli-
catessen across from the University in Berkeley.
She was nineteen and had sad eyes. That was the
first thing I noticed. I did not realize until
much later that she was also extremely beautiful. The eyes, however, had something that be-
witched me. The eyes hid something that
fascinated me incredibly and gave me the courage
to speak to her. She was a waitress in the
"Windmill", a deli run by a fat Dutchman, who
spoke English badly and laughed loudly at his
own jokes. He used to prepare salads with a
cigarette hanging from the corner of his mouth

and a sweaty forehead. One of his ham sandwiches was a complete meal and his prices were adjusted to the wallets of the students from across the street. He was a hearty, jovial man without a grain of evil. Everybody liked him because he was able to welcome each customer as if he was a long-lost brother, finally reunited with his family. Even if you came every day. Last year I was in San Francisco for a contract and I took the time to stop by. He was dead. There was a new owner who tried to make the same sandwiches, but without success. There was nothing wrong with the quality, but the laughter was missing.

Your mother had only been working there for fourteen days when I met her. In retrospect I am very glad she found such a wonderful boss, because few people had ever treated her in a nice way in the years before. Life had dealt her a crooked deck, almost from the beginning. Therefore the sad eyes, that intrigued me so, before I knew anything about her. I loved her so and I still love her with all my heart. The months that followed are still the best of my life. Not a day passes without me thinking of her. But I am a hired killer. I can be hired to do away with people, permanently, if their existence is too much for other people. That is my job, my profession. It is the only thing I know how to do. Your mother is too good and dear for this world, certainly too good to share her life with a hired killer. I did not want to cause her sorrow. I loved her too much for that.

Athens, Friday, April 27, 1984
    "Smith here. Is this 89219432?"
    "Aha, finally."
    "I have to be careful."
    "I know. Are you in New York at the moment?"
    "No."

"Well, I don't have to know. I want you to do something for me. And fast."

"I set my own pace."

"Yes, we know."

"Name?"

"Joe Bacelli."

"Address?"

"Unknown."

"Alone?"

"Joe is never alone. He knows he's wrong."

"I'll think about it. I call again in a week."

"Time?"

"11 PM, next Friday."

That is how this contract started and I will record for you, day by day, as a sort of diary, what happened. Consider it a small compensation for all those nights that I was not there, with you and your mother, at the dinner table. When I could not tell you what had happened during the day, as fathers ought to do. It is useless to tell you exactly what happened before. When I started this letter on the 21st of April, I did not know I was to receive a contract. As a matter of fact, I did not know myself, that I would ever again accept a contract. I had made up my mind. I had decided differently. The only reason I accepted was because I had started this letter. One more time, I decided, just one more time, just to write the diary.

After that conversation I replaced the receiver, opened the door of the small telephone booth and paid the man behind the counter. I paid with a handful of drachma and left the stuffy building of the OTE, the Greek telephone service. I was glad to leave the building. All buildings of the Greek telephone service stink and none have air conditioning. Even in the summer, with temperatures around 100 degrees, the windows are closed. They cannot be opened. Rusted shut, or painted shut. I was relieved to be outside. The traffic of the city, dominated by seven million kamikaze pilots, roared around me. Everyone who owns a car in Athens is certifiable. It always reminds me of the old joke about the pedestrian who was asked how he had reached the other side of the street. The answer was: "I was born here." Athens is a rotten city. You must come and visit the Acropolis, look at it long and intently, marvel at the knowledge and artistry. Then leave as quickly as possible. There is nothing else the city has to offer. If you are suicidal, but lack the courage to jump out of a window, the city offers the best chance in the world to die in a traffic accident.

I walked down a few streets and entered the office of Olympic Airways. I joined the end of a queue, but that does not mean that you wait your turn. Not in Greece! Whoever has the biggest mouth is the first one to be waited on. You have to get used to that, but after a few times waiting in line for nothing, you adapt quickly. When I managed to get the attention of the lady behind the counter I heard that there was still one plane to Rome, that day. I had hoped for that and everything I might need for the contract was in my luggage and ready to go. I bought a ticket and paid in cash. I do not own credit cards, too easy to trace. I had three passports with me for this trip and had the ticket issued in the name of Frank C. Johnson. A rather common name, but it happened to be the one on the grave in Kenilworth, England. The real Frank Johnson died in 1956. He was then about nine months older than I, at the time. Once you have the name, it is just a matter of a short trip to London to get a copy of the birth certificate. With that, a few passport photo´s and a "convenience" address, you can have a British passport within a few weeks. I have a total of eight British passports, all valid. True, I spent a considerable time in English cemeteries. Also, of course, each identity has its own disguise and character. I have noticed that I adapt my behavior, almost subconsciously, to the person behind whose identity I happen to hide. I live myself into a role. Not only my appearance and movements, but also my speech patterns adapt to the role I am playing. Perhaps I would have made a good stage actor. But that was impossible in the environment in which I grew up.

I left Olympic Airways and tried to snag a taxi. I was lucky and half an hour later I was at the airport. I checked in and that night at ten o'clock I was in the center of Rome. I took a room in one of the most expensive hotels, not from extravagance, but as pure self-preservation. One of the most important rules in my profession: always travel first class, stay in the best possible hotels. Cheap hotels are too often checked and are too small. You cannot hide in the crowds. Also, strangely enough, few people suspect the guests in expensive hotels of criminal activity. And of course, the more expensive the hotel, the more likely it is that a large percentage of the guests are criminals. But they are not recognized as such. An expensive hotel offers the best sort of camouflage when engaged in illegal activities. It is now a little past midnight and I am going to bed.

Rome, Saturday, April 28, 1984

In my profession it is of the utmost importance that nobody knows who you are. No name, no address and nobody has ever seen me. Anonymity assures a long life. I cannot be reached by mailbox, nor post office. I would have to pick up the mail. I could be followed. With disastrous results. A go-between is out of the question. Remember, a lot of my clients would love to know my identity. Because I know a lot! I know enough to put hundreds of high ranking politicians, or criminal bosses, in jail for the rest of their lives. I have kept a careful log of their names, addresses and the circumstances of the relevant contracts. The judiciary forces of a number of countries would be highly interested in the information I could reveal. Many a "higher-up" would not sleep another wink if he thought I was about to open my mouth.

As it happened, about three week ago there was a yacht under Panamanian flag in the bay of Serifos. The "Paradise." Almost 180 feet long and with a permanent crew of ten. Probably valued at about $30 million with maintenance costs of at least $2 million per year. I happened to be on the quay when she entered and the next day Petros and I, in his fishing boat, sailed around her. It was lunch time, the stewards in white uniforms stood along the rail on the poop deck, hands on the back, eyes staring in the distance, seeing nothing. The owner, surrounded by a number of male prostitutes was stuffing his face. Coffee was being served from solid gold pots, while the owner fondled his boy friends. I knew him, but he did not know me. I knew everything about him. Solidly married to a wife he has not seen for years. A mock marriage. That is the way in Italy. He is the most depraved homosexual in the Western hemisphere. Everything about the man is repulsive.

He is first cousin to Riccardo Mannucci of the Cosa Nostra, known from the Pizza Connection, an organization that has imported more than $1.5 billion (wholesale!) of heroin into the United States. One of the few that cunningly escaped arrest earlier this month. More than eighty arrests, among them bosses such as Don Gaetano Badalementi and "uncle" Pietro Alfara. I knew them all. Not personally, because I always avoided that, but I knew everything about them.

I know too much. If the queer on the "Paradise" had known who it was that circled his yacht in a fishing boat, he would have befouled himself. Because he is also on my list. Twice I have executed a contract for him.

When you get this letter, my documentation will be with the police. You will never get to see that. If you ever found out about the names I recorded, you would not live another day. Even if you were protected by both the FBI and the CIA, you would still not be safe. Because there are leaks everywhere. But I do want you to know that the people I killed were no loss to mankind, to the world. It was all scum. I would have been killed myself, long ago, if I had not maintained a careful record as life insurance. I made sure they knew. In certain circles they knew about me, knew I existed, but how could they reach me? I will explain that to you.

To begin with, you should know that my clients would just as soon remain anonymous themselves. I have developed a fail-safe communication system that is based on bank numbers. The people I do business with, all have secret bank accounts in Switzerland, Luxembourg, the Caiman Islands and such. All bank accounts identified with numbers. Not even the bankers know who owns the accounts. Orders for payments and withdrawals are made by telephone and a secret code is used as identification. Of course, the code is changed from time to time as an extra security measure. I too, have such an account in Geneva. Therefore a client may, without divulging the sender, deposit an amount in my account. So, the bank account number is the only thing that my clients know about me. But, as I said, the bank does not know who I am. Of course you ask how the client gets my account number. That is rather simple. Over the years the number has been "rumored" around and passed on to friends and relations. Also, over the years I have built up a certain "client pool" that is large enough to keep me busy most of the time. The connections between politics and organized crime are disturbingly more prevalent than you would like to believe. So, there is never a shortage of clients. The client sends me two checks. There is one week difference between the dates of the first check and the second. This is to make sure I know the difference between the first and the second. Via those checks, an amount is deposited to my account that does not exceed three numbers before the decimal. For instance, the first check may be for $257.89 and the second may be for $23.12. When these numbers are placed in sequence, for instance 257892312, I have a phone number. The sender has been identified as Mr. Smith and the city is indicated on the deposit. For US numbers I wind up with 10 digits (area code and number) and for European cities this will differ.

But I know the number and the city. I call the client and hear the name of the victim to be, as well as any particulars the client knows about the victim. I then take at least a week to locate the exact whereabouts of the victim, my "contract". I try to flesh out the information I already have. This is the most dangerous time for me. I must always be alert for a trap. The only time I am vulnerable, is when I have been enticed to a certain location for a fictitious contract and they are waiting for me. The contract is then used as bait to get me to move. It has been tried, once or twice, but I seem to have developed a special sixth sense for those instances. Usually, however, my clients know about my "life insurance" and refrain from meddling with me. In the world in which they live, nobody trusts anybody else. In fact, I exploit the fears that occupy every "boss" or "padrino". The most loyal lieutenant can become a deadly rival. They know that better than any-

217

body, because they gained power themselves through betrayal and corruption.

If somebody within their organization must be liquidated, it is usually unwise to use their own personnel for that, because there is a danger in that policy. It might give the wrong people ideas. Therefore the only solution: to hire an outsider to take care of the ticklish situation. Preferably an outsider they know about, who can be trusted and who has a reputation of delivering. The fear for their own skin guarantees me a long and safe life. They know that I am their only reliable source for a liquidation in their own organization and they know that I will always remain an outsider. The fact that I learned as much about my clients is a matter of deduction and clear thinking. I know all the families and their branches. I made a study of that. Primarily for self-preservation. But it is even more important, of course, not to use the knowledge I have. It must remain a threat only.

In any case, as soon as I have made contact by phone, we have a tentative contract. A perfect agreement, neither party supposedly knows who the other is, and nothing has been written down. After I have looked over the situation for about a week, and I am certain that the victim will be no loss to mankind, I call back. I then tell them my terms. It can differ. I have accepted contracts for as low as $50,000 and as high as $150,000. The importance of the victim, the danger involved, the risks, they are all factors to be considered. And I want to get paid for my services accordingly. I set the price and it is not subject to negotiation. The full amount must be transferred to my account within five days. As soon as I have confirmed receipt of the money, I start the job. Usually I estimate a time frame in which the contract will be completed. I will not be rushed. The moment somebody demands that I complete a contract within a specified time frame, I refuse the contract. I have my own methods and I will let nobody interfere. Also, I do not furnish interim reports. If I notice that they are trying to check up on me, I cancel the agreement and disappear. Those are my terms and my reputation is such, that I can permit myself to be that independent. They know I can be trusted. Strange, come to think of it, especially in an environment where nobody can be trusted.

Rome, Sunday, April 29, 1984

When I left the hotel at ten thirty in the morning, perhaps encouraged by the fine weather, I decided to walk part of the way, before I took a cab to the Piazza Colonna. At that time of the morning, on a Sunday, most Italians are still asleep and the city-scape is not dominated by the Alfa Romeos and Lancias. A breathing spell. You have time to appreciate the beauty of the city, something you can seldom do when you have to watch the traffic at all times, just to survive. Every facade is interesting and there is, so to speak, a piece of art at every corner. Everything in this city is of historical significance and you will constantly be amazed. It is frightening to think that our Belgian ancestors were still hunting wild boar with bows and arrows when this was already a city of more than a million inhabitants. They already had apartment buildings with multiple floors and the noise of the traffic was only slightly less than in the modern world. I always find it a strange thought. I walk here, but two thousand years ago, someone else walked here. Possibly also on his way to a meeting. Millions of people who, by pure coincidence, have never seen an airplane, or a car.

This will be my last contract. I told you that already. The last time that I prepare myself, after receiving the checks. I feel it must be so. I am still in good health and condition, but I notice that a number of things I used to do without thinking, now take some special attention and effort. I notice myself becoming forgetful, my memory for facts and faces is not what it used to be. I still have my sixth sense, an animal instinct, that warns me of danger. But I trust it less. I do not take the same thoughtless risks I used to take in my youth. Reason seems to take over and I wonder if that is a good thing in all cases. I am more and more aware of the danger and sometimes I am afraid.

Musing along those lines, I had arrived at the Piazza Colonna with the column honoring Marcus Aurelius, dating from 180 AD, as physical proof that in the past, too, people feared being forgotten after death. Those in power built their temples, had marble statues made in an attempt to buy eternity. But all that is left of them is stone. Stone that cannot speak, think, or exercise power. To the North is the palace that was once commissioned by the fabulously wealthy Chigi. Across, one of the few tea-rooms of the city. I passed the Corso to the corner of the Via Monte Catini in the direction of the restaurant, "Il Falchetto" and sat down on the terrace. I ordered a cappuccino and waited. The man I expected to find was not yet at his post.

In the paper I read an extensive obituary about Count Basie who died in Florida, the day before yesterday. He was seventy nine. One of the few jazz musicians who did not have to depart this vale of tears prematurely because of booze, or drugs. That man was, and is, an idol of mine. I have all his records and some have been played so often, they are almost ruined. Everything that genius ever recorded, I have in my house in Serifos. Only a few years ago I was fortunate enough to attend one of his concerts in Los Angeles. He was already confined to a wheel chair at the time. But you forgot all about the wheel chair when he started to play. That is truly a beautiful career. That is real immortality. The pillar of Marcus Aurelius just stands there. You can look at it. But you can still hear Count Basie, now and a thousand years from now.

When I looked up from my paper, I saw the man I was waiting for. In the old days, before the proliferation of pornography, he used to sell postcards from his inside pockets. They were Swedish, it was suggested at the time, with a wink. The man had not changed. He has not changed in the twenty years that I have known him. Some people are born old and stay that way. I knew he was rich. But he was also a scrooge, for himself and for others. I think he counts his money in the millions of dollars. Probably under his mattress. Yet, every day he is in the Piazza with his post cards. People buy them out of pity. It is whispered that he owns the entire street where he lives. But he lives in a basement. The street full of whores, pimps and other outcasts with which Rome has been so generously blessed. He knows everybody and knows where everybody is. He is a mine of information.

I called the waiter and paid the check. I stood up and walked in the direction of the postcard peddler. I waited until a number of tourists were crowded around him and then approached. I bought a card and wrote a name on it: "Salvatore Navonna" and the phone number and room number of the hotel. I returned the card to him with a bill of 10,000 liras. Without looking at me, or acknowledging me in any way, he looked at the card and raised five fingers. I expected that, I showed him three fingers and he nodded. We had done business like that for years. I gave him another two bills which he quickly put in his pocket. Less than two hours later the phone rang in my hotel room. I picked it up and heard a well-known, gruff voice:

"Who is there?"

"Roberto." That was the name by which he knew me.

He became less gruff and said enthusiastically:

"Aaaah, Roberto! Dio mio! What are you doing in Rome?"

"Niente, sempre niente, you know me, Salvatore, I never do anything."

"You dirty Congolese, you're not in Rome for nothing."

"I want to talk to you, Salvatore."

"Of course you want to talk to me. I want to talk to you, too. When?"

"Eight o'clock, same place?"

"Aha, you remembered! Ristorante Portofino. I'll be there, Roberto, and I'll show you the most beautiful women in Rome."

"Yes, like last time."

"You just wait, buddy, leave that to me. I'll see you at eight. Make sure you wear silk shorts, the girls love it. Arrivederci."

I hung up and smiled. Salvatore would never change. I knew him from the Congo. We had fought together in the mercenary army of Jacques Schramme. All the scum of Europe in one bunch. Now they had spread all over the world and had become my most important sources of information. None of my old buddies was made for a nine-to-five job and they all knew how to keep their mouths shut. There was an unwritten law in the jungle: you took care of each other. That band was never broken. We were all mercenaries together and you fought in order to eat. Everybody belongs to some network of comrades who have shared a piece of history together. We happened to be a group of criminals, disillusioned and outcasts with the same violent background.

Call them what you will. A sect, a church organization, a club.

In the Portofino not much had changed, either. Since time immemorial the place had seldom
been cleaned, never been painted. The boss hated
every form of modernization with a passion. He
had never considered plastic bunches of grapes
for the ceiling and empty Chianti bottles went
in the trash. Certainly he was not going to put
candles in them as table decorations. There were
the same chairs and tables and still the same
waiters. The boss was still in the same place
from which he could oversee the kitchen, the
waiters and the cash register. His spaghetti and
macaroni was not from a package and the stove
was black from the grapevines he burned in it.
The place was full when I came in. Salvatore was
waiting for me at a corner table. I had not seen
him for years. He had grown old. His hair and
the small moustache (model 1920) had turned
gray. Errol Flynn would have looked like that,
if he had not died so young. His eyes lit up
when he saw me and he came over with outstretched arms. He embraced me and kissed me in
a way that only Italians can do with grace and
style. We northern Europeans cannot do it, and
we will never learn, either. It embarrassed me a
little. I stuttered a bit. I can never force
myself to press my lips against a stubbly cheek.
We sat down and Salvatore talked. The old light,
I remembered it so well from the early days, was
back in his eyes. After we had spent the first
hour rehashing memories from the Congo, he became more serious after the second bottle.

"Tell me, why are you in Rome?"

"I´m working on a case and I need information"

"Dangerous?"

"Possibly a family quarrel."

"Mafia? Cosa Nostra?"

"Is there anything else, in this country?"

That got him going.

"No, you're right, Roberto. Italy is sick. Nothing works anymore. They're everywhere. Invisible. It's ruining it for everybody. Sure, I got a few girls, but they want to be in the business. I don't force them. I don't import teenagers, and younger, from Thailand. Sure I have an illegal gambling place and a guy that will take the rap. But that's what I pay him for. And I pay him real good and he knows the risks. If they ever close me down, I'll be back in business within weeks, maybe at the same location. If it lasts only four months, I've got my money back, and then some. But the mob spoils it for everybody. I've two sons, nine and ten, but I don't mind telling you that I burn a candle everyday, hoping they won't have to mess with the business. Roberto, you know I don't give a rat's ass for the church, but yet I burn a candle. Every day, Roberto. You know, it don't hurt and maybe it helps. Crazy, right? But it's nothing but fear, old buddy, just fear. They're everywhere. Heroin, cocaine, pills, you name it. Tons and tons, whole shiploads!"

"I know." I said.

Then he became uneasy. You understand, I'm trying to be as accurate as possible. Even if we did not use the exact words, you may be sure that it was something very similar. He asked:

"What are you working on, Roberto? Let them go to hell with their money. Go back to your island and stay there."

"This is the last time."

"Famous last words. I've heard them so often. But I can tell you, they've been pretty nervous, the last few weeks. You know they picked up more than eighty of them a few weeks ago? Even some of the big boys!"

"I know, But I've recorded twenty years of history and carefully documented it. If something ever happens to me, they'll grab another five hundred."

"Do they know that?" he asked.

"They do, if they're smart."

Then he looked me straight in the eyes and lowered his voice. He whispered:

"Roberto, I don't know what this is all about, but I want to help you. If you have to kill one of them, I am your man. You can count on me. I'll do anything to get rid of the scum. Understand, it's not just for you, but also for myself. Consider it a down-payment. My life has been such, that I can't exactly expect a warm welcome, upstairs, you know. I count on nothing, that way I won't be disappointed. But I want to do it for my sons. I want to do something, Roberto. Something worthwhile, to protect them. Perhaps that's what's expected of me, like that rubbish with the candles. Call it faith, who cares." His eyes begged me to understand.

"Joe Bacelli," I said.

"Aha, from the Tandello family, Mannucci e Lovallo"

"Know about him?"

"Oh, yes. Where is he now?"

"That's what I wanted to find out from you."

"He's been banished?"

"Perhaps, maybe he fled. Who knows. But I don't care about that."

"What do you want to know about him, Roberto?"

"Everything, Salvatore, everything. Where is he? How is he protected, habits, you name it."

"I'll see what I can do. Will you be at the hotel?"

"For the time being."

"Is that wise?"

"Nobody knows me."

"Not yet! But be careful, Roberto. I have a good address for you, if you want it."

He took a piece of paper from his pocket. I read it, memorized it and returned it to him. He took his lighter and burned it.

"You'll never know if you'll need it," he said. I thanked him.

"Give me a few days, and I'll have something for you," he said.

"How can I reach you?"

"Every morning at eleven in the Bar Corone."

"I know it."

"I'd like to go with you. Like old times, know what I mean?"

"Salvatore, I'll think about, but I prefer to work alone."

"I understand." He seemed to regret it.

It was almost midnight when Salvatore asked for the bill. He would not let me pay. We left the restaurant and he admonished me to be careful, when we parted. He disappeared down a dark alley. Thank God, he did not kiss me.

I took a cab back to the hotel and I asked for a Rome phone book at the reception desk. I found the number of the Bar Corone and memorized that as well. I went to bed and thought about you two, as always.

Rome, Monday, April 30, 1984

The knock on the door woke me. Although nobody knew about my contract and nobody knew my identity, I was instantly alert. I stood to the side of the door and turned the key. The door opened and a voice said: "Buongiorno, signore. La prima colazione." A waiter came in and set the table for breakfast. I tipped him and he left.

After breakfast I showered and dressed. I did not shave and the clothes I put on were a little less elegant than those I had checked in with. I left through the garage and in a public bathroom I put some make-up on my face which made me look less reputable. I then took a cab to the center of the city. After paying off the cab, I found a shop for second-hand clothes. The place smelled of moth balls. Nobody took any notice of me while I searched the racks. I looked like the usual customer for such a shop. I was looking for something that would be English in appearance, green and brown. It had to be used, but not worn-out. A bit old fashioned, preferably, but not so old fashioned that I would look ridiculous. I was almost certain I would have to go to Sicily. That is where the family members go, when they have to go underground. No place on earth offers them better protection.

I wanted to use the passport of Neville James Footman. He too, had died long ago, in 1935. "His" profession was archeologist, a visiting professor at Cambridge. I even had a letter of recommendation from the University, complete with verified Italian translation, signed by the Italian ambassador himself in London. You can be sure that everybody going to Sicily will be scrutinized. A dried out English professor, armed with a small spade, looking for antiquities, is not an unusual sight on the island. It seldom raises an eyebrow. It was the type of disguise that I used often for this sort of preparations. As long as one takes care to obtain the disguise locally, there is little danger. In the case of eventual customs checks it simply would not do to be found with eccentric clothes in my luggage when I am supposed to be travelling as a businessman.

Much to my surprise, I found an old pair of plus-fours in the racks. Green corduroy with thinner spots where thinner spots are supposed to be. That was it. I found a beige jacket with leather patches to match the outfit. I selected a number of shirts and some other items and put

them all on the counter, along with an old rucksack that was to be my luggage. The man behind
the counter looked at me, started to count the
items and said:

"150,000 liras."

"110,000," I countered.

"Prego, signore, not possible," he cried.

"Bene, non `e possible. Arrivederci." I
walked away.

"Signore, 130,000 liras. Contento?"

"125,000 liras."

The deal was made. I had played the game as
he expected. The price had come down from
150,000 liras to 125,000 liras, a difference of
about twenty-five dollars. The few liras were
not at issue here, but if I had not haggled, he
would have found it something to remember. I had
to try and avoid that as much as possible. At a
tobacconist I bought a pipe and a bag of stink-
ing, English pipe tobacco. Now I would even
smell like an Englishman. I then stored everything in a locker at the railroad station and
went back to the hotel.

I am trying to write this as detailed as
possible in order to give you as complete a
picture as I can. I hope you will not be bored.
Mine is not a honorable profession, you know
that. One can hardly boast about it. You certainly cannot discuss your father's career with
your friends. I have done nothing you can be
proud of. I have never been able to be there for
you, like other fathers. I have not been able to
help you with your homework, I have not been
able to see you play, if you were on the school
team and I have been unable to grumble when you
came home too late from a party. We never did
anything together. I wish I could have taught
you to drive, on a lonely back road somewhere.
Or taken you fishing. I could not teach you how
to shave. Often history repeats itself. My own
father was down the mine, or in the bar. Under

the ground, or under the influence. All he ever
gave me was beatings and a big mouth. There were
four of us at home, I was the youngest. Marie
was the oldest. She took care of the house when
mother died. I hardly knew my mother. Marie was
my mother. Marie is dead, too. She sacrificed
her young life to a family that could not be
saved. It was hopeless. My oldest brother, Paul,
married at age seventeen. I never heard from him
again. I did know Gerard well, we were buddies.
We slept together in a single bed that was seldom changed. He contracted pneumonia and died
shortly after. I can still hear his labored
breathing and coughing and the death rattle when
he died next to me. I was only six at the time
and there was a war on.

When the priest came he told us it was a
punishment from God. Mother´s death, too, had
been a sign from heaven. I can still vaguely
remember her. I have only one picture. Marie, my
sister, is the only one who told me about my
mother. I loved Marie. She used to take me on
her lap and tell me stories. I was not aware, at
the time, how terrible her life really was. I
was just twenty one when the news of her suicide
reached me in Leopoldville, Congo. Only four
months earlier she had accompanied me to Antwerp, to see me off. I can still see her waving
on the quay. The police doctor established that
she was pregnant. She was not married and had
never had time for men. There could be only one
reason for her suicide: my father.

Suddenly you realize a number of incidents
from the past, strange incidents that you soon
forgot because life was bad enough as it was.
Also, so many things were simply not discussed
in the Roman-Catholic town where we grew up. But
there, in the jungle, I suddenly knew. My father
was also the father of her child. He had used
her all those years and we had left her to bear
that cross alone. We, Paul and I, could have

229

known, if we had shown a little more interest in her. But we were too busy with our own flight. He into an early marriage and me as volunteer for the Congo. When she waved to me for the last time, she could only return to a dilapidated, dirty house with a drunkard who used her and humiliated her. She lived to be thirty years old and that bastard is still alive and gets a pension from the Belgian government. Marie and my mother, two women I loved so much and gave so little. It was not possible in the case of one, and I forgot in the case of the other. The third woman was your mother.

I left her because I loved her. How could I ask her to live with a criminal? There was a good chance that I would wind up in prison. I could not go back anymore, at the time. I was in it up to my ears. I would always be on the run, I knew that and I had reconciled myself to it. Then your mother entered my life. Five years late. We only spent six months together. During that time I tried to lead a normal life. I even tried a few jobs. But my past would not leave me alone. Also, what could I achieve in a regular job? I don't know enough of anything that would enable me to make a career in "civilian" life. What could I offer her? A life in a rented apartment and a car on payments? I could not even offer to marry her, because all my papers were false. And I could not tell her. My name was Robert Dubour during those days. A name I still use, because it is still "respectable". I have never attempted any contracts under that name and always lived as an upstanding citizen. I can even renew my passport at the Belgian Embassies and Consulates.

My real name is Jean Louis Dupre. If I had tried to marry your mother, the American authorities would have checked the antecedents of Robert Dubour most carefully and I would have been discovered, found out. When she was pregnant with you I foresaw a dim future for you. But I wanted you to have a carefree childhood and prospects. I did not fit in that picture. The only option was for me to leave and to make sure that your mother would have the means to care for you and to finance a good education. I could not make that sort of money in a regular job. As Neville James Footman I bought her a house, without telling her about the landlord. All these years she has promptly paid the rent into a bank account in San Francisco. When I allow Mr. Footman to pass away, soon, it will be discovered that he left her the house in his will. When I left I promised I would take care of her financially and I have done so. At the moment I have more than $5 million in a numbered bank account in Switzerland. That is for her and later for you. My will is with a lawyer in Ireland and by now you know the name. I have an agreement with my lawyer that requires me to call him every three months, to let him know I am still alive. In my profession you have to be prepared for anything. If I fail to contact him in any three months period, he has been instructed to open my will and to take all necessary steps to execute the will and to handle it according to my instructions. He will also send you this letter.

I hope, however, that I will be able to send you this letter myself. As I told you, I am working on my last contract. Between now and your 21st birthday I will devote myself to try and erase the traces of the past. That is possible, but it will take time. My private wish is to meet you some day and that, perhaps, we can make up for lost time. You are just thirteen at this time and before long you will be attending College, start your studies and prepare yourself for the future. The coming years, also, will pass me by. But in my imagination I see your campus, as I know it only from films. I try to imagine what you look like. Perhaps you look like me. I fantasize about the nice girls you meet and who cluster around you and your convertible, the one I give you for your eighteenth birthday. I imagine you in your classes and can see you as quarterback for the school team. I envision you as the most popular guy in school, able to do all the things I would have liked to do, but missed out on. You are blond and athletic, almost six feet tall with wide shoulders. You usually wear faded jeans and fashionable shirts, as a concession to your mother, who likes nice shirts. You have healthy teeth, well maintained by a Berkeley dentist. Just like me, you are bit impatient, but much more carefree. And in my phantasies I always want you to love your mother very much.

You are the only one who reminds her of me. Everything I ever meant to her, she sees in you. Oh, how I would love to see her again. I dream about growing old together, despite the missed, wasted years. But perhaps she is now happily married and we may both have changed so much that we could not stand each other, anymore. But, maybe, we could get to know each other again and I might be able to provide some part of your roots, roots you know nothing about. I will be there when you get married and we will have the best and biggest wedding celebration in Berkeley. Together we will paint the house you bought and I will spoil your children, my grandchildren. I will be the best grandfather in California and I will love your mother until the day I die.

Palermo, Tuesday, May 1, 1984

Salvatore called last night. I do not know where he gets his information, because he has no contact with the Mafia, but he told me that Joe

Bacelli could be found on Sicily. He is visiting a friend on Favignana. Of course, "visiting" is a misnomer. He is hiding. Again "hiding out" like that is not all that unbearable for these guys. They are free as a bird, are received everywhere as if they are royalty and the bad part is, that they actually believe that. There are too many people in this world who are never tormented by a bad conscience, or tender feelings. But as long as they have not run afoul of a Mafia family, they have nothing to fear. I never could get used to that. They are known to the police and yet they are untouchable. The community on the island is so close-knit, everybody knows everything about everybody else and they all know exactly what can and what cannot be discussed, and with whom. Because even in Sicily, and especially in Palermo, there are some people who are still on the side of the angels, who fight against the Mafia and its cohorts. But in some way two opposite and contradictory communities live together, without knowing much about each other. The majority of the five million inhabitants of the island are law abiding citizens, who have jobs, who are friendly and try to raise their children as best as possible. Fathers who take their sons fishing and mothers who gossip with their daughters. But the reign of terror, perpetuated by a violent minority, causes all to be deaf, mute and blind. Therefore Joe Bacelli and the other "guests" can enjoy a carefree vacation that can last as long as their crimes are great.

At eleven this morning the train left Rome for Sicily. In Villa San Giovanni in Calabria, the train goes on the ferry to Messina. From there it is another few hours to Palermo. I arrived at nine. A roundabout way to travel, the plane is faster and almost the same price. But first of all I like traveling by train and second, it fits the character I am impersonating. A

British archeologist in search of the past. I
speak Italian. I started to learn it in the
Congo. One of my buddies was from Sicily. Because of that I have a slight Sicilian accent.
One day he was gone. Probably killed and eaten
by his captors. But the Sicilian accent has been
of some use to me over the years. In a South
African prison I studied Italian grammar. Now I
speak Italian with a British accent, because the
job requires it. I sound ridiculous. The British
seem incapable to learn any language well. They
are either too lazy, or their vocal cords are
unable to reproduce the right sounds. I am staying at a small inn behind the Santa Caterina
Church, while I am writing this part of the
letter. It is past midnight and it is quiet in
the streets. I am in the lion's den, surrounded
by a dirty city, consisting mainly of neglected
buildings.

Tomorrow I go to the Archeological Museum at
the Via Roma. It has been established in a former monastery and the exhibit halls surround the
old courtyard. There I will feign interest in
the Egadi Group which consists of five islands:
Favignana, Levanzo, Marettimo, Formica and Ma-
raone. I will report to the learned curators
with my letter of recommendation from Cambridge,
which will clear the way for me and they will
point out the most interesting archeological
features of the archipelago. They will also inform the local authorities, apprise them of my
arrival and request the necessary cooperation.
Just camouflage, of course. I just want to make
sure that the local cop knows who I am and what
I am doing. That way he will not be suspicious
when I roam around the interior of the island
with my small spade. Because there I will find
Joe Bacelli. I know the name and the general
area. That is all. I will have to survey the
local situation in person. I may have to ask
questions. As the average stranger I would not

get far. Now they can inquire about me and I will just be one more eccentric Englishman. I will be able to become part of the landscape.

Perhaps I will meet Joe Bacelli. I can sit on the same terrace with him and pass the time of day. Nothing suspicious about that, under the present circumstances. Perhaps you will find this strange, but I like to meet my victims. I love it. To have a conversation with somebody knowning exactly how long he has left to live. I know his background, know what he has done to others. I feel like a judge and a jury. Strange, really, because I respect the judiciary. But some people have managed to escape the responsibilities of civilized society. The normal judiciary process is too slow and too lenient for such people. Even if they were to be locked up, they would still cause new victims from their prison cell. Their thinking is so twisted that they cannot be rehabilitated. They are strangers to pity and remorse. No government on earth has the means to cut out this cancer in the community. The system does not work that way. And that is a good thing. No government should be more criminal than the criminals, no society can afford to sink that low. The state would lose all credibility. But somewhere, well hidden in the darkest corner of our soul, resides a merciless avenger. Just barely held in check by civilization, justice and cowardice.

Meanwhile it is almost three o'clock and I am still wide awake. That happens more and more. My thoughts, my memories keep me from sleeping. So much occupies me, so much more is unclear. I have forgotten so much, but I want to remember. I want to remember how it was and how it came to be. The images are vague and far away. Who was my mother and what did she do? How did her lips feel, when she kissed me as a child? Did she laugh a lot, or was she sad? She walked the same floors in the small house in Belgium, where now

235

a Turkish family lives and breeds. From the small window in the attic room where my brother Gerard and I slept you could see the enormous slag heaps which stretched toward the railroad line. The trash and waste of decades piled in heaps and where weeds hardly grew. Loose rocks on a sandy bottom that turns into dangerous mud slides when it rains. Mountains made by men and therefore unreliable. An avalanche has never happened, as far as I know, but it is always possible. Not too long ago, one of the slag heaps started to slide and buried an entire blue collar neighborhood. Because the slag heaps are always close to the homes of the workers, never next to the homes of the shareholders. They have real mountains where they can ski and where their children can have affairs with the ski instructors. Although I was born in the hospital in Brugge, we lived in this miserable mining town that is not even on the map. On the map you will only find the name of the mine. But across from the mine entrance, where the mining engineer lives, you will find no slag heaps. Nor will you find them in the street behind him, where the Mine Manager lives. He would not be able to grow his thirty six varieties of roses on a slag heap.

Often I stood in front of that house, my face pressed against the bars of the fence. I looked at the long driveway, the millimetric lawns around the enormous house and the bushes and flowers and gardens maintained by a full-time gardener and "volunteers" from the miners. That is the way things were, then. Sometimes I saw children play on the lawns, children my own age. I wondered what the inside of the house would look like. Did their father come home drunk and looking for a fight? Did he beat his wife and children? Did they have a broken pool cue behind the door? Did they sit at the top of the stairs, shaking with fear, like my sister and brothers? Or did they have a special room where they could hide? That room, for instance, underneath the beautiful blue roof of the tower? The room with the round window that intrigued me so. What was that room like? Did it have toys? Could you play there?´

I can clearly see my father´s face. As far as I know he is still alive, but I do not want to see him. I do not know where he lives, or about his health. I think he went back to Brugge, after the mine closed. I cannot care less. For me he died the day we cast off the lines of the ship in Antwerp that would take me to the Congo. I well remember the bar where I had to find him. I would walk past the houses that were black with coal dust, past the miners that had just finished their shift. Big, blackened men, who laughed without joy. Their mouths as red holes in their blackened faces. Of course there were no showers. I walked past the long, gray wall that encircled the grounds of the mine, almost to the end of the village to the bar, the "Miner". Nobody looked at me when I came in. An eight year old boy was not unusual in that place. Because I was not the only one who was sent "to get father for dinner". The place smelled of beer and nobody ever laughed. The owner´s wife sometimes gave me some candy, or an ice cream in the summer. She would always wink at me when she did that. As if we shared a secret. I would pretend she was my mother. My father would hardly acknowledge me when he saw me. I wonder if he ever looked at me. I believe not. He never came at once, he would always "come later". His breath stank of booze and his eyes were watery. He would steady himself against the long, gray wall as he stumbled home.

The rows would start as soon as he entered through the back door. Usually it was Paul who would get the first blows, or Marie. I would disappear to my regular hiding place, behind the washtub in the shed. A big, wooden tub on three legs. There I waited until things calmed down. We had long since stopped screaming. We endured pain as if it was expected. It was part of our life. Marie liked to read and she had borrowed a book from a neighbor. I cannot remember the title, but it was a thick book. I was twelve at the time. She was reading when father came home. He got angry. After he had cursed her, I saw his legs pass my hiding place to get the pool cue. I knew what that meant, I had seen it so often. In the afternoon Marie had read me a story from the book and had promised to read me some more that evening. It was a nice story, I remember that. Then I heard the sound of the blows and then the door of the stove that served for heating and cooking. He threw the book in the flames. Marie wailed in agony, said that it was not her book, she had to return it. That was the first time I left home.

That night I hid in the portico of a grocery store a few streets away. A poor street where a few small shops managed to survive. I saw the last people leave the bars and I saw the beer signs switched off. At night it was the only light in the street. The street was dark and deserted. I cannot remember another time that I felt as lonely as that night. And I know about loneliness. Despite the cold, I must have fallen asleep, because I was found the next morning by Mr. Berg, the owner, when he came to open the shop. He took me inside and his wife gave me breakfast. He must have informed the priest about the conditions at home, because he came that same afternoon. I forget what he said but even as a twelve year old I recognized them as hollow phrases, facile placebos. I can still see him in my mind's eye, with his big stomach, round cheeks. I remember his clammy hands when he left and he repeated once again that we should pray often.

Favignana, Thursday, May 3, 1984

Everything went as planned. I arrived in Favignana this morning and introduced myself to the local constable. He had been notified by Palermo and was very helpful. He is a typical Italian macho, kissing the feet of those above him and bullying everybody else. But he did have a large map of the island in his pigsty of an office. On that map I pointed out the various areas I wanted to explore. He nodded, feeling more and more important. In passing I pointed to the area of the Alfonso Franchi estate. There Bacelli was "hiding out". He told me everything I wanted to know. Within half an hour I knew how large the area was, what was private property, how to get where. I invited him to lunch and he greedily accepted. I spent two hours on a terrace with him, in the middle of the village. Everybody who passed greeted him, some jovially, most submissively. Within a day the whole island would know about the crazy Englishman. As I said, he was very helpful. The more they know about me, the less suspicion I will create.

After lunch he took me to a small inn and carried my luggage. We parted as old friends. Loaded down with map, camera and binoculars I left for my first reconnaissance. It took more than an hour to reach my objective. I walked down roads bordered by small, stone walls. It is a hard life for the farmers. The ground is arid and rocky. Here and there I saw a farmer. Once in a while a car, or a donkey's cart would pass. I recognized the house from the cop's description. A straight driveway, bordered by tall cypresses. A closed gate at the end of the driveway. Two men with shotguns guarded the gate. The gardens immediately surrounding the house were closed off with a fence. The property looked like an oasis in the center of a barren desert. Only the roof of the house could be glimpsed between the palm trees. About fifty yards away I saw an opening in the stone wall and I followed the track that ran parallel to the driveway. After another fifty yards I saw the side of the house and part of the terrace in front. Two men were seated on the terrace. I used my binoculars to study their faces. They were unknown to me. As I told you, I have made a study of the Mafia families over the last twenty years. I have also collected a large number of photographs, but those two were not yet in my collection. Although I had seen neither before, from the description I had received, it was clear that Joe Bacelli was the one on the left. It was quiet. Apart from the two men at the gate, I could discover no other guards. I worked my way around the house, looking for hidden cameras. I found none. I also failed to detect any dogs. The gentlemen must feel safe.

I went back to the spot from where I had first observed them and remained for several hours, watching. From time to time a woman appeared, apparently a maid, who refreshed their drinks. Around five, Bacelli stood up, yawned and went inside. A little later he appeared behind a window on the second floor. Just before I could focus in on him, he closed the curtains. I presumed he was taking a nap. Carefully I worked my way back to the road and returned to the village. At the inn I explored the possibilities for leaving and entering unnoticed. There was only one entrance and a back door from the kitchen. There was always someone in the kitchen.

My room is on the second floor with a window on the side of the building. I always carry a mountain climbing rope in my luggage. If there is no other way to disappear unnoticed for a few hours, I use it as a last resort. I would rather find a better way, because the rope will have to stay where it is while I am gone and anybody could see it. Therefore I decided to explore the building, start a conversation here and there, meanwhile checking for alternate routes. There were only a few guests. Next to me was an Italian couple and in the room at the end of the corridor two vacationing girls from the North of Europe. The communal bathroom was also on the second floor and there was an additional powder room on the ground floor. This space had a window that came out on a small court yard behind the kitchen. It was filled with crates and things.

I came in at nine tonight and asked for the key to my room. I gossiped a little with the owner and shared a glass with him. About nine thirty it was dark enough and I said goodnight. I walked in the direction of the stairs and when nobody was looking my way, changed direction for the powder room. I left through the window and forty five minutes later I was back at the spot where I had first observed Bacelli. I saw no signs of life. Shortly after midnight I heard a car and I could see the lights between the cypresses. The sound of voices and of the gate being opened. I saw two men climb the wide steps to the terrace and enter the house. A little later the outside lights were turned off. About an hour later the light went on in the room where I had seen Bacelli before. Again I watched him close the curtains. Then all was dark. I walked back to the inn and re-entered through the window in the powder room.

I am now back in my room and writing this part of the letter. Tomorrow I will check again, to verify the pattern. If there are no changes, I know enough for the time being and the British archaeologist will wave goodbye to this island. I will call 89219432 and tell him that I accept the commission and I will demand $75,000 for the job. Rather high for a such a relatively easy job, but that is my business. I'll go back to Serifos. Before leaving Rome for Athens, Neville

241

Footman will book a flight on British Airways to London. The ticket will not be used. I will be back in Greece the day before. My suitcase and different clothes are in a locker in Rome. It will be only a matter of moments to change the eccentric Footman into businessman Frank C.Johnson. In Athens I get rid of the glasses, pull on a sweater instead of the jacket of my three-piece suit and I'll muss my hair. I'll show the passport of Robert Dubour to go through customs. Then I'll take the ferry back to Serifos. There I will plan the finishing details for the liquidation of Joe Bacelli. I'll use a Winchester with silencer. I have a number of weapons stashed away in various banks around the world. In San Francisco, New York, London, Rome and of course, also in the house on Serifos. The weapons can all easily be dismantled and fit nicely in a regular briefcase. I know the peculiarities of each and every weapon and I never miss. It sounds like a boast, but it is the truth.

I picked a strange profession and I would not recommend it to anybody, especially not to you. I would like you to study, gain respect and enjoy what you do for a living. I feel that the sense of accomplishment, something about which you can later think with satisfaction and gratitude, something like that is very important for the development of a human being. Appreciation by others, acceptance by your surroundings, those are the things that make life worthwhile. Every person wants applause. No matter how humble, or seemingly unimportant the work may be. My job does not provide for applause. Nobody pats me on the back when I have accomplished an assignment successfully. Everything is anonymous and secret. Sometimes, after I have killed some piece of dirt, an article appears in the papers, outlining his misdeeds. That can give me a warm feeling. But I cannot discuss it with anyone. I cannot be proud of it, or boast about it. And yet, we all need that at times. But there is so much injustice and so many criminals in this world. Therefore I do not regret what I have done over the last twenty years. I have cleaned things up. Garbage is collected by the Sanitation Department. I remove human garbage. As they say, it is not much of a job, but someone has to do it. So let me be the one. I have relieved the world of 213 criminals who would have caused untold misery if they had stayed alive. I was in a position to prevent that. It is no more than a drop in the ocean, I know, but every drop counts. After all, it is unbearable to think that nobody should be able to catch, punish and kill that scum. That they should be able to live in liberty and without risks. Do they deserve that? It would not be fair, if they did not have to learn the meaning of fear. Let them be afraid. Let them surround themselves with body guards. Let them lay awake at night, waiting for the bullet that will end their filthy life. It is a wonderful thought to know that they, too, know that the bulletproof glass they hide behind is no protection. That is why I do not regret what I have done. I am proud of it. Too bad nobody else knows. Just you.

Favignana, Friday, May 4, 1984

I am being followed! I am certain. Although there is no logical reason to suspect it, my instinct tells me it is true. I am not positive, but there is that feeling. The way someone looks, the fact that I see someone twice. There is no "shadow" in the strictest sense of the word, that would be too obvious. That is not their style. They are far too intelligent for that. Because I am not dealing with stupid people. Even the butchers, the "soldiers" in Mafia

243

terminology, are not dumb. They can hardly write
their name and they have never heard of grammar,
by they do understand their job. That makes them
so dangerous. They are just like rats. It is
usually the head that betrays. Incomprehensible,
really. The "padrini" and the "capi" are cunning, intelligent people, but they do not seem
to be aware that their soldiers are hardly pre-
sentable in polite society. That is almost always true. They all have degenerate, criminal
faces. Also, the man wore the wrong clothes for
that time and place. He stood out. If he had
worn a pair of work pants and a T-Shirt, I would
not have noticed him. But I could not miss him.
A dark blue suit, too tight around the shoulders
and a bulge under the arm. On a sunny day on
this island, nobody wears a suit. But you see,
that is how they betray themselves, through
their background. He simply refuses to wear old
clothes, his father wore work clothes, that
evokes bad memories. He sees it as a humilia-
tion, a regression. So, he wears the wrong
clothes at the wrong time in the wrong place.
And his face does not match his clothes. He is
not carefree enough to be a tourist and too
lonely to be a local. I did not see the man at
the house I was watching. He also was not on
guard duty at the gate. Also, how can he know
that I am after Bacelli? But he does follow me.
   Nevertheless I spied on the house again,
last night. I am reasonably certain. Bacelli
goes to bed around twelve thirty and is momentarily silhouetted against the light as he
closes the curtains. That is enough for me. The
distance is about 350 feet, perfect for a Winchester 125. His head reaches just below the
center of the window. I will have to be quick,
there will be no time for a second shot. The
silencer will muffle the noise of the shot, but
I must take into account that the falling body
will make a noise in the house. It is an old

building, probably wooden floors and inadequately soundproofed. The sound of the falling body will be heard. They will investigate. I am sure they will recognize the sound at once, they have heard it so many times. I will have to concentrate on my getaway. There is no ferry after midnight, which means I will have to spend the night on the island. Not a pleasant thought. The island is too small to provide an adequate hiding place and you can bet your life that the few people who take the ferry in the morning will be thoroughly scrutinized. Also, I have to take my "shadow" into account. Usually I cancel a contract at once, if I see something I do not like. I should do that this time, as well. But there is a problem. This is my last job. I told you that. When this job is finished I will try to erase the past and perhaps I will be lucky enough to spend a few years with you and your mother. I told you how I imagine that.

If my "shadow" is who I think he is, he will be in the way. It would mean that somebody, a family, or an individual, has tracked me down. I cannot allow that. Especially not now. This trail must be obliterated. Anybody who penetrates behind my disguise, must be eliminated. I know he did not follow me to the house, nor did he visit my room during my absence. Nothing elaborate, just some "invisible" tape on doors and windows. The seals were not broken. To merge with the night is one of the tricks I picked up in the Congo, it is almost second nature to me now. I will keep my eyes open, tomorrow. I will take the ferry to Trapani, the bus to Palermo and then the train to Rome. He must be really good, if he does not stand out, then.

Tomorrow I will be unable to write. What I have written so far, will be mailed tomorrow. Not from the Favignana Post Office, but from Rome. A registered letter would be too noticeable, here. Somebody might remember the address, because it might be the only piece of registered mail in a month. At the main Post Office in Rome, at Piazza San Silvestro, it will just disappear in the flood of mail.

Strange, I wrote the letter today, tomorrow it will be mailed, but you will not receive it for more than eight years. Will I be there, then?

Now I go to bed and I wish I could sleep for eight years straight.

Serifos, Sunday, May 6, 1984

I saw him again when I took the ferry, yesterday. The fact that he knew I was leaving that day, must mean that he spoke to the inn keeper, perhaps put pressure on him. I did not see him in the bus from Trapani to Palermo, but as I stepped onto the platform for the Rome train, I saw him at the ticket counter. I stood behind a pile of freight and watched him. He walked along the entire train and climbed in at the end. A few minutes later I saw him descend from a carriage at the other end. I saw him stand there, looking at the train and then, obviously having come to a conclusion, he entered the carriage. I saw him behind the window, almost in the center of the carriage. It was not very busy on the platform and I waited until seconds before departure time. Then I quickly climbed into the train myself and made my way to the carriage in which I had seen my "shadow". He was seated to the right of the center aisle. He was alone. He was obviously shocked to see me, additional proof for my suppositions.

"Buongiorno," I said with a heavy British accent. I placed my rucksack in the overhead net across from him. He turned pale, growled something and was obviously ill at ease. This type of criminals is used to kill their victims from

246

a distance, or as part of a group. Eye contact makes them nervous.

"Have you visited Favignana as well?" I asked.

"Why?"

"Oh, I thought I saw you there."

He moved uneasily in his seat. The bulge under his left arm became more pronounced. That meant he was right handed. He was facing the engine. I would be an easy target if I were to sit opposite him. If I were to sit down next to him, at his left side, I would be on the side of the weapon. Even more dangerous. Therefore I took the lesser of two evils and sat down facing him, with my back to the engine. Three gentlemen sat down across the aisle. I heard the whistle and the train started to move.

"Been on holiday?" I asked.

"No." It sounded sullen.

I enjoyed myself. The man was at a loss about what to do in this situation.

"Family visit?" I persisted.

"Sort of."

"I am from England. I was on Favignana for research. I'm an archeologist. My name is Footman."

"Great."

"You're from Sicily"

The tension could be cut with a knife, but I enjoyed myself. He knew who I was, but he did not know that I knew he knew.

"No," he answered.

"Where are you from?" I nagged.

"Rome."

"Aha, Rome. A beautiful city. I live in London, myself. Not bad, but Rome, Rome is the cradle of civilization."

"Yes," said the man and it was quiet for several minutes.

"Do you mind if I smoke?" I asked and showed him my pipe.

"Go ahead."

I wondered how he wanted to finish this business. It could be that he only had orders to follow me, not to kill me. But I could not count on that. I had to expect the worst. I lit my pipe and poisoned the air with the obnoxious smell of English tobacco. The killer across from me stared out of the window with dull eyes and did not speak. Meanwhile I pestered him with stupid and naive questions. He was visibly irritated. It would make him nervous, I was certain. After about an hour, I said:

"Do you know which way is the toilet?"

"That way," he said and pointed.

"Thank you."

I stood up and walked in the indicated direction. At the end of the carriage I saw the door with the sign "Gabinetto". The narrow door jutted into the corridor at an angle. Inside the stool was placed opposite the door. I positioned myself on the left, between the door and a minuscule wash basin, leaving the space in front of the stool unoccupied. Then I waited. It was just an idea, but I would know soon enough. I heard the door to the platform slam and footsteps. Three quick shots and the stool was shattered into a thousand pieces. There were three holes in the door. It was over in less than five seconds. I heard footsteps again and the carriage door slammed into the frame. Then all was still, except for the monotonous sounds of the wheels. Well, now I knew! That was the goal! They had tracked me down and somebody wanted to eliminate me. It could be my client, or someone who had heard about the contract. Both were a possibility. I left the toilet and went to the dining car. The small tables were set and there were few passengers. I ordered a cappuccino and an extensive English breakfast, with ham and eggs, according to character. Just as the waiter placed the plate in front of me, I saw him. I stood up and called to him:

"Are you having breakfast, too?"

He was frightened, wanted to turn away, but I was quicker. I took him by the arm and shoved him through the door of the dining car. We were standing on the plates over the coupling between carriages. Leather, pleated walls moved around us. Quickly I took his pistol from the shoulder holster. The man was so startled by the speed of my actions that he recovered himself with difficulty. Seeing me in the dining car, had totally confused him. I used those few seconds, the time that he was briefly confused, to my best advantage. Another lesson from the Congo. In a man-to-man battle, life depended on seconds, on instant action. I am always amused by fight scenes in movies. If that was for real, one, or both of the contestants would be dead in seconds, or less. Unless strict rules are governing combat, such as in a boxing match, no fight lasts more than moments. Not, if the participants are professionals. You just get one chance only, and you better use it. First the surprise, then the coup de grace. I pushed his own pistol into his kidneys and directed him to the nearest toilet. Inside I hit him hard in the stomach and, groaning and clutching his belly, he sank down on the stool. I locked the door and pistol whipped him. In immaculate Italian, with a slight Sicilian accent, I asked who sent him.

"Go to hell!" he said.

Again I whipped the barrel of the pistol across his face. Slammed the grip against his lower jaw, which broke a few of his teeth, and repeated my question:

"Who sent you, asshole?"

His head hung down and he mumbled a few curses. I took a black nylon cord from an inside pocket and wound it around his neck. He made a rattling sound as he tried to breathe. With a quick snap I broke the adam's apple. He was dead almost instantly. I washed my hands, cleaned the pistol on the outside with a paper towel, opened the small window and tossed the weapon out. I left the toilet and locked the door with one of the gadgets on my Swiss Army knife. The sign above the doorknob announced: "occupato".

I went back to the dining car and sat down at my table. My ham and eggs were now cold.

This afternoon at three I arrived on Serifos. I missed the last ferry, last night, and I spent the night in a hotel near Piraeus. I am worried about the man on the train. I cannot be sure how much they know about me, the place I live. It irritates me. I always felt safe on this island and I would like to keep it that way. I thought about everything and reconstructed my actions over the last few weeks, but cannot discover the mistake, the leak. Only Salvatore and the client know about my contract. Salvatore does not talk, I know that. Yet, I will call him at the Bar Corone tomorrow. He will be there at eleven. Perhaps he can discover the identity of the man on the train. Of course I searched him, before I left the toilet, but found nothing, except some money. He had no luggage. That is not surprising. It is obvious that he had orders to kill me. But how did he know it was me, and how did they spot me? Was I spotted in Rome? Except for Salvatore, I only had contact with the picture postcard seller on the Piazza Colonna. Be he did not know who I was.

The question is whether they want to protect Bacelli, or just want to eliminate me. They know, or should now, that I kept records over the last twenty years. Perhaps they want to get hold of my records. But then they would not kill me, but would try to discover the hiding place. Kidnapping would be more productive, in that case. But they are not after that. I simply do not understand it. This coming Monday I will call 89219432 in New York. Three days late. I will find out what he has to say for himself. Under the circumstances I do not feel that I can cancel the contract. If the orders come from my client, then the only way to discover more is to fulfill the contract and be extra alert. This has never happened before. I spoke at length with Petros, earlier today. In a manner of speaking, I trust Petros with my life. He does not know what I do for a living, but he knows it is not exactly charity work. I asked him if he felt like a long trip with "Christina". It is probably the best solution. I mentioned the Caribbean. His eyes glistened at the thought and he was ready to pack at once. It may be the only solution: to disappear for a year, or more. Away from Europe. I have always wanted to take my boat there and spend some time among the islands. Perhaps now my wish has become a necessity. In any case, during the coming days we will prepare her for a long voyage. We need a few pieces of modern navigation equipment. The sails were replaced only last year. Petros will start with provisions. We can take it easy on our way to the Canary Islands and from there to the Caribbean at our leisure.

Petros is also a loner, like me. Financially he has been a little less lucky. He is a wonderful, warm man, with a childlike devotion to anyone who accepts him as he is. That has not happened often during his sixty years. He was born in 1924 on a ship, the "Tommaso di Savoia", en route for Rio de Janeiro with Greek immigrants. His mother died in childbirth and there were no other children. His father married a Brazilian and he was sent to an orphanage until he was sixteen. He ran away and joined a Greek ship to Athens.

For years he sailed on the deep water and he made his home, such as it was, on the island of Spetsai. He never again saw his father and the rest of his family was wiped out by a Turkish bombardment. You see, we have a lot in common. Together we are in the same hole and we hold on to the same edge. The first time I met him, we understood each other. That has never before happened to me with a man. He is a friend, a real friend. I love him. Not sexually, but it is love. Men, especially older men, should be able to love each other. Why should men not be able to love each other without being homosexual? I never understood that. Women have female friends. They have friends of the same sex for life. They love them like their own sisters, perhaps more. Petros is more than a brother to me and I know he feels the same about me. We leave each other free in all things, but enjoy each other's company and laugh a lot, together. We are each other's true and faithful sheepdog.

Serifos, Tuesday, May 8, 1984

When Petros left with his shopping list for the supermarket on the quay, I picked up the telephone and called. As usual, I will try to give you the gist of the conversation as accurately as possible.

"Smith here."

"I had expected you to call sooner."

"There were problems."

"I heard about that."

"So, you know about it?"

"Yes, you may consider it a closed incident."

"You call it an incident? I could have been killed."

"I'm sorry." The man in New York did not sound sorry.

"Kiss my ass, Mr. whoever-you-are! I think you'd better find someone else," I answered.

252

"Listen, I told you it's a closed incident. You may rest assured that those responsible will answer for it. You can be sure it won't happen again."

"What sort of guarantee do I have?"

"None. Except you can trust me."

"Not much of a guarantee, don't you agree?"

"I understand. It's all I can do."

"Who was the bastard?"

"I don't give names."

"I'll find out."

"That's your business. I only repeat that I have given you a commission and I want the contract executed. You can trust me."

"I have to know who's behind it, before I proceed."

"That's your decision. I can only promise it won't happen again."

"So, you know who it was and who sent him?"

"Yes, I know. But again, you don't get any names from me. I can only guarantee you that it wasn't me. That's all."

"Are they looking for something?"

"You won't hear me say that. You know, better than me, what you have in your possession. I can only tell you that it doesn't interest me. It's your right to provide for your own life insurance. I'd do the same. But I'm sure you will never interfere with us. You've proven that, over and over again. If you did want to play a trick on us, you're smart enough to know we can always find you, eventually. But there's no reason to worry about that. I trust you. Name your price and complete the contract. We're talking about a traitor, dangerous to us, and maybe to you."

"Why me?"

"Because they've found you once. But I don't know where you are right now, and neither do they."

253

"But, Mr. X, how can you control the characters who are behind this?"

"You must trust me in that. I trust you too,
don't I? We've been talking on the phone for
more than five minutes. I could have assumed
that after the incident on the train, you'd already contacted the cops, right? This is, as far
as I know, the first time that anyone tried to
interfere in one of your missions. So, would it
be too far fetched if I assumed that you informed on us, in exchange for a full pardon.
Just for revenge? Out of revenge, or out of fear
for what has happened. If I weren't sure you
could be trusted, would I stay on the phone with
you? More than five seconds? Let alone five minutes. Let's face it, both our numbers can be
traced in less than sixty seconds. That's tech-
nology for you. But I speak to you, because I
know I can trust you."

"That's nonsense. I already have your phone
number. All I'd have to do is pass it on and
they know who you are."

"First of all, you won't do that and second,
we've taken steps, you know. This is a so-called
"sleeper" number. A number that has never been
assigned. It's just a matter of making the right
connections in the nearest switching system. If
you know how, and you have the right people,
it's a small job. After our conversation the
connection will be removed and the line will be
dead."

"Well, then you don't have to worry about it
being traced."

"You're right. They certainly won't find a
name that belongs to the number. But they can
determine where the receiver is located. But,
please believe me, the incident was caused by an
over-eager partner. Name your price and I'll
deposit the money, as agreed."

"Seventy five thousand."

"I'll double that, as a sort of damage claim, a bonus for the inconvenience. Also as a token of trust. As you know, trust is a serious thing with us."

"Agreed."

I replaced the receiver. Although I had not thought about it myself, in those terms, he was right. If he had known that I was about to be killed and if he had heard that the attempt had failed, I would have been unable to reach him. Period. It was proof positive that he was not the one who had given the orders to have me killed. The question remained, however: Who was responsible? Perhaps, as he assured me, he had them under control, but I would be a fool to depend on that.

I called Bar Corone at eleven fifteen. I heard the noises in the bar when it was answered. I asked for Salvatore and whoever answered the phone said: "Un momento." A few moments later I heard Salvatore's voice.

"Hey, you old Congolese, where are you?"

"Home."

"Problems, Roberto?"

"All over."

"Goddamn," he said and started to whisper: "Let them go to hell, Roberto, I told you. It's war. Another four were shot down in the last few days. They're killing each other. Listen to me, buddy, their nerves are in shreds. They tippytoe around. Stay out of it!"

"You're right, Salvatore, but I have to finish one job and then I'll be a puff of smoke in the distance."

"What you want from me?"

"Last Friday a man was strangled in the Palermo-Rome train. Try to find out his name and his family connections."

"I'll look in the paper. I'm sure it was in there. If there's no name, I'll find out. Call me tomorrow, same number, same time. OK?"

255

"Fine and thanks."

"Asshole!" he said emphatically and hung up.

The rest of the day Petros and I worked on "Christina". That was nice. Petros has always maintained and nurtured the vessel while I was gone. This time, too. She is immaculate. I love her. She is beautiful. She has gorgeous lines and is forty seven feet long. The hull is a shiny black, with a white stripe and mahogany super structure. She is now fifty five, but she looks like a young girl. She gathers admirers in every port and you just know she revels in it. Crazy, I know. But everybody is entitled to some eccentricity. It would be wonderful if you could learn to love her too. Just imagine, father and son and an old sailboat. But I am starting to dream again and it starts to resemble a commercial for some exotic place.

Serifos, Wednesday, May 9, 1984

I am afraid. For the first time I am afraid. The "incident" in the train worries me. Although I am convinced that my client had nothing to do with the attempt on my life, I cannot help but wonder if he does indeed have enough influence to stop future attempts. I have to know if I am safe on Serifos and I can only find that out myself. I can hardly ask the local constable. His name is Takis and he is a good guy, but of course, he does not know about my background. If they have discovered my whereabouts and they intend to kill me, how do they plan to reach the island unnoticed? There are just two possibilities. By plane, or by boat. For starters I will watch the arrivals on the ferry every day. I have to know who comes to the island. I assume that I will be able to recognize the types that are after me. I have a certain instinct for that and that sort of scum has a habit of betraying themselves rather easily. They will be Italian, I can be sure of that. The tourist season is slowly starting up, but that type of visitors is easily recognized from the luggage, the cameras and the expectant faces. They are but a few. Those that I do suspect, I can easily follow to one of the few, small inns on the island. I can easily keep an eye on them, there. Couples are by definition excluded. If they come, there will be two men. Luigi Alfara was here a few weeks ago with his yacht. In the context of what I now know, that may have been a little early in the season. Could there have been another reason? Luigi is a slippery octopus with tentacles in a number of families. I could name a dozen with which he is associated. I will have to question the Harbor Police, carefully, to see if anybody left the "Paradise". As far as I know, she stayed just one night, because I could see the ship from my window. But that does not rule out the possibility that she may have anchored at the other side of the island. It is a bit too coincidental, but perhaps my nerves are on edge. Nobody knows where I live. Not even Salvatore. He knows I live on a Greek island, but not which one. There are about a thousand Greek islands, so he can only guess.

I have never been afraid of death. Not in the Congo, when it was a daily companion and not after that. After death you just fall back in the same deep, black hole where you were before you were born. I am not curious about the future. I have no desire to know what happens in the millions of years after me. I will not miss a thing. I did not miss the years before my birth, either. I have walked this earth for forty nine years and have seen and experienced things that someone from the Middle Ages would not have dreamed about. I will never know the experiences of someone to be born in 2178 AD. But I do know what my brother Gerard has missed.

257

Because I live in his time. A time to which he was entitled but did not receive. My sister Marie would have been fifty eight tomorrow. She would have had twenty two years more than my mother. All unlucky people. How is it possible that people can cause each other so much grief when they have had hardly one happy day themselves? Even people from the same family. Why and because of what, did my mother die? I remember what I was told, at the time. But is it true? What did life mean to her? If her life had been different, would she have had the will to live on? It cannot be coincidence that the members of just one family all have had such short lives. Somebody is to blame for that.

Of course, I should have protected Marie when I was old and wise enough to do so. But I was selfish, I only thought of myself. I could have saved her, but I was not there when she needed me. Perhaps she could have met a nice guy and have had children she loved. I do not even have a picture of her. I wonder if she has ever been photographed. Who thought enough of her, to preserve her for posterity? Who wanted to keep her photo? Nobody? As if she never existed. As if her dear voice that sang me to sleep and told me stories had never sounded. We had no camera at home. My father used to spend most of the money on booze. For him it was bad enough that we existed at all. I never wondered, even then, why there were no pictures of any of us. What did Gerard look like? The image has faded, the face is gone. Sometimes I still see the piece of ground where we went together, to feel safe. A few square yards of weeds at the bottom of a slag heap. That was our haven, at the end of a dead-end street.

Serifos, Sunday, May 13, 1984

It was a rotten day, today. I did not feel well when I woke up. It has happened before, it just seems to happen more often. It is raining and the sky is low and gray. I do not like gray skies, they make me sad. I should have stayed in bed. But I will not. I feel too useless that way. Thoughts chase themselves through my head. I cannot shut off the computer in my head. A mistake of the Creator. We should have had a switch, at the right side of the temple, to turn thoughts on and off. But then, most people have no need for such a switch and creation too, took into account the will of the majority. A matter of marketing.

This morning I was at my regular spot, near the curvy road, above the pier where the ferry docks. I have spent early mornings there and I have observed arriving passengers through my binoculars. Nothing untoward has happened, yet. When the ferry left again I walked down to the village and passed two boys with rucksacks. I heard them speak Flemish. I have not heard that language for years. Somehow it made me feel good and it made me curious. Before I realized what I was doing, I engaged them in conversation and offered them a drink on the terrace near the quay. We talked for almost an hour and then I walked them to their bed-and-breakfast. Because I knew the owner, I was able to get them a special rate. They gave me a Belgian newspaper and I started to read it. I should not have done that.

It had to happen. May 11, 1984! It was front-page news! Now, twenty four years later. Our own King Boudewijn was receiving President-Marshall Mobutu. Or rather: Mubutu Sese Seko Kuku Ngwendu Waza Banga (he who impregnates all chickens like a rooster). When I saw the photo, there on the quay at Serifos, it all came back to me. I was twenty one and was doing my

National Service. I was offered the "opportunity" to become a professional soldier, if I signed as volunteer for the Congo. I received special training and was promoted to Sergeant. It was 1957 when I arrived in the Congo. We were stationed at the Kamina garrison. It was a relatively quiet time and I was able to become expert in all forms of killing. I learned to handle everything that could be used as a weapon, from an Uzi to a knife. I lived the life of Riley, had my own servant and the native females were plentiful, cheap and insatiable. I practiced survival techniques in the jungle and man-to-man combat in the savannahs. I liked the life so well that I re-enlisted and I wound up in the Force Publique, under General Janssen. A native Congolese Army, under command of white, Belgian officers. Again a relatively quiet time until the political situation changed so drastically during 58-59 that you could cut the tension with a knife. I felt the end was near and I was not about to wait until our own soldiers would cut us to ribbons. The contempt with which the whites had treated the Congolese for more than eighty years, the degenerating discrimination and the appalling differences in opportunities, would have to be avenged. That was very clear to me. The beginning of this uncontrolled and uncontrollable revenge had started and would continue.

I deserted and a few months later I became a mercenary. I only knew one profession and that was fighting. Killing. Should I have gone back to Belgium? Nobody was waiting for me there. I was not homesick and I had no desire to go back. That came later. But I never thought about later. I lived from day to day.

I have a distorted view of mankind. I know it, but there is nothing I can do about it. It cannot be true that everybody is bad, but I find it hard to believe the opposite. I heard of a man once, who professed that at least fifteen percent of the world's population was irrevocably evil. I think the percentage is too low. I look around on my island and see normal people, who work and live and breed. That is my world and everything is different here. It is not right that I am so suspicious and that I approach almost everyone with distrust. I have to break that habit. I must forget. I was so long a part of a different world. I must learn to think as if I had a carefree youth, a loving mother and a caring father. I could have become that sort of man if I had been allowed to live in a clean and warm house, if I could have become "Uncle Jean" for the children of my brothers and sister. I sometimes feel that all is not lost, but I am running out of time.

Corinth, Wednesday, May 16, 1984

This morning we left the island of Aiyina and sailed through the Corinthian Canal. We are now moored on the quay in Corinth. Petros is in town, shopping for a few items. It is a few days since I called Salvatore. He told me that the man on the train was Carlo Barinne, a member of the Lovallo family. He was not sure about the connection, but he warned me. He is a good man.

I am writing at the chart table. For the first time in days. I keep asking myself if I should ever have started this letter. I recall too many things, things that make me sad. For the first time in my life I am in flight. We're sailing to Gibraltar via Sicily. We should be in Gibraltar in about two weeks, wind and weather permitting. From there it takes only a few days to the Canary Islands. There we can wait to make the big crossing in September, or October. In passing I will finish the job in Sicily. I have accepted it. I have thought about it, long and hard, but decided that I should. I can trust my client. I am sure of that. I do not have to fear him. Whether I complete this mission, or not, those who are after me, will keep after me. Also, there is an extra $150,000 in my account. I hate to make refunds. But after this job, I will disappear. I have become a refugee, a fugitive. A strange realization which disturbs me. I closed the house in Serifos and I wonder if I will ever see it again. If one of the families is after me, it can take years before they catch me. But they have memories like elephants. They know Dubour and they know about Footman. I must find another, "clean" name. How will I ever explain all this to your mother, if I ever meet her again? The past will always haunt me. Will she accept it? Once she knows who I am, what I have done, will she still remember me as the "nice" Robert Dubour she knew twenty years ago?

You will receive his letter on your twenty first birthday. As I said, I will either deliver it in person, or my lawyers will forward it. In either case you will let her read this. Then she, too, will know everything about me. I hope she can forgive me. But it is no small thing to ask, it is almost impossible. I cannot expect her to understand. I will be doomed to remain a runaway from her, and all others. I am starting to realize the futility of this letter. How can I expect you both to receive me with open arms? I started by saying that I would tell you all about myself, that I wanted you to know what sort of man I was. That was my intent. I never expected this to become a plea for rehabilitation, a confession.

I do not want to ask forgiveness. But when I think back about what I have written so far, that is exactly what I have done. I have let myself be ruled by feelings. I should not have told you that I still love her, still think of her, everyday. I do not want this to become a

Jeremiad. What it comes down to, is that I have burdened you with something that is my own doing. Please do not feel regret. I am the only one to regret things. Think about it, everything I have told you, could be lies. Or I could have twisted things to make myself look good. Perhaps subconsciously. Perhaps I am just a common criminal but I have created excuses for myself I have started to believe as the truth. I do not know. I do know I have a son and you are my son. But am I really interested in you, or have my fatherly feelings been thwarted? Do I want to prove something? Do I want to forestall rejection? I do not know. I think it is love, but am I fooling myself? How can I expect anything from you after having neglected you for twenty one years. I have not lifted a finger. I have done nothing to help you, or your mother. I soothed my conscience with a house and a monthly allowance. Almost like a parking ticket. What good does it do you when I tell you I am sorry and what does it help you when you know that I think about you, everyday? Thinking is easy, nobody can read your thoughts and it makes a wonderful excuse. You can write it down and use the most flowery language.

When your mother reads these letters, she will not be able to control her tears. But is that not a cheap success? Did I subconsciously hope for that? Did I calculate in advance that I could use that sort of reaction for my own purposes? And is not the forgiveness she would give me based on half truths? When you are twenty one, I will be sixty five. Is that not the age when a man looks for the protection of a home, where he can live his last years in peace, when the urge to roam has died in his breast? Why should either of you believe what I have written? It is stupid to think that you would and I marvel at my own delusion. What have I accomplished? I have placed a number of words in some sort of sequence.

Petros is dead and I am back on my island.
The bastards blew him up, along with "Christina". Why did they not catch me? He was not a
part of anything. It happened in a small bay off
the island of Favignana. I had left the ship
only half an hour earlier and I walked along the
road above the bay. I could still see the anchor
lights on "Christina". As I was about to turn
off toward my target, I saw the enormous flame
and a little later I heard the explosion. It was
terrible. She was ripped asunder and sank within
minutes. The last thing I saw was the anchor
light that remained on for a long while, even
under the surface. Then it disappeared. I ran
back, stood on the shore, used my binoculars,
but could not detect any sign of life. Soon the
last ripples disappeared and the sea was once
again as smooth as glass. A few pieces of wood,
that was all. Not a trace of Petros. They killed
him, murdered him. They deliberately killed him.
Because if they knew it was my ship, they had to
know he was on board. But they could not have
cared less. They probably waited for me to go
ashore. Perhaps not. Maybe I was supposed to be
killed at the same time.
I am at my desk, going over the chain of
events, again and again, but there is only one
conclusion. It was a warning. But from whom?
They now know where I am and I wanted that. It
is the only way to discover the identity of
those that are giving the orders. They will
come. It was definitely not my latest client, as
I discovered that night. After I had gotten over
the shock, I pressed on to the Villa Franchi. If
the occupants of the house were involved with
the explosion, I would be able to discover evi-

264

dence of it there. But everything was as before. The terrace was deserted. The house seemed quiet and asleep. No extra guards, on the contrary, there were no guards at the gate. I found the spot between the rocks I had staked out earlier, assembled the Winchester and mounted it on the stand. I aimed the rifle at Bacelli's window, the cross hairs just below the center. Everything went off very smoothly. At fifteen to one, the light in the room went on, Bacelli appeared in front of the window, spread his arms to close the curtains. For the last time.

Next day I was able to leave the island without any difficulties. That was very strange. I had prepared myself for a manhunt, but nothing pointed in that direction. That could mean that the other occupants of the house were already aware of Bacelli's liquidation. Therefore others must have blown up "Christina". Salvatore had mentioned two names: Mannucci and Lovallo. I know that Mannucci is the big Cosa Nostra boss in New York. My client is also in New York. Perhaps a little too coincidental? My client could have been Mannucci. Lovallo and Mannucci are related. The bonds between the two families are very strong and of long standing. I cannot imagine that Lovallo would cross Mannucci in any way. Mannucci's second son is married to a Lovallo daughter. The late Joe Bacelli was a cousin by marriage to Mannucci, just like Luigi Alfara, he from the yacht that anchored in Serifos bay, only a few weeks ago. Although powerful enough in their own rights, both were relatively low in the hierarchy of the families. Had they planned a "palace revolution"? A revolution that was prevented by the two padrini, or one of them? I had received a commission to kill Bacelli. Most probably from Mannucci. That leaves Lovallo and Alfara. What do they gain from my death?

Because they want me dead! The "incident" in the train points that way and also the explosion of "Christina". But no matter how I figure, I cannot discover any sense behind it all. Mannucci clearly indicated, during our last conversation, that he is aware of my life insurance. If he had wanted to trap me on the Bacelli job, I would have been dead already. Perhaps he is after the files, but it does not seem that way. Somebody wants to kill me. And whoever wants to kill me, could not care less about the records. And that is extremely strange. Without my lists, my value is absolutely nil.

One thing is certain. Whoever they are, or is, knew that I would come and they knew about the boat. In that case they know who I am and where I live. That is why I came back. To wait for them. I mounted my telescope in front of the window, covering the harbor. With my binoculars I spy out the mountains. They must arrive in the harbor and then they have to walk the twisting path to the chora. There is no other way.

Now I am a prisoner in my own house. It has come to this. Petros is dead. When I arrived by ferry this afternoon, nobody asked after him. That occupies my mind a lot. He was a stranger in his own country. Nobody misses him, because he did not belong. He was even denied a decent funeral. I should be alert, but I seem to lack the strength. Like an elephant that separates from the herd in order to die. Is this my final resting place? Over the last few weeks I told you what I think and what I thought important. I was near the end. Is there a Providence, after all, that has enabled me to complete this for you? I could have been dead, long since. But that did not happen. I did have the opportunity to tell you everything. Tomorrow morning, against my better judgement, I will mail this letter from Serifos. Just as a precaution. I have no idea what the coming days will bring.

Perhaps I will intercept them and I will fire the first shot. My aim will be true. Perhaps I will survive this. But then what?

I do want you to know that you two have never been out of my thoughts, out of mind. Sometimes I doubt my own honesty, but I would like you to believe this. It cannot be true that I fooled myself all these years and that I have indulged myself in wishful thinking. I know what I feel and I know the intensity of my feelings. How many feelings of regret I have had to absorb? I have learned to live with longing for the impossible. If this is to be the end, so be it. I probably clung to false hopes and idealized expectations. Perhaps I should not think this way. Most especially not at this moment. It will destroy my will to resist and will make me a sheep, ready for the slaughter. I must resist that feeling, that inclination. I must continue to hope. You could have given me the strength I now need so much. But I cannot call you, or visit you. Not yet. Petros, too, is no more. I could turn to him when I felt low. If I could just tell you one positive thing about myself, would that help? If I told you that I was able to love a number of people, like Marie and Petros, my brother Gerard, your mother and you. People I loved truly and for whom I would have sacrificed anything, given the chance. Who have never been out of my thoughts, but to whom I could never say how I felt. Does that make me a criminal? Does that make me evil? Does a real criminal have feelings? Can a true murderer, a killer, love anyone? If you have any feelings at all, if you know what "love" means, you cannot kill innocent people, you cannot kill people who are not your enemies, who have never harmed you. As they did to Petros. I could never do that. Perhaps I should describe myself as a common man with an uncommon profession. Would you then believe I love you?

I am an invalid without crutches.

SERIFOS, Tuesday, May 22, 1984

Nothing has happened and I dare to hope
again. What I feared yesterday is not forgotten,
but I am no longer preoccupied by it. It no
longer rules me. I feel capable of winning and
am able to think about you again and to fantasize about later. Who knows, everything may yet
be resolved and perhaps there will be time for
many things, perhaps I will be allowed to grow
old with her. I imagine that I will then tell
her, every day, about a day of my life when we
were apart. And she will be able to tell me
about one of her days. Every day we shall have
something new to talk about. It will take at
least twenty years before we run out of things
to talk about. I will be 76 and she will be only
60. But together we will have at least forty
years of memories. Memories we can argue about,
whenever we mix up the dates. Together, we will
spoil our grandchildren and sneak them extra
pocket money, despite your protestations. She
will tell me not to whine about my little maladies and infirmities and I take her on short
trips with the car. For the last time we shall
travel to the places where our memories were
formed and where we can recognize nothing. Once
a week she will dress in her best clothes and I
will proudly show her off in the best restaurants. The doctor will still allow us to eat
anything. People will look at us and wish that
they, too, could grow old as gracefully as we.
She will scold me about the size of the tip and
on the way home I take the wrong turn. I will
hold her hand when we cross the street and I
will have a little list, written in her own dear
hand, when I go shopping. She makes sure that I
wear a scarf when it is cold and I will squeeze

fresh orange juice for her, when she is in bed
with the flu. Daily we will tell each other that
time flies and you will tell us not to be boring. She will decorate the house with fresh
flowers from our garden and I polish the car
once again. In Spring, I paint the picket fence
and together with her I

ADAMS & GERRARD, SOLICITORS
5 ST. STEPHENS GREEN
DUBLIN 2

TELEPHONE (01) 9264589   D.D.E BOX 99

JAMES H. ADAMS
WILLIAM H.E. GERRARD
BARRY J. O'SULLIVAN
MIKE S. O'FLAHERTY

                              Our Ref: AD/RS
                    Your Ref: November 5, 1991

Mr. W.A Camper, Warden
Los Angeles State Prison
2178 High Road
Los Angeles, California, USA

Concerning: Inmate 37489
        Jon-Jon Lucas / 11/30/1970 / Berkeley, CA

Dear Mr. Camper:

In regard to a written agreement (see enclosure) between our client, Jean Louis Dupre (born on February 22, 1935 in Brugge, Belgium and deceased on May 22, 1984 in Serifos, Greece), and our office we request that you convey enclosed letter to the above captioned inmate.

The letter consists of 58 pages and is addressed to Jon-Jon Lucas, born on November 30, 1970 in Berkeley. Mr. Lucas resides in your facility under Inmate number 37489.

At the express wish of the deceased, you are requested to deliver the material to the recipient on the day of his 21st birthday, which will be this coming November 30th.

There are no further costs or considerations connected to the conclusion of this case.

Sincerely,

[James H. Adams]
James H. Adams, Esquire

*Glossary of some uncommon words:

andrangheta (Italian slang): A mafia-type organization originating in Calabria.

ascoltami (Italian): "Listen to me."

buongiorno (Italian): Good day, or good morning.

Calabria—A province in Southern Italy.

camorra (Neapolitan slang): A mafia-type organization originating in Naples.

Campania—A province in Southern Italy.

capo familia (Italian): the head of a smaller Mafia family, a family within the extended famiglia, headed by a *padrino* (or Godfather).

Carabinieri—A military organization with police powers. Members of this elite force are specifically selected from police and military units. The *Carabinieri* also supply SWAT (Special Weapons and Tactics) teams to regular State and Municipal police forces.

chora (Greek): A village with the same name as the (Greek) island on which it is situated.

Circondario Marittimo—A district of the Water Police. It patrols inland waters and harbors. Not to be confused with the Coast Guard (Guardia di Finanza) which also performs Customs duties.

colazione (Italian) breakfast.

Cyclades—An island group in the Aegean Sea, southwest of Athens.

Dio—God.

Dio mio—My God.

Force Publique (French): A military organization with native troops and non-commissioned officers and led by white (mostly Belgian) officers, immediately after the achievement of independence by the former Belgian colony of Belgian Congo, now called Zaire. Eventually entirely staffed by Zaire citizens.

Gianni (Italian): short for Giovanni (John).

Interpol—INTERnational Criminal POLice Organization, to facilitate co-operation and exchange of information between various police forces of most countries in the world. Headquarters are in Paris and the general assembly, the supreme authority in the organization, meets annually in different capital cities. Interpol has its own communication network to various affiliated countries. Interpol specifically does *not* consist of "super" police officers, but acts as a clearing house for information on international crime. Interpol has *no* jurisdiction in its various member countries, but relies on the cooperation of the affiliated police forces.

ispettore (Italian): Inspector, a rank equivalent to Lieutenant.

Livadi—the "second" city on Serifos.

Kithnos—An island in the Cyclades.

Mikonos—An island in the Cyclades.

May 1—or "May Day" celebrated as "Labor Day" in many countries that were under a communistic influence, or had a largely communistic population.

Mezzogiorno—A region in Italy, comprising a number of southern Italian provinces.

Milos—An island in the Cyclades.

mousse de truite (French): trout mousse, a mousse made with trout.

nessuno (Italian): nobody.

niente (Italian): nothing.

omerta—The code of silence imposed on Mafia members. To speak of "Our Thing" (Cosa Nostra) is forbidden. Breaking the code of silence will result in death or vengence (Vendetta).

padrini (Italian): plural of padrino.

padrino (Italian): The chief, or Godfather of an extended Mafia family, consisting of two, or more subordinate families.

pensione (Italian): A cross between a "bed-and-breakfast" and a residential hotel. Limited meals are generally available, but no menu. Rooms can be rented by the day, the week, the month, or by the year.

pizzo (Italian slang): "Protection" money.

prego (Italian): please.

prima colazione (Italian): first meal, or breakfast.

Questura Centrale—Headquarters of the (Italian) State Police, independent from both the Municipal police and the Carabinieri.

ragazze e ragazzi (Italian): Guys and dolls.

Serifos—An island in the Cyclades

scusi (Italian): Excuse me, I'm sorry, etc. Used in various ways to either apologize, or express regret.

succo di frutta (Italian): Fruit juice.

Taunus—A car model produced by the Ford factories in Germany, specifically for the European market.

Tyrrhanian Sea—The sea enclosed by Italy, Sicily, Sardinia and Corsica in the Mediterranean.

VDT(s)—Video Display Terminal(s), or computer "screen(s)".

About the Author:

Henk Elsink (ELSINCK) is a new star on the Dutch detective-thriller scene. His first book, *Tenerife!*, received rave press reviews in the Netherlands. Among them: "A wonderful plot, well written." (De Volkskrant), "A successful first effort. A find!" (Het Parool) and "A jewel!" (Brabants Dagblad).

In the United States, *Tenerife!* has been called "a fascinating study of a troubled mind." (*Mac Rutherford*, Lucky Books). The author has been called "crafty and inventive" (*Timothy Hunter*, Cleveland Plain Dealer) and "sharp and concise" and "one cannot help but fall under the spell of this highly original author." (*Paulette Kozick*, West Coast Review of Books).

After a successful career as a stand-up comic and cabaretier, Elsinck retired as a star of radio, TV, stage and film and started to devote his time to the writing of books. He divides his time between Palma de Mallorca (Spain), Turkey and the Netherlands. He has written three books and a fourth is in progress.

Elsinck's books are as far-ranging as their author. His stories reach from Spain to Amsterdam, from Brunei to South America and from Italy to California. His books are genuine thrillers that will keep readers glued to the edge of their seats.

TENERIFE! by Elsinck

Madrid 1989. The body of a man is found in a derelict hotel room. The body is suspended, by means of chains, from hooks in the ceiling. A gag protrudes from the mouth. He has been tortured to death. Even hardened police officers turn away, nauseated. And this won't be the only murder. Quickly the reader becomes aware of the identity of the perpetrator, but the police are faced with a complete mystery. What are the motives? It looks like revenge, but what do the victims have in common? Why does the perpetrator prefer black leather cuffs, blindfolds and whips? The hunt for the assassin leads the police to seldom frequented places in Spain and Amsterdam, including the little known world of the S&M clubs in Amsterdam's Red Light District. In this spine-tingling thriller the reader follows the hunters, as well as the hunted and Elsinck succeeds in creating near unendurable suspense.

First American edition of this European Best-Seller.

ISBN 1 881164 51 9

A fascinating work combining suspense and the study of a troubled mind to tell a story that compels the reader to continue reading. **—Mac Rutherford, Lucky Books**

. . . A wonderful plot, well written — Strong first effort — Promising debut — A successful first effort. A find! — A well written book, holds promise for the future of this author — A first effort to make dreams come true — A jewel of a thriller! — An excellent book, gripping, suspenseful and extremely well written . . .
— A sampling of Dutch press reviews

MURDER BY FAX by Elsinck

Elsinck's second effort consists entirely of a series of Fax copies. An important businessman receives a fax from an organization calling itself "The Radical People's Front for Africa". It demands a contribution of $5 million to aid the struggle of the black population in South Africa. The reader follows the alleged motives and criminal goals of the so-called organization via a series of approximately 200 fax messages between various companies, police departments and other persons. All communication is by Fax and it will lead, eventually, to kidnapping and murder. Tension is maintained throughout and the reader experiences the vicarious thrill of "reading someone else's mail".

First American edition of this European Best-Seller.

ISBN 1 881164 52 7

Elsinck has created a technical tour-de-force: This high-tech version of the epistolary novel succeeds as the faxed messages quickly prove capable of providing plot, clues and characterization.
      — Publishers Weekly

This novel by Dutch author Elsinck is so interestingly written it might be read for its creative style alone. It is sharp and concise and one easily becomes involved enough to read it in one sitting. MURDER BY FAX cannot help but have its American readers fall under the spell of this highly original author.
      — Paulette Kozick, West Coast Review of Books

This clever and breezy thriller is a fun exercise. The crafty Dutch author peppers his fictional fax copies with clues and red herrings that make you wonder who's behind the scheme. Elsinck's spirit of inventiveness keeps you guessing up to the satisfying end.   **— Timothy Hunter, (Cleveland) Plain Dealer**

. . . Riveting — Sustains tension and is totally believable — An original idea, well executed — Unorthodox — Engrossing and frightening — Well conceived, written and executed — Elsinck sustains his reputation as a major new writer of thrillers . . .
      — A sampling of Dutch press reviews

DeKok and the Somber Nude
Baantjer

The oldest of the four men turned to DeKok: "You're from Homicide?" DeKok nodded. The man wiped the raindrops from his face, bent down and carefully lifted a corner of the canvas. Slowly the head became visible: a severed girl's head. DeKok felt the blood drain from his face. "Is that all you found?" he asked. "A little further," the man answered sadly, "is the rest." Spread out among the dirt and the refuse were the remaining parts of the body: both arms, the long, slender legs, the petite torso. There was no clothing.

First American edition of this European Best-Seller.

ISBN 1 881164 01 2

Baantjer's laconic, rapid-fire storytelling has spun out a surprisingly complex web of mysteries. **—Kirkus Reviews**

It's easy to understand the appeal of Amsterdam police detective DeKok. **—Charles Solomon, Los Angeles Times**

DeKok and Murder on the Menu
Baantjer

On the back of a menu from the Amsterdam Hotel-Restaurant *De Poort van Eden* (Eden's Gate) is found the complete, signed confession of a murder. The perpetrator confesses to the killing of a named blackmailer. Inspector DeKok (Amsterdam Municipal Police, Homicide) and his assistant, Vledder, gain possession of the menu. They remember the unsolved murder of a man whose corpse, with three bullet holes in the chest, was found floating in the waters of the Prince's Canal. A year-old case which was almost immediately turned over to the Narcotics Division. At the time it was considered to be just one more gang-related incident. DeKok and Vledder follow the trail of the menu and soon more victims are found and DeKok and Vledder are in deadly danger themselves. Although the murder was committed in Amsterdam, the case brings them to Rotterdam and other, well-known Dutch cities such as Edam and Maastricht.

First American edition of this European Best-Seller.

ISBN 1 881164 31 4

Murder in Amsterdam
Baantjer

The two very first "DeKok" stories for the first time in a single volume. In these stories DeKok meets Vledder, his invaluable assistant, for the first time. The book contains two complete novels. In *DeKok and the Sunday Strangler*, DeKok is recalled from his vacation in the provinces and tasked to find the murderer of a prostitute. The young, "scientific" detectives are stumped. Soon, a second corpse is found. At the last moment DeKok is able to prevent a third murder. In *DeKok and the Corpse on Christmas Eve*, a patrolling constable sees a floating corpse in a canal. Autopsy reveals that she has been strangled and that she was pregnant. "Silent witnesses" from the purse of the murdered girl point to two men. The fiancee is suspect, but who is the second man? In order to preserve his Christmas Holiday, DeKok wants to solve the case quickly.

ISBN 1 881164 00 4

The two novellas make an irresistible case for the popularity of the Dutch author. DeKok's maverick personality certainly makes him a compassionate judge of other outsiders and an astute analyst of antisocial behavior
　　　　—*Marilyn Stasio*, **The New York Times Book Review**

This first translation of Baantjer's work into English supports the mystery writer's reputation in his native Holland as a Dutch Conan Doyle. His knowledge of esoterica rivals that of Holmes, but Baantjer wisely uses such trivia infrequently, his main interests clearly being detective work, characterization and moral complexity.　　　　—**Publishers Weekly**

Both stories are very easy to take.　　　　—**Kirkus Reviews**